THIS BLOODY WINE

This Bloody Wine

KAY AND TERRY HALLAGAN

Mallard Cove Publishing

To our family, who encouraged and
supported us all the way.

First Printing, 2021

ISBN: 978-1-7369582-1-6

Library of Congress Control Number: 2021938175

Chapter 1

Toni heard a scream. Someone cried out again, low and sorrowful, like a trapped animal. My God, it was her own voice! She kicked out with her feet, raised both arms to protect her face and connected with something hard—and wet.

She opened her eyes and saw it. "It's blood! It's blood!" Toni screamed, curling up and clutching her knees. It was hard to breathe; her throat and lungs hurt, as if she had just run a mile. A hand came into view, which caused her to recoil. When she recognized it as Mark's, she relaxed. He laid his hand on her shoulder and gently stroked her upper arm.

"Toni, it's only wine," Mark said. "I was pouring you a glass. Then you shouted and bumped into my arm. I spilled some on the floor." He knelt down next to her, avoiding the red stain on the white carpet, and held her hand. "You poor thing! You were whimpering like a frightened kitten. Here, let me wipe your hand; it's wet with wine."

She let him dab her hand and wrist with a paper napkin.

"Don't worry," he said. "I'll clean this up. That must have been quite a dream."

She pushed herself up into a sitting position. She couldn't stop shivering and her teeth were chattering so badly she couldn't speak. Mark put a crocheted throw over her shoulders and hugged her. It took a full minute for her panting to slow to a calmer and more regular cadence. She could feel the warmth of Mark's arms and chest radiating through the throw; this gave her the strength to brave an attempt at speech.

"It was a terrible dream—a nightmare! I don't even re-member falling asleep."

"You must have dozed off, Toni. I was in the kitchen and I brought in a bottle of wine. All of a sudden you started moaning, screaming and thrashing around."

"Oh Mark, it was so terrible. Blood all over our house . . . splattered everywhere. It was so real."

Mark squeezed her even tighter and kissed her on the neck. "It's okay. I know you had a bad day. I shouldn't have badgered you like that."

She sobbed quietly for several seconds more, and then struggled out of his grasp. She stood up and said, "Let me get something to clean this up." Mark objected, wanting to do the cleanup himself, but she overruled him. She needed to work at something, anything, to get her mind back to normal. Mark let her go without arguing. He was a won-derful husband; he always seemed to know what she needed—and when to give her space.

"It was just a dream. I don't know why it seemed so real," Toni said as she scrubbed ineffectively at the at the crimson stain spreading out on the plush living room carpet. This would require a professional carpet cleaner. "I'm sorry if I spoiled the moment. I don't know about you, but I've lost my interest in the wine."

Mark re-corked the wine. "It can wait," he said.

"But that's the special, twenty-dollar-a-bottle merlot that you just bought. Don't you want to—"

"Toni, forget it; it's just wine. I thought it might smooth things over, sort of as my way of apologizing for snapping at you earlier." He helped her up from the carpet, wrapped his arms around her and hugged her tightly. "It's so rare that we argue. I feel really bad. I'm sorry."

Toni rose up to kiss him. "Let's forget about that for now. The kids are asleep. Let's go to bed."

*   *   *

Toni disentangled herself from cuddling with Mark and looked at the bedside clock. It was 2:00 a.m. She closed her eyes but couldn't get back to sleep. Mark was right; it was so rare that they argued. Was tonight's argument her fault or his? Not that it mattered. She wished it had never happened and she was pretty sure Mark felt the same. He had questioned the wisdom and timing of her spending big bucks to expand her business. She had retaliated—perhaps unfairly, she admitted with 20-20 hindsight—with a complaint about his excessive traveling. His law firm always had him flying here and there to litigate crucial cases.

Had she been wrong to take offense at Mark's questioning of her business plan? She had such a big vision of putting two companies together successfully. It would work well; she just knew it! But Mark had criticized what he called her "desperate attempt" to piece together these two businesses. He found it hard to understand why she couldn't have stayed in her little office.

This new merger was eating up their savings like a ravenous mistress. She had thought things would get better last month or this month for sure, but so far it hadn't happened. She was beginning to worry. This business of hers . . . has it become an obsession? She couldn't let this hurt her marriage or, God forbid, her kids. She prayed that it would soon work out.

The next thing she knew, she felt Mark roll out of bed. The sky outside the window was no longer dark. She must have fallen asleep despite her worries. Unless she had missed it, he had not given her the normal passionate embrace before getting out of bed. Was he lost in his own thoughts or was he holding a grudge about last night? Toni heard the shower go on.

When he emerged from the bathroom dressed only in boxers. her heart took a sharp jab at her ribs. He was handsome even with disheveled hair. His trim and well-muscled five-ten frame still gave her longings to drag him back into bed. He turned and looked at her.

"Good morning," he said. "Sorry to be in a rush, but I've got to get to the airport."

"Mark, don't go," she said. "Please don't go. That dream I had was so real. What if it's an omen?"

"Look, darling, I know you're upset. But I have so much to do; I've got to go." He pulled on his black socks and continued dressing. But he stopped while buttoning his shirt. He walked over, sat down on the bed next to her and gently brushed back her hair. "I can understand how you feel, Toni. But remember, it was just a dream. Remember that. It was just a dream."

"My brain tells me that, Mark, but my heart is telling me it was more than a dream. Don't forget Caesar's wife. She warned him and look what happened."

Buckling his belt, he took a deep breath, closed his eyes for a second and then looked directly into her eyes. "Toni, I told you last night. I have no choice. This deposition is vital. My case is coming up; I have to do it. Anyway, I'll be back tonight. I promise."

As she watched him brush his hair, she ached for a hug or a word or two to tide her over until he came home.

"I'll call you from Midway when I get in. It's liable to be a mess out there. In addition to the normal Friday travel rush, storms are forecast for Texas. I'll keep you updated." He was carefully tying the red striped tie she had given him for his birthday. "The tickets for the Mahler concert are in the desk. Be ready when I get here, OK? Did you get a sitter?"

She nodded. "Wish we were going to Michigan."

"We'll go tomorrow." His tone warmed a little. He leaned over and kissed her forehead lightly. "Hope today goes better."

"Me too." She stifled an urge to wrap her arms around him and keep him home for a few more seconds. Instead she looked away. "Have a good trip."

Toni heard the front door close quietly. The children would not be up for another hour. She fluffed up her pillow, pulled the covers back over her shoulders, and closed her eyes. After a few minutes of trying to sleep, she gave up and shuffled out to the kitchen, where she was surprised to find the coffee made and orange juice poured. She wondered if he had taken time to eat.

Chapter 2

Peter Jacob "PJ" Conroy strode out of Chicago's Union Station swinging his overnight case and whistling softly. For a Friday in October—Friday the 13th, he reminded himself—the weather was surprisingly nice. Skies were clear and the wind was blessedly calm for the moment. He merged with the army of clerks, paralegals and secretaries in their relentless drive eastward. The morning rush was underway. On a normal day, he wouldn't have used the 'L.' Chicago's elevated train was more suited to the common man. His preferred mode of transportation was his Mercedes two-seater. Today, however, after some time at the office, he had to fly over to Detroit and the 'L' was the best way to and from the airport—no hassles with traffic.

PJ swarmed into the surging force of the crowd, bypassing the donut shop on the corner. He reminded himself that Toni had ruled out sugary, high-fat foods for the staff meeting. She was providing fresh fruit. Ugh. He was sure she'd even bring granola bars.

He had reason to be pleased with himself. Today's conference in Detroit had given him an excuse for a holiday. And, was he ever ready for one! All the good behavior of the past few weeks had grown stale. He needed a break.

Heather had unwittingly endorsed his plans as she hugged him when he ran for the train this morning. She had said, "Enjoy," which was an unexpected suggestion coming from his wife. That had almost made him feel guilty. Of course she had meant the business trip but for him the real enjoyment would come tonight.

The upcoming software conference promised to be a real drag. But he had to put in an appearance to give the company some visibility and maybe secure some new contracts. He hated Detroit, but he had figured out a little diversion to make it a fun weekend, or at least a fun Friday night with a sexy young blond. She was much too young for him. However, during his last visit to Union Pier, he had seen how she had looked at him—sizing him up, as if he were a side of beef. Evidently, even though his curly hair was beginning to grey, his boyish face, six-foot height and lean body still had the ability to attract younger women. All those early morning workouts were paying off; he was tanned (okay, so it was artificial), lean and in better shape than the average forty-five-year-old. To celebrate all these good thoughts, he lengthened his stride, passing others on the sidewalk and hoping they would be a little jealous of his youthful gait.

He hadn't quite figured out how to get over to Union Pier from Detroit. Driving was out of the question; that would take three hours. As a minimum, he had to register for the conference this afternoon. Then . . . what? Drive the rental car three hours over to Union Pier? Wait! They had commuter flights from Detroit to South Bend. Even in those puddle-jumper propeller-driven planes, it couldn't take more than an hour. Then he could rent another car and drive the forty-five minutes to Union Pier. That would give him an extra hour or two to sip a glass or two of fine wine with this young thing—and perhaps get to know her much, much better.

As P.J. rounded the corner on Michigan Avenue he experienced a tug of pride. So far, 1989 had been one of his best years ever, in both the business and romance departments. The merger with Toni had been a great move. Although no contracts had been signed yet, he had lots of promising irons in the fire. He was right where he belonged, occupying a prestigious Michigan Avenue address. His gift was to put the right iron in the right fire. Okay, that meant he was really just a salesman for Toni's software. She had the brains—and the looks too, if the truth be known—to design software for their clients that vastly improved any business's efficiency. He drifted back to the "looks" part of his assessment. Shame on him! What did looks have to do with her proficiency as a software designer? But, hell, she *was* easy to look at. Petite, shapely, perfect face, looks great in heels—and happily married. A man had a right to dream, though, didn't he?

He was sure they were building a business to rival Beacon and Beacon, the advertising company of his rich and successful father-in-law, old Mr. Corrigan. He couldn't explain exactly why, but he was still jealous of Adam Corrigan's meteoric rise to the top of Beacon and Beacon's marketing department. He should stop being jealous of a dead guy. Heather would have a cow if she knew he was having these thoughts about her dear departed father. But really, it's tough competing against a ghost.

In the elevator to the 20th floor, PJ forced those troubling thoughts out of his mind and tried to let in some happy ones. On a personal level, his investments were tantalizingly close to paying off in a big way. Was it luck or good judgment that he was positioned to cash in on a really big opportunity? He flashed back to his prof's comments in business school. *"You want gigantic returns on your investments? Well, then, be prepared to take gigantic risks. By the way, that's how people get rich."*

He preferred to call it "speculation" or "educated guess" rather than "risk." That last word had such negative connotations. He had gotten his foot in the door on a truly spectacular real estate deal, thanks to one of the cronies he had met while peddling Toni's software. In a few weeks the announcement would come out about the new stadium, and *voila!* Who owned the land in that area? Good ole' PJ! After a speedy elevator ride, he opened the door to Simplified Data Systems and tried to avoid swaggering down the hall to his offices.

Chapter 3

Toni paced around her desk. Coming in early had been a mistake; she was too worried to concentrate on work. The radio news said hurricane-force winds were buffeting the Houston area. Flights would be delayed or canceled. Mark's would probably be one of them. Well, as she had once heard from an old pilot: *A delay is better than a disaster.* It didn't take a genius to figure out that many airline crashes were related to severe weather. Mark would be okay, wouldn't he? Oh, God, she just knew that stuff with the tub had been an omen! Maybe a cup of tea would settle her nerves.

In the conference room's small coffee and snack area, Toni put a bag of Chamomile tea into a cup and poured in boiling water. While it steeped, she decided to cancel this morning's staff meeting. She just couldn't handle it to-day. If she postponed it until Monday, PJ could report on his conference. Before returning to her office, she carefully took her first sip of tea and stepped closer to the board room's massive corner windows. Below was a magnificent view of Grant Park.

She took great pride in this park and was sure that all of Chicago's 7.3 million residents would agree with her. Every-one she knew used the park's 300 beautiful acres as an escape from urban congestion. It was so relaxing and invigorating to look out to the east and see . . . nothing—nothing but Lake Michigan. For her, at least, Grant Park had always provided a welcome respite from being crammed into a high-rise apartment building, an old brick multi-family house or working in an equally crowded downtown office.

Toni had fond childhood memories of walking Grant Park's miles of winding paths and multiple playgrounds bordered by green grass. As an adult, she had developed an appreciation for the park's historic structures. Her favorite was the rococo wedding cake-style Buckingham Fountain, which was often surrounded by locals as well as tourists, all jockeying for position for a good family photo. She had spent many an afternoon or evening at one of the multiple performing arts venues in the area. And, now that the kids were old enough to appreciate fine art, she looked forward to showing them the Art Institute of Chicago. In addition to the fine arts displayed inside, the building itself was a piece of art, a 100-year-old masterpiece of Beaux-Arts architecture.

Early morning sun highlighted the park's autumn leaves and bright flowers. A small flotilla of sailboats had emerged from the lakefront marina, their sails struggling to catch the unusually calm morning breeze. Farther out in the lake, there seemed to be evidence of Chicago's famous wind; Toni could see white sails fully inflated, contrasting with the bright blue waters of Lake Michigan. This view was worth every penny of the high rent; it was a stress-reliever. She chuckled. Could she get a tax write-off for this room if she called it a necessary medical expense—stress therapy?

How had she gotten here, to this fancy new office, twenty floors high in one of Chicago's most prestigious buildings? Not so long ago, she had been a part-time waitress, saving every dollar—make that every dime—to pay for undergrad and grad school tuition. Today she was standing in a conference room—*her* conference room—no longer the little girl from a two-flat on Chicago's North Side, but the co-founder and CEO of Simplified Data Systems, the city's newest consulting firm. She owed a lot to her parents. They had told her the sky's the limit, and here she was, in a skyscraper, standing in lavishly remodeled offices so new that her parents hadn't even seen them yet.

Toni resolved to bring them up here soon, maybe for her thirty-fifth birthday, which was coming up next month. She envisioned birthday cake, candles, maybe a little champagne, hugs and handshakes all around. Mom and Pop would be proud of her. God, they had already bragged to the whole neighborhood about their little girl. Pop had told her just the other day, "I got to telling Bill, just down the street, 'I don't really get all this computer stuff. I just know Toni has pioneered a new data processing system that streamlines health care administration, especially for low-income populations. Heck, that's why she named it *Simplified* Data Systems!'"

The problem was, she was not a born salesman; her initial presentations had been disasters. Maybe she should have hired her dad to promote the business instead of merging with—

"Good morning, my dear! And how are you this fine day? Say, for an Italian lass you look mighty good in the wearin' o' the green."

"Oh, hi, PJ. I didn't hear you come in." He could muster up a brogue on demand and it usually made her laugh. Today it was all she could do to force a smile. "I was just thinking about you."

"Really? And why would that be?"

"Let's go down to my office," she said, trying another smile. When she stepped inside with PJ behind her, she asked him to shut the door. "Well, I was just thinking about the merger and how critical your sales expertise is to our success. But there is one thing that—"

"By the way, Toni," he said, "would you sign a check for me—for expenses, you know?"

Her smile disappeared. "That's what I want to talk about." He was not going to understand what she was about to say. PJ came from money. His wife had inherited the Beacon and Beacon fortune. He lived well, with fine wine and gourmet dining every night. Though Toni had never visited their home, she knew it was on the lakefront up in Highland Park. His two daughters attended high-priced Eastern colleges.

"Look," she said, "I didn't want to bother you with this before your trip, but we are a little short of cash right now. Our start-up expenses have been ridiculously higher than expected. I had hoped the hotel and plane tickets would cover the cost of your trip." As soon as she said that, she realized how ridiculous it must sound to PJ. How was he supposed to eat or to wine and dine prospective clients?

"But Toni, I thought we were in great shape. My sales leads have been really promising, right?"

"Yes, they have. But that's all they are right now—sales leads, not money in the bank. Not yet, at least." She took a deep breath. "How much do you need?"

"Oh, fifteen hundred ought to do it," he answered with a smile.

She opened her purse and fumbled for the business checkbook. Her big ring of keys got in the way. She pulled it out and tossed it on the desk, where it landed with a crash loud enough to startle PJ.

"Sorry," she said. She opened the check register and looked at the handwritten balance— $1,105.22. She looked at PJ and said, "I'm sorry, the most I can give you right now is five hundred."

"Tell you what," he said. "Let me write a personal check for five thou and you write the expense check for fifteen hundred. We'll call it a loan to the business and that should handle things 'till business picks up. Let's not have you worrying about these details." He pulled out his checkbook, scratched out a check and put it on the desk.

Toni stared at it. "Are you sure about this?"

"Sure. We are both confident that things will pick up soon, right?

She shrugged.

"Right?" he repeated.

She picked up the check and put it her drawer. "Right. By the way, I thought we'd postpone the meeting until Monday. You can report on the conference."

"Good," he said. "I'm off to Detroit in a few minutes. So, you and Mark are going to Michigan tomorrow?

"Yes. Mark's due back from Texas at 4:00 p.m. Then we're going to the Mahler concert with some friends. We'll probably get a late start tomorrow, but I am so looking forward to the weekend over in Union Pier. We really love that place; it's quiet and peaceful and sort of small town-ish. When we go there, our stressful lives in Chicago seem to fade away, if only for a day or so."

PJ said, "Enjoy the evening. And, don't worry; the money will begin rolling in soon. This partnership of ours, it's like a marriage made in heaven." He walked out.

Marriage! That reminded her of Mark and their argument yesterday. She knew he wanted her to succeed, but who could blame him for worrying? She had cashed in some IRAs and fed the money into office renovations without telling Mark. When he had noticed the penalty for early withdrawal, he had blown up. She had tried to explain, to tell him she wasn't risking their future. Simplified Data Systems was going to make it. PJ had all kinds of proposals out and she knew they'd pay off. They had a good product and once they were launched there would be no more problems.

She spent the rest of the day at her desk with only a short break for a brown-bag lunch in the conference room and a brief trip downstairs to the fitness center. The phone rang just before quitting time. "Simplified Data Systems, this is Toni."

"Toni, it's Mark! Things are crazy down here due to bad weather. I've been delayed, then canceled, and then re-booked to arrive at O'Hare instead of Midway. I won't get in until 8:00."

"So, I guess we'll miss the concert."

Mark said, "To hell with the concert. Let's go to Michigan tonight. And, let's forget yesterday. I'm truly sorry. By the way, I'm no Caesar."

"I agree with you. Ah, maybe not about the Caesar part, but about going to Michigan tonight. I am desperate to get away from the rat-race in Chicago. I'll have everything ready when you get here." She could feel herself relax. She had just joined the TGIF club. "Mark, you don't know how great it is to hear your voice." They said their good-byes. She went home and packed for the weekend. Toni had their station wagon at the curb, loaded with suitcases and kids already in pajamas and buckled in, when Mark climbed out of his cab.

"Can't I even change?" he asked.

"At Union Pier," she said.

*   *   *

Toni parked behind their house and shut off the engine. She poked Mark on the shoulder. He must be really tired; usually he was too nervous about her driving to fall asleep. When he opened his eyes, she said, "Here we are, my love. Our Union Pier getaway cottage awaits us!"

He yawned and stretched. "Wow, sorry for dozing off; the early morning meeting and then all the stress of traveling . . . but I'm refreshed now. Ready for a romantic late-night date with the love of my life."

"Yeah, me too." Toni said. They worked together to get the kids into their room and tucked in. Allen fell asleep clutching his baseball glove and mumbling something about the Cubs never winning a pennant. They put a sleeping Emily into her bed and surrounded her with an entourage of dolls and stuffed animals. Mark brought in their luggage and said he'd change into comfortable clothes while she got out a block of cheese and some crackers for a late-night snack. And, of course, she couldn't forget the bottle of very rare Caymus Vineyards Cabernet Sauvignon that Mark had given her as an early birthday present. Tonight, she would have preferred Chardonnay. Red was just going to remind her of the dream.

"Hey Mark!" she called, hoping he could hear her from the bedroom, a half-floor above.

"Yeah?"

"Why don't you get your fancy new jetted tub going? Don't bother getting dressed. I'll open the wine, we'll climb into the tub together, sip some wine and . . . one of us will try to seduce the other."

"Right-ho!" he shouted, feigning a British accent.

Toni arranged two glasses on a silver tray, uncorked the wine, and poured it. After picking up the tray, she glanced down at the plate of cheese and crackers and decided that would have to wait for later. She headed up the stairs. At long last, she would get to enjoy their newly remodeled, elegant master bath. At the top of the stairs, Mark, a thick white towel wrapped around his waist, grinned at her. He looked good.

"Toni, you are over-dressed," he said. "Why don't you set that wine down and slip into, ah, something more comfortable?" He bent down and twisted the faucet handles. Water gushed into the tub. He reached down with one finger and pushed the button to start the jets.

The motor in the tub roared as if it were a DC-10 revving up for takeoff. A fine mist of red liquid exploded out of the jets and sprayed everywhere. Mark was instantly covered in—my God . . . oh, no! Blood was spraying everywhere! She cried out, "Mark!" The tray tilted and, before she could react, the bottle of wine and the two full glasses crashed to the tile floor. The noise was deafening. Mark was shouting something. God, he was barefoot and broken glass was everywhere.

"Mark, Mark! Turn it off! Turn off the jets!" She pointed at the button. He didn't seem to hear her. His ears were probably still ringing from the jets and her screams. But he noticed the broken glass, gave her a brief nod and pushed the button.

When it got quiet, she said, "Don't move! There's broken glass all over the floor."

The frothy red liquid made a sickening, bubbling noise as it dripped down the sides of the tub and gurgled down the drain. The musty, metallic smell was shockingly similar to what she had heard about the smell of . . . it had to be—

"My God!" he shouted. "My God, it *is* blood!"

"Are you bleeding?"

Mark reached out for her but, noticing that his bare arms, lower body and towel were covered with blood, he drew back. The bathtub behind him still hissed with red bubbles, as if it were a wild animal warning them to stay away. He was shaking.

"Mark, Mark!" she screamed, "are you hurt?"

"I'm not hurt. If it's blood, it's not mine. But what the hell!" He dropped the bloody towel from around his waist, grabbed another one from the rack and began to wipe himself.

Toni steadied herself. "Mark, what on earth is it? Is it the plumbing?"

"Not likely," he replied, taking a glance into the tub and at the blood-splattered walls and floor. "It looks like Jack the Ripper had a real struggle in here." He glanced into the mirror and shuddered. "I've got to get some of this stuff off." He took another towel from the rack and carefully walked over to the sink. After that, I—"

"Wh . . . what do we do? What? What?" She stuttered her words and couldn't control her trembling.

"Can you take that last towel and help me move the broken glass?" Mark said. "After that, we'll get you cleaned up."

You mean . . ." She glanced down to see spots of blood on her skirt and blouse. "Ugh. Yuck."

Mark had already cleared a path from the tub to where she stood. He put his hands—now clean, thankfully—on her shoulders and said, "Come on. Let's get changed. Then, we'd better call the police."

Chapter 4

Mark squeezed her hand tightly as they went downstairs to the kitchen. He took a deep breath, reached for the wall-mounted phone and dialed 911. Unbelievably, it took four or five rings for someone to answer. Toni wondered how 911 could be so busy up here in sleepy little old Union Pier. Finally, someone answered in a deep voice loud enough to make Mark recoil and move the handset away from his ear. Toni could hear it easily.

"911, what's your emergency?"

"Please come," Mark pleaded. "We have a terrible problem. We . . . we—"

"What's the problem?" the voice growled.

"There's blood . . . there's really blood in our bathtub."

"Is someone injured?"

"Not that I know of. But my wife is frightened and my kids . . . oh, God, the kids."

"Just give me your address, sir. We'll get there."

Mark gave him the details and hung up.

Toni said, "The kids!" and rushed up the stairs to their room. She could hear Mark right behind her. She opened the bedroom door and saw Allen and Emily, snuggled in their blankets, sleeping soundly. Allen still cuddled his baseball mitt. Emily shared her covers with her family of dolls. She shut the door carefully.

Mark hugged her from behind and whispered, "Thank God. Wow! Take it easy, Toni. I can feel your chest heaving. Your hands are shaking. Take some deep breaths. They're safe. We're safe."

Through the hug, she could feel his heart pumping. His heart rate was probably as high as hers. He unlatched his arms and led her by the hand into the living room. He helped her get seated on the couch.

"Wait here," Mark said. He stood and looked up the stairs toward the master bathroom. "I'm going to clean up that broken bottle of wine and the glasses and such. I don't want the police to think we were just drunk. Let me get a mop, a broom and—"

She pushed up off the sofa.

Mark said, "No, no, you just wait here. I'll take care of . . . oh, hell, c'mon. I know you. You can't sit still at a time like this."

They worked together to clean up the wine spill and the broken glass. When the broom, dustpan and soiled rags had been put away, they returned to the couch but, before they could sit down, flashing red and blue lights appeared outside their front window. Car doors opened and were slammed closed. An officer appeared at their front door. Mark hurried over to greet him before the officer rang the bell or shouted something to wake the kids.

"Somebody here called?" the officer said after Mark opened the door.

"We have a bathtub full of blood!" Toni said, cutting off similar words from Mark.

"You're okay, though?"

"Yes," Mark said. "And so are our two kids. They're asleep up there." He pointed up the stairs. "So please try to be quiet. They don't know about this yet."

"Bathtub full of blood. No injuries. Well, that's a new one." The officer pushed past Mark. "Just so you know, my partner is outside checking things out. Now, let's take a look. Where is it?"

"Up those stairs," Toni answered.

They went up the stairs in single file to the bloody bathroom.

"Never saw anything like this around these parts before!" the officer said.

Toni suspected it was the fancy jetted tub that merited astonishment, not the bloody contents.

"I'm Officer Lechner," the policeman said. "Oh, and here comes my partner, Officer Baker. Outside clear, Carl?"

The second officer nodded. "All clear. I did notice a broken security light, though."

Officer Lechner said, "Carl, why don't you check out the rest of the house while I check out this mess? Mister and Mrs., ah . . ."

"Harrington," Mark said.

"Mister and Mrs. Harrington will wait here with me. "Oh, Mr. Harrington, please point out to this officer which one is the kids' room. He'll try to be quiet. Two kids, right? Ages, please?"

Mark said, "An eight-year-old boy and a six-year-old girl."

Toni gulped when she saw the second officer unsnap his holster before leaving the room. The first one—Lechner—must have noticed her anxiety.

He smiled briefly and said, "Don't worry, ma'am. Everyone will be safe with us here."

Mark left the bathroom for a moment to show Officer Baker the kids' bedroom. Officer Lechner, meanwhile, bent over the tub and sniffed—but did not touch—the red stains. He stepped back and surveyed the red spots on the wall and floor.

When Mark returned, Lechner pulled a notepad from his back pocket and a pen from his shirt. "Okay," he said, "I'd like to get some things down for the record."

He confirmed their names, home and work addresses in both Union Pier and Chicago and their phone numbers. He asked what time they had arrived tonight and what they had done when they first entered the house. When had they first noticed the broken security light?

Mark looked at her. She shook her head. "Neither of us noticed it was out," he said. "It was on and undamaged the last time we were here, which was what, about ten days ago?"

"Just a few more questions," Officer Lechner said. "then we can get out of this room. I call tell it's uncomfortable for you both."

Mark reached out and squeezed her hand. Toni said, "I'm okay with this. Go ahead."

"How did you discover the, ah, the stuff in the tub?"

Mark said, "Toni was downstairs. I was up here. I . . . we . . . were getting ready to enjoy the tub. I turned on the water and then I got, ah, distracted by Toni coming up the stairs. When I pushed the button to start the jets, blood gushed out all over everything—and I mean, everything! Officer, it sure smelled and looked like blood to me."

"Did you see anything in the tub before you pushed the button?"

"I am so sorry to say this, but, like I said, I was looking at Toni coming up the stairs. I know it sounds stupid, but I just pushed the button without looking into the tub first."

"Don't worry, sir," Lechner said. "Now, Mrs. Harrington, tell me what you saw."

"I was coming up the stairs with . . ." Oh, oh. She'd blown it. Now she'd have to admit spilling the wine. This was serious business, though. Honesty was the best policy. "I was coming up the stairs, carrying a tray with a bottle of wine and two glasses. I had just reached the top of the stairs. When Mark pushed the button and blood jetted out, I think I screamed. The tray and everything on it fell to the floor. The bottle broke and the glasses shattered into a million pieces. The jets were roaring. We just stood there, speechless and scared."

Lechner looked at the floor.

"Mark was barefoot," she said, "so we had to clean up the broken glass. But I swear, we never took a single sip of that wine."

"Can you show me where you put the broken glass and the rags you used to clean up?" Lechner asked.

"Sure," Mark said. "It's downstairs, along with another bag with a couple blood-soaked towels and Toni's skirt and sweater, which got splashed with . . . well, you know."

Lechner wrote something in his note pad and said, "Why don't you two go back downstairs and wait for me in the living room. Officer Baker will sit with you. Please don't touch anything you don't absolutely have to. I'll grab some samples from this tub and, ah, the walls and floor and be down to join you in a few minutes. Excuse me." He stepped out onto the landing. "Carl, are you down there?"

"Yeah. The house is clear."

"Okay, I'm sending the Harringtons down to wait in the living room. Sit with them while I get some samples from this tub."

Toni and Mark sat side by side on the couch. Officer Baker sat in a chair opposite them, eyeing the tray of cheese and crackers.

Mark said, "Go ahead, have some. We seem to have lost our appetite."

Baker leaned forward, reached out for a cracker but pulled his hand back. "Better not. This might be evidence." He leaned back in the chair and folded his hands in his lap.

They watched Officer Lechner make two round trips up and down the stairs and out to the police car. When Lechner returned to the living room, Baker stood up and said, "Charlie, can I talk to you for a moment? In private?"

The two policemen had a brief conversation in the kitchen and returned to sit with them in the living room.

Lechner, notepad in hand, said, "Officer Baker noticed a couple things outside." He glanced at Baker and smiled. "There was one curious rabbit, who evidently gave Carl quite a start, but no harm came to either Carl or the rabbit."

Baker said, "Aw, Charlie, did you have to tell 'em about that?"

"Don't worry." Lechner winked at them. "Their lips are sealed. They don't even know about the fact that you drew down on the poor bunny with your .38."

"Aw, Charlie . . ."

"Forget it, Carl. It won't go into the report." Lechner turned his attention to Mark.

"Mister Harrington, on a more serious note, Carl—Officer Baker—did find some broken glass under the security light and we will investigate that."

"Probably some teenagers smashed it," Baker said. "Parents never keep track of their teenagers anymore. They run around smashing lights, drinking beer, breaking into houses."

"Also," Lechner said, "Officer Baker noticed another house on the other side of the back yard that seems to be on your property. Tell me about that."

"We rent that to a couple from town," Mark answered. "I don't think they're home tonight. At least their car wasn't there when we drove up."

Lechner asked for the tenants' names and Toni told them. She retrieved their phone number from the address book on the kitchen counter. After copying this into his notepad, he said, "Carl looked at all the windows and doors and found no sign of forced entry. Are you sure the house was locked?"

"Positive," Toni said. "I did it myself before we left last week. I distinctly remember setting the alarm and hearing the tone saying it was armed."

"Ah, the alarm," Lechner said. "That's a very good point. Thank you, Mrs. Harrington. We should check with the alarm company. Darn it, why didn't I think of this before? May I have the contact information for your alarm company?

After Toni gave him the information, Lechner asked permission to use their phone. He returned from the kitchen a few minutes later and consulted his notes. "Well, there it is. The system was disarmed at 7:33 p.m. and rearmed at 9:08 p.m."

"There you go," said Baker. "One of your pals is playing tricks on you. Halloween is coming up, you know. You summer people all have friends up here, don't you? Is there anyone you know who's up here right now and could have done this?"

Mark snapped back at him, "Listen now, our friends couldn't do a thing like this. This is too ugly to be a prank."

"Wait," Toni said. "Who could know the code? And, they'd also have to have a key. You said there is no sign of forced entry."

"Halloween, I tell you," Baker said. "You wouldn't believe the strange things we see this time of year, and not just from kids. Why, last year—"

"Okay, Carl, that's enough," Lechner said. He flipped through his notes. "Just a couple more things. Here's a receipt for the items we've taken into evidence." He handed it to Mark and then said, "Look, Mr. and Mrs. Harrington, I appreciate the fact that the mess upstairs is really horrible, especially if it turns out to be real blood. I can understand how you would be shocked and frightened. I promise you this. We will investigate this thoroughly—very thoroughly—and get back to you as soon as we know anything. But I have to tell you, lab analysis of the red substance in your tub may take a few days."

"Okay. Thank you," Toni said.

"One more thing. Do you two feel safe staying here tonight or would like us to help you find temporary lodging?"

That was a very good question. Toni looked at Mark, who shrugged.

"How do you feel about it?" he asked her.

She asked Lechner, "Can we clean up the bathroom?"

"Yes, we have good samples and I took some pictures. Since there is no direct evidence that a crime has been committed, we have no cause to seal off and preserve the scene."

"Well, then," she said, "Mark, if you agree with this, I think we should stay here, mainly so as to not disturb the kids. We'll try to have it all cleaned up before they wake up."

They all stood up. Officer Lechner handed a card to Mark and said, "Call me anytime. I'll have a patrol car drive by about every two hours for the rest of the night."

Toni was not sure if it made her feel safer or more at risk to know the police were going to swing by every few hours. After the patrol car had left, she sat back down in the living room and eyed the "potential evidence," the plate of cheese and crackers.

She looked at Mark, who raised his eyebrows.

"No way," he said.

"Believe it or not," Toni said, "all this stress has given me an appetite. But no wine. Please no wine! How about a nice glass of water before we do the cleanup?"

A few minutes later, they pulled some fresh cleaning materials out of the kitchen closet to replace what the police had confiscated and went to work. It took over an hour, but now the master bath was clean. Somehow, though, neither of them could stomach the thought of sleeping in their own bed, so close to the formerly bloody tub. They pulled a double sleeping bag out of the closet and rolled it out on the floor next to the kids' beds. Mark crawled in first and Toni followed.

In a tight embrace with Mark, Toni closed her eyes and wished for sleep. Wouldn't it be nice to wake up and find that this had all been a bad dream, just like the other night?

She needed a do-over of today—one without the discovery of a bloody jetted tub. Just as she was falling asleep, she flinched, which woke Mark.

"What?" he said.

"Nothing, honey. I guess I was dreaming, reliving that moment where I spilled the wine before we even had one sip."

He rolled over to face her and pulled her close. "Let me kiss your troubles away." After a passionate kiss, he said, "You know, they say that danger increases a man's libido." He pressed up against her, closer still.

"Mark! Shhh! The kids!"

"Oh. Forgot where we were. You're right. Good night, Toni. I love you."

"I love you too." How could he think of a thing like that tonight, here, in the same room as the kids? It *was* a little flattering, though.

Chapter 5

For the second night in a row, Toni had trouble sleeping. Thunder as loud as cannon shots followed by bright lightning flashes had forced her awake. Wind howled through the trees; she heard a few large branches crack and fall to the ground. There would be some yard cleanup duties tomorrow. Although they were two blocks inland from the beach, she could hear massive waves battering the shore. The final straw for Toni was the onset of a typical southwestern Michigan lake effect rainstorm. Sheets of sideways rain mixed with ice pellets or hail beat against their bedroom window. She was now officially wide awake.

She thanked her lucky stars she was on the zipper side of the sleeping bag. As quietly as possible, she unzipped the bag far enough for her to crawl out, stood up and glanced at the kids' bedside clock. 5:00 a.m. Gee, she had gotten a whole three and a half hours' sleep. After a trip to the bathroom, she decided to stay up, make some coffee and do some thinking. She looked down at Mark and over at the kids; they had slept through it all.

Just as the coffee maker finished its job, Mark appeared in the kitchen doorway, wearing a thick white terrycloth robe that matched her own.

"Well," Toni said, "your timing's good."

"Couldn't sleep," he said. "No wife to cuddle with."

"Me too. That is, I couldn't sleep either. My mind is going a mile a minute." She got out two mugs, poured coffee and put out cream and her favorite raw sugar.

She sat in the breakfast nook facing Mark, both hands wrapped around her hot mug; the warmth was comforting. "I've been trying to think this through, this tub thing. Trying to look at it from every angle. First, I thought about what that officer said, the guy who almost shot the rabbit, what was his name?"

"Baker, I think."

"Yeah, him. He's the one who speculated that it was a prank. I only know one person who could possibly do that. You have three guesses as to who that is."

"Oh, oh," Mark said. "You have me at a disadvantage, I haven't even had a sip of my coffee yet." He raised his cup but hadn't quite gotten it to his lips when he said, "Jack? No way! Even Jack wouldn't play this type of ugly joke."

"Even though—"

"Yes, yes, Toni, I know what you're going to say. Even though you suspect him of sending us 288 rolls of toilet tissue in giant cartons from Montgomery Ward. He never actually confessed to that."

"Oh, please. You were there. He winked at me and said I should just consider it as a housewarming gift for our new apartment! Nobody else we know would think of such a thing."

"Even if he did the toilet paper prank," Mark continued, "he wouldn't consider something as gross as dumping blood into our tub. I've known him ever since we were juniors rooming together at Notre Dame. Okay, I admit that in his college days he was known as somewhat of a party animal, prankster and instigator of all sorts of wild schemes. Unlike . . . ahem . . . unlike me, who stayed in to study even on football Friday nights, Jack was always one to put beer and girls—not necessarily in that order—in front of academic pursuits. But even back then he had a serious side. He loved to debate political issues, was active in student government, wrote a column for the university newspaper, and so forth. And then, when his romance with Jeri blossomed, he was a changed man. He only had time for her. In fact I, his best pal, felt neglected. The pranks stopped."

Toni nodded and said, "Yeah, I can't see Jeri letting him get away with putting blood in our tub." Jeri had told her they'd dated each other since high school. They had essentially gone away to college together, with Jeri at St. Mary's College, a ten-minute bus ride from Notre Dame.

"Did you know that Jack and Jeri celebrated their nuptials at the Basilica of the Sacred Heart on the Notre Dame campus?" Mark said. "It was quite the ceremony. Then they had some very challenging years with Jeri at the University of Chicago Law School and Jack a low-paid fledgling reporter. Finally, Jeri's record as editor of the Law Review swept her into a comfortable career as a corporate lawyer at Montgomery Ward. Since Jack was just a struggling freelance writer until he got hired by the *Chicago Dispatch*, it was Jeri's income that gave them the means to buy the place over here at Union Pier."

""Okay," Toni said, "so your friend Jack's almost a saint, but with his history, I still have to suspect him."

"Wait! He's innocent; I'm sure of it! He and Jeri are back in Chicago. Remember? We were supposed to meet them at the concert last night."

"Hmm . . . you're right," she said. "Even Jack O'Connor wouldn't be silly enough—or stupid enough—to arrange all this by sneaking back and forth between here and Chicago."

Mark said, "You know, I believe they are coming over to Union Pier later today. Let's invite them to celebrate your early birthday dinner at Miller's. Once we're there you can cross-examine him right at the table."

Toni nodded. "Sure, that'd be great. You know, in one way, if he did do it, I could relax a little. Now, I don't know . . . was it someone else we know? Was it kids? How did they get in? Why us?"

Neither she nor Mark came up with any plausible answers to these questions. They would just have to wait for more information from the police. Mark suggested a pre-dawn, intimate breakfast for two and set about making some scrambled eggs, sausage and toast. While he was at work, Toni poured some orange juice, drank coffee and made some plans for the day. They needed to get out of this house for a while. If the weather cleared, she would suggest a walk on the beach with the kids.

By 8:00 a.m., sunrise had revealed a clear and calm day. Toni volunteered to assume chef's duty for the kid's breakfast. "That will not be a challenging undertaking," she said, and immediately regretted her choice of words. "Ugh. Bad choice of words. As you lawyers like to say, let me rephrase. Breakfast for the kids will be easy." She opened a cabinet, pulled down a box of dry cereal and poured it into two bowls. She selected two bananas from the fruit bowl. Adding paper napkins, spoons and glasses of milk, she said, "*Voila!*

Mark stood and puffed up his chest. He said, with an exaggerated south Texas accent, "Ah must object, your honah!

The prosecutah has not established a connection between the bathtub and a murdah, nor has she established the need for (he pronounced it 'foe-ah') an undertakah." He sat down and exhaled deeply.

Two sleepy-eyed kids appeared at the kitchen entryway. "Who was that talking?" Allen asked.

Toni gave them both a hug and said, "That was just your dad, making one of his usual bad jokes. Now, sit down, please, and have your breakfast." She bent down and whispered in Mark's ear, "Ah hope your objection is sustained, darlin'"

*   *   *

Once the family had gotten cleaned up, dressed and on the way to the beach, Toni could feel her mood change for the better. This was a clear, crisp and colorful Saturday, the kind of fall day that only the Midwest can produce. Not a single remnant of the storm intruded on the blue horizon. Their giant, stately maple tree hadn't lost any limbs after all and, in spite of last night's winds, quite a few bright orange leaves remained on the branches. Of course, many other colorful leaves had not been so lucky; their yard was carpeted in a thick multi-colored blanket that would require some serious leaf raking. Perhaps they could bribe the kids to do that. They would, of course, enjoy jumping into the piles of leaves, thereby redistributing them all over the yard, but that was okay.

Mark pointed to fallen tree limbs in the neighboring yard, just to the north of their rental cottage He said, "Looks like we got lucky. All the wind damage seems to be over there. But it looks like nothing fell on the house itself.

What's the story with that place, anyway? It seems to be vacant."

"My understanding is, it's under renovation," Toni said. "The last time we were over here, there was just one guy working on it. I think it was the owner Ruth's nephew from Chicago. He told me his aunt had fired the previous contractor. You remember Ruth, right? Tall, matronly-looking black lady? Single or widowed, I think. We met her at the party last summer."

"Oh, yeah. She lives in Chicago too, doesn't she? A nurse." He looked ahead to see the kids were already at the crosswalk for Lakeshore Road. "Hey, kids," he called out. "Wait for us!"

Once she had descended the long set of stairs which provided public access to Lake Michigan, Toni relaxed, knowing the kids could roam safely on the white sandy beach that stretched as far as they could see in both directions. Most trees along the bluff sported yellow and red leaves, while others were still as green as they had been in midsummer. They played tag on the lonely beach and tested the autumn waters with their bare toes—it was much too cold for anything but toe-dipping. Toni asked that they turn back after a mile of walking north. After all, that meant another mile walking in the soft sand to get back to their start point. Normally she would go farther, almost up to the Nine Cranes Inn, a fancy waterfront bed and breakfast about a half-mile mile ahead. But today, after a very stressful night with almost no sleep, there was no way.

After a pleasant hour of Saturday morning TV cartoons for the kids and newspaper reading for the adults, Toni declared it was time for an early lunch. Mark volunteered to make sandwiches but Toni reminded him he needed to contact Jack and Jeri, invite them to dinner, and make reservations. By the time he returned and reported success, she had lunch prepared and the kids seated at the table. She tried to act normally for the kids' sake. When they asked to be excused, she made sure they had their jackets on and sent them outside to rake—that is, to play in—the autumn leaves.

Once Allen and Emily were engrossed in the leaf project, Mark turned to her and said, "Well, that was a nice walk. Took our minds off last night. What shall we do now?"

They became kids again themselves, first flopping down in piles of leaves with Allen and Emily and then helping bag them. The rest of the afternoon was spent watching Notre Dame football on TV and reading.

Chapter 6

After dropping the kids at the sitter's house, Mark got them over to Miller's Country House restaurant in record time. Jack and Jeri were already seated when they entered the dining room. Their favorite table was centered in an alcove facing a picture window. Outside was a placid pond and a small wooden bridge; the scene reminded her of Claude Monet's famous water gardens in Giverny. Flowers, many of which were still in full color, and green perennial leafy vegetation surrounded the pond. Red begonias were still blooming. Silvery dusty miller leaves, fading but not quite done for the season, lined a stone path leading up a grassy knoll. As daylight faded, Toni looked back at Mark and her two longtime friends. This was a perfect setting in which to de-stress.

After handshakes and hugs all around, they studied the menu and made their choices. Their server suggested the house red vintage wine would be a match for all their entrées so Mark ordered a bottle.

Mark said, "Guys, I have some disturbing news to report."

Toni pursed her lips. So much for de-stressing.

At the word "news," Mark had garnered Jack's full attention. Jack was, after all, a reporter for the *Chicago Dispatch* and, according to Mark, could sense a juicy story from a mile away. Jack leaned forward, elbows on the table, eyebrows raised.

"Last night—of course we had to skip the concert, you know that—we arrived here very late and found someone had broken into our house and filled our new jetted tub with what appeared to be blood. Actually, I am ashamed to say that I turned on the jets before I even looked in there and blood shot everywhere. We were up all night answering questions from the police."

Jeri said, "Oh, my God!" and grimaced.

Jack, on the other hand, whipped a note pad out of his blazer pocket faster than Wyatt Earp had ever drawn a gun. A pen appeared in his other hand and he peppered them with questions without even pausing for them to answer. "Blood? Police? In your house? What time?"

Jeri shushed him when the waiter arrived with the wine. He poured four glasses, placed the bottle on a silver stand near the table and departed. Only minutes later, he returned with their appetizers. All of them had chosen salads of one form or another.

When the waiter left, Jack resumed his rapid-fire questions, aiming first at Mark and then Toni. He scribbled notes in shorthand. When it was Toni's turn, she summarized, beginning with her trip up the stairs, her shock at seeing the red-smeared tub and her dropping of the wine-laden tray. From the looks on Jack's and Jeri's faces, Toni judged that neither of them could be the perpetrators of this terrible event.

"Wow!" Jack said. "That's an unbelievable story." His expression of sympathy faded. "Hey . . . this is not a joke, is it? You're not trying to pull a fast one on me, make me look like a news-hungry fool?"

"No, Jack, it's all true. Anyway, you've never needed our assistance to look foolish."

Jeri snickered.

Jack grabbed his chest with both hands as if shot by an arrow. "Ouch. That was cruel."

Mark reached over his shoulder for the wine and refilled Jack's glass first, then the others. "No hard feelings, my friend, but I'd really like to change the sub—"

"Excuse me, sir," a young waitress said. "Sir, that bottle belongs to my table here, to these people. Yours is over there, on your other side."

"Oh. Uh, I'm very sorry. You'd better get them another bottle. Put it on my bill.

The waitress looked down at her shoes and gulped. "Do you know, sir, that's a Château Clerc Milon—at $51 a bottle?"

Mark swallowed hard and gave a brief glance at Jack. Toni was sure it hurt him more to see the glee in Jack's eyes than it would to pay the $51.

"Please, just get it," Mark hissed.

The waitress brought a new bottle and placed it on the stand beside the other couple, who were so wrapped up in conversation that they never realized what had just happened.

At that moment, Jack brushed back his thick red hair, stood up with the full glass of fifty-one-dollar wine and puffed up his freckled face. He reached for a breadstick, stuck it between his lips as if it were a cigar, and said, in his best Churchillian voice, "Let us raise our glasses to this

Island, these brave people and this Empire! Cheers!" He drained half the glass.

Jeri glanced at the nearby tables and her cheeks reddened. Toni saw that patrons within earshot had their glasses in the air. Several of them said, "Hear, hear!"

Toni looked at Mark and laughed, sincerely, for the first time that day.

"What?" Mark snapped at her. "What's so funny?"

"I know you," she said. "I know you just calculated how much Jack's gulp of wine cost you."

"Arrggh!"

At that, they all had a good laugh.

Jack bowed to his audience and sat down, still gnawing on the breadstick. He smacked his lips. "Say, that Château Clerc-whatever is pretty darn good." Then he motioned them to lean forward. He gazed at each of them in turn and whispered with an exaggerated conspiratorial flair, "Pssst! I'll bet it was just a cheap Beaujolais in your bathtub. Just a bloody vino."

Toni could see Mark's features soften under the spell of his jocular friend. That was all well and good, but what about her own needs? "Jack," she said, "I know you mean well, but after last night, I could go a whole year or so without hearing the words, 'blood.' Or 'bathtub.'"

"But . . . hey, I didn't say that, I said—"

"Or any of their derivatives, tenses, synonyms or whatever. Please."

Jack put the breadstick down and said, "Okay, no more jokes, at least for a day or two. But seriously, can I write a story about this? It'll sell a lot of papers."

Mark said, "You'd better check with the police first. Try Officer Lechner from New Buffalo Police; he seemed to be the senior of the two who came to investigate."

Thankfully, their dinners arrived, effectively halting conversation for a few minutes. Jeri, bless her heart, chatted about last night's Mahler concert and other upcoming music and theater events back in Chicago. Toni vowed to plan another double date with Jack and Jeri to attend one of these. They discussed Chicago's and the state's latest political intrigues—always plentiful—until the waiter came to clear away the dinner plates. They all declined dessert.

Mark summed up their condition to the waiter. "The meal was so great and the portions so generous that we are all pleasantly stuffed."

"If we aren't having any more wine or after-dinner coffee," Toni said, "we'd better collect our children."

The four of them said their goodbyes in the parking lot.

Before Mark started the car, Toni said, "Mark, let's not go back to the house. It's all safely locked up and the alarm is set. Let's go back to Chicago."

"Great idea."

When they were halfway to Chicago, with the kids fast asleep, her guilt got the better of her. Was it because she was Catholic and wasn't supposed to tell a lie? Hell—oops, another sin—heck, if only she had chosen her words a little more carefully when Mark had asked her if she had locked up. She could have said something vague, like, "Don't worry. I locked almost all the locks." Or, "Honey, no one can get in. I locked up." That was technically, in the eyes of God, not a lie. Well it was too late.

"Uh, Mark? Honey?"

"Yes?"

"Just checking to see if you were getting sleepy."

"Nope. I'm wide awake."

"Great," she said. "Well, there's one little thing I should mention. Remember when I said the house was *all* locked up?"

He sat a little more erect and took his eyes off the road just long enough to squint at her. "Yeah?"

"Er, that wasn't 100% correct. Let's see . . ." She paused long enough to calculate. Eighteen windows, and two doors—one with the dreaded deadbolt and a separate lock-set—makes twenty-one. She rounded down for simplicity. "I locked 95% of the windows and doors."

She noticed his sharp intake of breath and the tightening of his hands on the steering wheel. Then he exhaled and smiled at her.

"Wow, Toni, you have missed your calling. You should have been an attorney. You sure know how to equivocate and seem to be an expert at splitting hairs."

"Honey, I am so glad you are being a good sport about—"

"What did you forget, Mrs. Harrington, Chief Equivocator?"

"Well you know the deadbolt on the front door? I couldn't lock that one because, ah, I seem to have misplaced my Union Pier key. It's not on my key ring anymore."

Mark was silent for several seconds. At least he wasn't huffing and puffing, swearing or trying to strangle the steering wheel with white-knuckled hands.

He said, "Toni, this is not good. I'm sure you know that same key unlocks every door in the house. And talk about bad timing! Really, think about it. Someone has dumped blood in our hot tub. The security light is broken. And now you tell me that your key is missing? When's the last time you used it?"

"Probably during our last visit, over a week ago."

"Hmm. Not much we can do about it now. Maybe it will turn up at home or in your office."

After a few more miles of driving in silence, Mark said, "Toni?"

"Yes?"

"Don't worry about the missing key. Don't let it ruin today, which was so much of an improvement over yesterday. Today seemed almost normal, don't you think?"

"Mark, I don't think we'll have a normal day until this mystery is solved."

Chapter 7

Rhonda Shain forced herself into a sitting position after she had silenced the second snooze alarm. It took a moment for the dizziness to subside. God, how she hated Mondays. Maybe she should call in sick. No, that wouldn't do; she was out of sick leave. She swore to never drink rum and Coke again, but there had been nothing else left in the house. She had drained the bottle of good wine Friday in a futile effort to dull the pain of being stood up. How dare he! She cursed herself for choosing to date PJ instead of accepting Ed Page's offer of Friday night dinner at his place. Both of them met her most important criteria: being rich. But PJ was just a smidgen more polished and seemed to have a better body.

Page looked even richer than PJ, if you could judge a man by the flashy gold chains around his neck, his fat wallet and a giant Rolex watch. Oh, yeah, and his car, a Lincoln, was more like a limo than a normal car. He wasn't a bad looker if you didn't mind his paunch. That was from too many free lunches from his constituents over in Chicago and maybe too many martinis. The fact that he was a middle-aged black man and she was a blond white woman in her twenties didn't bother her at all.

However, Ed Page was now on her shit list for refusing to finance her divorce. She had gladly accepted his invitation to lunch at the Red Arrow Café on Friday. Of course, he had wanted her as dessert but she had begged off with a lie. When she dropped the hint that maybe she'd be more available to him if he financed her legal fees, he'd gotten very evasive. He had given her $200 to "go buy something cute to wear; it will take your mind off your problems." Whatever. Screw him. She had taken the money, but would not give up on getting Page to pay for her divorce.

PJ, however, was fresh meat to her. She had met him at a 4th of July party last summer given by her landlords, Mark and Toni. He seemed to be in business with one or both of them. He was alone and had stared at her for half an hour before coming over to introduce himself. Within ten minutes, he had propositioned her, promising a wild weekend either here or in Chicago. But back then, her husband had still been around and she couldn't get away.

So, when PJ had called her at work Friday morning and suggested they get together for dinner and "whatever" that night, she had been ready, especially for the "whatever." She had left work early to prepare. By 7:00 p.m. she had her hair and makeup just right, had wiggled into her tightest and lowest-cut dress and had her high heels waiting for her at the front door. The bastard never showed! Called with some lame excuse about being stuck in a sales meeting in Detroit. PJ was now tied with Page for top ranking on her shit list.

Rhonda groaned. It was time to get moving. She had a piece of toast to settle her stomach and washed it down with Coke. She went into the bathroom, washed her face and pulled on one of her conservative sweater and skirt outfits. After applying a touch more makeup than normal to negate the ravages of a long lonely weekend, she grabbed her purse and walked out her back door. She heard a noise from the hedges and then footsteps. Someone was running toward her—fast.

Her first reaction was to reach into her purse for the can of Mace she always carried. When she looked up, she relaxed her grip on the spray can. It was Bernie, another one of her previous conquests. Although good in bed and fun to talk to, she couldn't get serious about him. He didn't meet the "rich" criteria.

He seemed to be running away from something. God, she hoped he hadn't cut off his hand or whatever doing the new floor in his aunt's house. He had all sorts of power tools over there.

He slid to a stop about ten feet from her, panting. His face was shiny with sweat. Once he caught his breath, he cried out, "Rhonda! Rhonda! Come quick!"

"What is it, Bernie?"

"Page's dead! He's dead! He's dead in our house!" He turned and started back for his aunt's house.

"Page? Page dead?" Rhonda hurried after Bernard. By the time she climbed the four steps to the porch, Bernie was standing on a piece of plywood nailed down over the big beams that supported the flooring. He pointed to an opening between two of the exposed beams.

"Look," he said.

She walked carefully up to the edge and looked down into the crawl space. There, between two thick beams, lay Ed Page, face up, partially wrapped in a big green canvas thing. His face was kind of shriveled. There was dried blood on the side of his face. Flies buzzed on and off his head and neck. Any doubt about his status was erased by the stench. He was very, very dead.

"The door wasn't locked," Bernie said. "I must have forgotten when I left Friday."

Rhonda spotted the Rolex on Page's wrist. This was an opportunity, if she could just overcome the grossness of the situation. Page won't need it, so why not? "Bernie," she said, "get the watch."

"Not me, baby. I ain't touching no dead body."

"You fool!" she yelled. "Page told me himself that watch cost $10,000."

"I don't care if it cost ten million. I ain't touching no dead body."

"Damn you, you silly bastard! I'll get it myself." She knelt down, reached Page's sleeve and pulled his arm up. Gingerly, she slid her fingers beneath the blood-caked wrist and pulled the Rolex over his big hand. She briefly considered the diamond-studded gold pinky ring, but Page's finger was too badly swollen to allow easy removal. "Wow, Bernie, he's cold. Now, help me roll him over."

"Uh, uh," he argued.

"Come on, help me. He's got a wallet stuffed with hundred-dollar bills, or at least he did on Friday. Why let the cops find it?"

Bernie looked around the room. He grabbed a two-by-four about six feet long and levered Page's torso over to expose his back pocket. "I still ain't touching this man."

Rhonda's hand was shaking, but she took a deep breath, reached into the pocket and slid out the wallet.

"We are rich!" Rhonda yelled in triumph after she looked into the wallet. "We're rich!" She found the snaps on the gold neck chains and unfastened them. "He won't need these." She stood up and put the watch, wallet and chains in her purse. When she turned to Bernie, she noticed his mouth was hanging open; he glared at her with wide open eyes.

He said, "Damn, girl, I always thought females, especially white girls, were fragile. But you're something else again. I say, even if we're rich, we're in big trouble. They'll hang it on me. Young and black. That's what happens. I'll have a terrible time. I don't even know where I was most of this weekend."

"What?"

"I got drunk Friday night after working on the house. Woke up in the van way out north by that bed and breakfast. It's a long story. Now this!" He pointed down at the crawlspace. "What are we gonna do?"

"Let's get back to my place and think this over," Rhonda said.

They hurried back to her house. Rhonda locked the door and told Bernie to sit down at her kitchen table. She put her purse on the table, pulled out Page's wallet and counted the cash.

"He only keeps hundreds in his billfold; there's forty-seven of them," she said. "I've never seen this much money. How about you, Bernie?

He shook his head.

"He must have smaller bills in his pocket," she said, hoping Bernie would volunteer to go back and take a look.

"I don't care what he's got. He can keep it. Not me."

"We'll let it go," she agreed. "I've got to get to work. I'll put all this in the trunk of my car."

"What about me?" Bernie said. "What'll I do?"

"You can't stay here."

"Where can I go? What can I do?" Bernie said, slumping in his chair. I can't go back to work on the house . . . unless I dump the body somewhere. No way I can handle that body or any dead body. Rhonda, help me. Don't leave me. I'm here alone."

"I've got to leave; I'm already late and can't afford any hassles at work. Don't be such a baby. Why don't you call your Aunt Ruth? Tell her, but leave me out of it." She stood up and picked up her purse. Let's get out of here, right now. I'll call you later."

Chapter 8

Detective Sergeant Bruce Markowski draped his sport coat over the chair back and rolled up the sleeves of his dress shirt. He tucked his tie into his shirt so it wouldn't get drenched with all the delicious drippings from his John Wayne Burger. He picked it up, not an easy task with the double meat patties, grilled onions, alternate layers of melted cheddar and swiss cheese, a tomato slice, and Norma's signature sauce. As he opened his mouth wide and brought the burger toward his mouth, his pager buzzed.

He ignored it and took the first delicious bite. And then a second, followed by two giant, heavily salted Heart Attack French Fries, a Norma's specialty. Art Wingo, the owner, had so far declined to tell him how those fries had acquired their name. However, using some police resources, Markowski had looked up the history of 911 calls from this address and gotten only two hits. One of them was a medical emergency two years ago, a heart attack. The patient's name was Art Wingo. He would leave it up to Art to tell him the story someday.

He washed all this great-tasting food down with a long sip of orange pop, during which his pager buzzed again. What were the chances it was for an actual crime, especially in his specialty? There hadn't been a murder up here in more than a year. He put the cup down and pushed the button on the pager. Cripes! He pushed back from the table and went to the counter.

"Art!" he called out to the owner. "I've got to use your phone. Police emergency. Can you box up my lunch, please?"

*   *   *

He used the gumball light and siren to get up to Union Pier in a hurry. Two Chikaming Township patrol cars, lights still flashing, were parked in front. He parked behind them and shut off his car, including the bells and whistles. The Chikaming cars were attracting enough attention. An officer he recognized was waiting for him. What was her name, though? He got out of the car and grabbed his crime scene bag from the trunk. As he approached her, he had his badge in hand in case she didn't remember him.

"No need, Detective. I recognize you. This way, please. Watch your step; this is some kind of a construction site."

Before she turned away, he got a glimpse of her name tag. Nelson. About two years on the force, if his memory was correct. She stopped at the bottom of the porch steps and waited while he gloved up and covered his shoes.

"I'll wait out here," she said. "Oh, one more thing. You might want to wear a mask. They tell me the stench is pretty bad."

"Great. Thanks." He rummaged in the bag for a mask.

Inside, he flashed his badge at three officers, all of whom he hadn't met. They repeated Nelson's warning about the site. Two-thirds of the wood floor and sub-flooring was gone, leaving exposed floor joists and a two-foot or so deep crawlspace. Below two of the joists rested a very large, apparently lifeless body lying on a green tarp. Markowski knelt down for a closer inspection and discovered that the green thing was actually a canvas tent. He studied the corpse for several seconds trying to read a facial expression, to let the poor guy communicate with him, help him solve the murder. Definitely a murder. His head had been bashed in from behind and there was a large patch of coagulated blood on his chest. Gunshot wound or a knife? He'd let the medical examiner figure that out. Getting no messages from the victim, he stood up.

"Sorry to begin with such an obvious question, but has anyone checked for vitals?"

"Yes sir," said one of the officers, Thomas, who seemed to be in charge. "No pulse. You've seen the wounds. He's been dead a long time."

"Medical examiner's on the way," a second officer said. "We didn't see the need for an ambulance."

Thomas said, "If you don't mind, Sergeant, I'd like to send these two back outside. I'll remain with you to answer any questions."

Markowski smiled but realized no one could see that due to the mask. "Sure, get some fresh air." They hurried out the front door, which was still wide open. He pulled out his notebook, walked around and made some notes and sketches. As with most construction sites, it was chaotic; sawdust littered the floor. Power tools and boxes of nails and screws rested on a makeshift table of plywood over sawhorses. Wood scraps lay everywhere. In short, this scene was a nightmare for evidence collection. Speaking of evidence—damn, he should have done this already—he asked

Thomas, "Can you get one of your guys to radio the State Police and get the Grand Rapids forensics team over here right away?" His local crime scene technicians were on the way, but he was going to need help from the big boys over in Grand Rapids—about an hour and a half away.

While Thomas stepped away to do that, Markowski squatted down to get another close look at the body. He had to kneel to reach it. Gripping the left sleeve, he carefully lifted an arm. It moved freely. That, in addition to the putrid smell, told him that rigor mortis had come and gone. This guy had been dead for at least 48 hours. As he lowered the arm, he noticed a fancy-looking gold ring on the victim's little finger. A diamond at least one carat in size was mounted at the top; smaller diamonds were mounted lower, but swelling had obscured that part of the ring. He pushed himself up and walked slowly toward the rear of the room, which had a wide arch leading to the kitchen and back door. The floor was still intact in this section and there were signs of recent activity here.

"Hey, Officer Thomas!" When Thomas came back into the house, Markowski asked, "Did any of you walk around back here?"

"No sir. We came in the front door and went no further back than where the body is."

The floor was trying to tell him a story. He saw footprints in the sawdust and evidence of sweeping or, perhaps, something being dragged from the back door to the living room. Why would someone sweep only this narrow section? He would ask forensics to pay close attention to this area.

He said to Thomas, "After the medical examiner confirms the death, can you make sure no one comes in here until the Grand Rapids forensics team has done its thing?"

After Thomas agreed to that, Markowski said, "Let's go outside. I'd like to jot down some details." Thomas suggested they sit in his cruiser, as the engine was still running and the heater was on.

Once inside the cruiser, Markowski said, "Tell me what you know so far. Start when you first got the call."

Thomas was pretty good at summarizing. At 10:46 a.m. he and Nelson, his partner, had responded to the call. A lady had reported a dead body. When they arrived, they saw two agitated people outside the house.

"The lady who called it in showed us the body," he said. "She owns the house. A younger guy, her nephew, had discovered the body when he arrived to do some remodeling work at 8:30 a.m. but, instead of calling 911, he called his aunt in Chicago."

"Say that again?"

Thomas said, "Yeah, I thought that was a little strange too. A guy finds a dead body but calls his aunt an hour and a half away. Anyway, I called for backup to preserve the crime scene. No one touched anything except for me, when I checked the victim for vitals."

"Okay. So, where are these two people right now?" Markowski asked.

"They're out in back in the nephew's van." Thomas consulted his clipboard notes. "Mrs. Ruth Smith. Black lady about fifty years old. The nephew's Bernard Smith, black male in his mid-twenties. By the way, they both seem to know the victim."

Markowski raised an eyebrow. "Why don't you take me back there and introduce me? When you get the rest of your notes written up, can you fax them to me?"

After stopping at his car to get two bottles of water, he walked with Thomas around the outside of the house and found the van empty. Its occupants were now seated at a picnic bench in the back yard. The sun had popped out from behind a cloud bank and warmed up the yard enough to make it tolerable, in fact almost pleasant, to sit outside. Thomas introduced them and went off to manage the arrival of the crime scene team. Markowski considered his options. Interviewing them inside the unheated house, with a dead body not quite removed yet, was out of the question. It was either here or at his office down in New Buffalo.

Ruth Smith was a tall woman with broad shoulders and thick arms. Her skin was very dark and her curly hair cropped and styled. Her dark blue suit, tailored white shirt, conservative jewelry and dark blue pumps led him to believe that she was a professional person, one who might have a leadership role. Bernard Smith was also tall but thin and dressed in a wool shirt with frayed cuffs and thick tan work pants, the kind with pockets and loops everywhere.

He introduced himself and said, "Mrs. Smith, Mr. Smith, I appreciate your patience. This must be a terrible shock to you." He watched for any reaction. Bernard fidgeted with his hands and wouldn't meet his eyes.

Mrs. Smith put her hands to her chest and said, "I about had a stroke when I saw him there; I know him, you see. We both do. But for the life of me, I can't figure out why he would be in my house, alive or dead."

"Would you each like some water?"

They both eagerly accepted and said thank you.

"I'd like to ask some questions, but we don't really have a good place for that except right here or down at Headquarters in New Buffalo. Are you comfortable answering a few questions here?"

Mrs. Smith looked at Bernard, who shrugged. She said, "Let's do it here."

"Okay, thanks. I'd like to interview each of you separately, beginning with Bernard. I understand it was he who first discovered the body. Is that correct?"

"Yes, sir," Bernard said.

"Mrs. Smith, may I suggest you wait in the van while I ask Bernard a few questions?" She agreed and said she didn't need any help getting over there. Markowski stood when she left, not an easy task when rising from a picnic bench.

He sat down and said, "Okay, Bernard. First, may I see your ID?" He copied down the information. "Now, tell me exactly what you saw."

Markowski let Bernard tell the whole story without interruption. He watched Bernard's eyes for "tells" and saw one or two indications of either reluctance or outright lying. He jotted down some notes about these. When Bernard reached the end of his story, Markowski said, "Thank you, Bernard. I'll have all this typed up into a statement, which you'll have to sign at the State Troopers' post down in New Buffalo. Do you think you could make it down there later today?"

"Uh, sure, I guess so. I'll be passing that way on my way home to Chicago. Won't be no more work to do here for a while, I guess. Does that mean you're done with me?"

"Yes, I think so."

Bernard exhaled, stood up quickly and said, "Do you want me to go get Aunt Ruth?"

"Yes, please." Just as Bernard turned to walk away, Markowski said, "Bernard, one more thing." The young man stopped and turned around to face him. "Why did you call your aunt first? She's all the way over in Chicago. Why not call the police?"

This time Bernard looked at him directly. "Detective, I'll be honest with you. I have a record, back in Chicago. Minor stuff, some theft, some fighting, but I know you'll check on me and you'll find it. Growing up in the projects, people like me—young black males—we don't want nothin' to do with the police. No offense. It just the way it is."

That seemed sincere enough. Markowski slipped in one last question. "Before you go, I'm curious about something. You said the body was cold. But you also said you didn't touch him. How did you know it was cold?" He watched the eyes again, which darted up and stayed there for just long enough for Markowski to know. Bernard was stalling for time—time to think up a lie.

"Well . . . man, he just looked like it. Like cold, I mean. It *was* cold in there."

"Okay, Bernard." He reached out and offered a handshake. "Thank you again. Now, please go get your aunt. Don't forget your water."

He felt a little sorry to put Mrs. Smith through the same routine of producing I.D. and telling her side of the story, getting the call and rushing over from Chicago to see Edwin Page dead beneath her floor. He made a few notes and, as he had done with Bernard, asked her to sign a statement later that day. "Finally, I just need a little more information on how you know the victim."

Mrs. Smith said, "Ed Page is a Chicago City Councilman who is involved in the budget process. He's also the Health Committee Chairman. I'm the Director of Public Health Nurses for the city of Chicago. Several times in the last few months, I have testified before the Council, pleading for more nurses in the projects. That requires money, which I am sorry to say, the City Council has not yet seen fit to provide."

"I see. And whose side was Page on?"

Mrs. Smith huffed once and said, "Not mine. There was always some other project that had grabbed his attention; in fact, it was a software company, Simplified Data something-or-other, that was his pet project. He pushed that and ignored my needs."

"Is there anything else you think I should know?"

"Actually, yes." She hesitated. Her chest rose and fell once, then twice more. She opened her mouth to speak but stopped.

Markowski waited, observed and speculated. Was she making up a story or was this something more innocent?

She filled her lungs once more, apparently having decided to tell a story that, by the way she grimaced and gritted her teeth, was unpleasant. "You saw the house, right? It's a mess inside. The new flooring is buckled; it was installed wrong. The new plumbing leaks. New doors don't fit right."

"Yes, I noticed," Markowski said.

"Well, it was Page's brother who did all that shoddy work; Ed Page was the one who convinced me to hire him. And the straw that broke the camel's back? According to my nephew, it seems I've been charged for lots of materials that never showed up. So I fired Page's brother and refused to pay a $9,000 bill for all that bad work and missing material. I know it looks bad as all get-out to say this, but it's the truth. Right now, I hate Ed Page. But I wouldn't kill him.

"The sad thing is, Page and I grew up in the same neighborhood, right there in the Chicago projects. He's older than I by several years, so as a middle school girl I used to, you know, admire him shooting baskets at Marillac House. That's sort of a hangout place for the local youth. But, now that I think of it, he probably didn't know I existed back then. God, that was a long time ago."

Markowski thanked Mrs. Smith and told her she and Bernard were free to go. He went back into the house to talk to forensics and the medical examiner. Out in front, in addition to the medical examiner's vehicle, multiple patrol cars and the New Buffalo crime scene van, there were two TV news vans, satellite antennas already up into position. It was shaping up to be a real circus. He found Officer Thomas and asked him to call in more officers for crowd control.

The medical examiner said the apparent cause of death was one of two things, either a stab wound to the chest or a blow to the back of the head. An autopsy would help her decide which one was primary. Her initial estimate of time of death was between 48 and 72 hours ago. She promised a speedy autopsy. He gave her permission to remove the body.

Bob Rookey, the local crime scene guy, reported that the victim's wallet was apparently missing. A back pocket was stretched and showed an impression of a fat billfold but the pocket was empty. The victim's left wrist had indentations from a metal watchband but no watch. Rookey had also noticed the solid gold, diamond-studded ring on the left pinky finger. Three twenties and four five-dollar bills had been found in the right front pocket of his pants. They also had recovered fibers from the back porch steps that appeared to match the green tent. More of these fibers, several footprints and some dark spots—possibly dried blood—had been discovered on the floor between the back door and the living room.

Mention of footprints gave Markowski an idea. "Bob, is there anything useable outside? Any drag marks? Footprints?"

"Nope. Makes me think that the body was placed here before Friday night's gully-washer of a rainstorm. That would've erased any good evidence."

"How can you be sure he wasn't killed right here in the house?"

Rookey said, "Oh, that's possible, but not very likely. Those wounds caused a lot of bleeding but I found no evidence of massive bleeding inside the house. Plus, there's the fibers on the back porch. My best guess is that the victim had already bled out before he was carried or dragged inside."

"About those inside footprints, did you get any useable pictures of them?"

"Yes. Looks like three people, very recent, probably from the people who discovered the body."

"Okay. Send me a full report ASAP. And thanks for the good work; please thank the rest of your team for me. Can you wait for the Crime Lab guys from Grand Rapids and give them a full briefing?" As Rookey walked away, he jotted down a note about *three* sets of footprints, underlined that with double lines and added a question mark. As far as he knew, there had only been two people in this house since the body had been deposited. He added one final note: *Why didn't they take the pinky ring?*

As was his custom, Markowski inspected the scene, inside and out, one more time before departing. Bernard was right; it was darned cold in the house, especially with both doors open. That reminded him of an important question which he had forgotten to ask Bernard. How did the body get into the house? Wasn't it locked? He made a note to ask Bernard about this later.

He left the back porch, heading for the picnic table, but stopped to survey the neighbors' houses. There wasn't a house on the north side, just a small city mini-park on the corner lot. To the south, there was a nice-looking house with a mother-in-law cottage on the same lot. He'd go around to the front and knock on those doors in a minute or two, after he wrote down a quick summary of his findings so far.

He sat at the picnic table and flipped open his notebook. It always helped him to do this while he was still at the crime scene, with observations still fresh in his mind. After scanning the notes and diagrams, he wrote a summary. He listed only the raw facts. *A body in the crawlspace. Two wounds. Estimated time of death: 48-72 hours ago (between noon Friday and noon Saturday). No murder weapon or weapons found. Reported by Ruth Smith. Bernard Smith states he found body at 0830. Call to 911 at 1045 by Ruth Smith. Forensics states it is likely the body was carried or dragged into house through back door. Some valuables apparently stolen. Awaiting coroner and State forensics for more analysis.* That was it for the facts.

It was too early for speculation, but something had just popped into his mind and he had to make a note of it before it was OBE'd. Using that term brought back memories of his rookie year as a trooper, when his partner, a man very senior to him, had used it. When he had asked, his partner had growled at him, "OBE'd, stupid! 'Overcome By Events.'"

Everybody knows that." Markowski had not heard it since, unless he was the one using it. But, in a profession filled with acronyms and three-letter abbreviations, it seemed quite useful.

Now, what was it that he had wanted to write down? He should have done that right away before he had gotten lost in memories. Oh yeah—the diamond-studded pinky ring. Why wouldn't a thief take that, along with the Rolex, wallet and gold chains? One possibility was that the perpetrator just panicked and ran. However, that theory didn't hold water since other items had been stolen, apparently by a person calm enough to remove the other stuff from a dead man's body. No, a more likely scenario was that the theft had occurred well after the murder, when the finger was swollen due to bloating. It would have taken a lot of balls to force a ring off that finger. On the page in his notes describing the pinky ring, he squeezed a note into the margin: *Victim robbed after bloating began? 48 hours plus?*

What was the next step? Knock on the neighbors' doors. He walked over to the main house and found no one at home. It was the same with the mother-in-law cottage in back. Markowski jotted down the addresses and resigned himself to look up their contact information back at his office. He really wanted to talk to them before the day was over. During the drive back to the post, he prioritized his next steps. First on the list was to learn more about the victim and the Smiths.

Chapter 9

The microwave dinged. Sergeant Markowski pushed the button to open the door and pulled out his partially-eaten John Wayne Burger and the rest of his fries. Regrettably, the almost full cup of orange pop had been diluted by melted ice. He drained the stuff into the sink and tossed the empty cup, lid and straw into the garbage can. After pouring himself some black coffee of undetermined vintage, he carried the mug and the Norma's bag down the hall to his office.

Alice Britt, an experienced trooper but new to the New Buffalo post, was approaching from the opposite direction. She pointed at the bag and said, "Ooh, I've heard of that place. Is it any good?"

"To die for," he said.

"Hah. No pun intended, I'm sure. Heard you caught a case."

"Yup."

"Well, I've got nothing on my plate at the moment, so if you need anything, let me know."

"Thanks. I will."

Once in his office, he took off his sport coat and made short work of the burger and fries. He removed the evidence—greasy wrappings and the bag itself—during a trip to wash his hands. That way the burger/French fry aroma, delicious as it was, wouldn't distract the Smiths, who were due in one hour. He used half of that time to do an online search for Edwin Page, Ruth Smith and Bernard. He read through a short biography of Mrs. Smith on the Chicago Health Department web site, a medium-sized rap sheet on Bernard—petty theft, but no history of violent crime—and great number of links and news articles about Chicago City Councilman Edwin I. Page.

One item on Page's results caught his attention. Page owned a house in Union Pier! Why hadn't he thought of this already? The address was just a few blocks up the beach from Mrs. Smith's place. He needed to get over there right away, but he didn't want to postpone the Smiths' appointment.

He picked up the phone and dialed Britt's extension. She answered on the first ring. "Trooper Britt, are you still available to help out—right now?"

She agreed to run up to Page's house, secure the site, and look around. He reminded her to coordinate with the Chikaming Police. He'd meet her there with a search warrant as soon as he was done with the Smiths.

With that crisis under control, Markowski returned to the search results for Page and discovered a police report from last year that described a fatal crash involving Page's vehicle. A teen-aged friend of Page's son had been behind the wheel; the son had been a passenger. The lone occupant of the other car, a Union Pier resident, had been killed. Excessive speed and driver inattention by the teen had been the cause. Page himself had not been in the car; he had not given the kids permission to use the car, a Lincoln. He printed out a report on this and all his other research, pulled out a fresh file folder and slipped everything inside. With a black marker, he wrote, "Page Murder" on the tab and set the thin folder on the desk. How much thicker would it get before this thing was solved?

Markowski pulled out his notebook, flipped it open and turned to a new page. He wrote down a few questions in random order. *Where did the murder occur? Where is/are the murder weapon/s? Who had a motive? What was Page doing in that house? Who was the last person to see him alive?"*

His pen was poised to write down more questions when a secretary knocked on his door and said, "Detective, your four o'clock appointment is here."

"Thanks," he said. "I'll come out and greet them. Do you have the statements typed up yet?"

"Yes, they're on my desk. I'll get them."

He decided there would be no harm in bringing both of them into his office at the same time. Once they were seated in front of his desk, he thanked them for coming and handed the typewritten statements to them. "Please read these and, if they are correct, sign them and we'll be done."

Ruth finished first, signed hers and handed it to him. Bernard reached for a pen.

"Oh, wait, Bernard," Markowski said, "don't sign yet. I forgot to ask you a couple important questions earlier." He paused to assess Bernard's reaction to the possibility of new questions but saw nothing significant. "When is the last time you were in the house before you discovered the body?"

"That would be about 5:00 p.m. Friday, when I closed up work for the day."

"Okay thanks," Markowski said. "Now, when you arrived at the house today, did you enter from the front door or the back?"

"The back. I always park my van in back."

"This next question is important, Bernard. When you got there today, was the door open or closed? Locked or unlocked?"

Bernard said, "Sh . . . shoot." He rubbed the back of his neck. "I knew you'd ask this! The door was open about a foot or so. Honestly, sir, I can't remember about—I can't say for sure if I locked it or even closed it before I left on Friday."

"That's fine, Bernard. No problem." Markowski made some notes on this and had the secretary type up a revised statement with the new information. Bernard read that, nodded and signed it.

"Thank you both so much for your cooperation. I am sorry this terrible thing has happened in your house. But I hope you understand that the house is now a crime scene and you won't be able to get back in there for a day or two. Mrs. Smith, I'll call you the moment we can release it back to you." He handed both of them a business card. "Please call me if you have anything else to help me solve this—anything at all."

He gave them a decent interval to depart, then hurried out to his car and drove to Page's Union Pier house, which was about a half-mile north of the crime scene. It was a big one, on the higher-income side of Lakeshore Road, prime beach front property. It was set back from the street by a long, narrow driveway lined with maple trees which had just lost their leaves. Two stories were visible at street level and a lower third level jutted out over the high-bank waterfront slope. Alice's patrol car was parked behind one from the Chikaming Township Police. He peeked into the decorative windows of the garage and saw a large white Lincoln Continental. Markowski got his evidence kit out of the trunk and walked over to introduce himself to the Chikaming officer.

The officer said, "The other trooper walked around to the waterfront side of the house. She's already rung the bell. No one seems to be home."

Trooper Britt appeared from the south side of the house and met him at the front door. "The front door is unlocked but I didn't go in."

"Have you seen any security cameras?"

"Nope," she said.

They both put on booties. Markowski added gloves; Britt already had her gloves on. He opened the door and walked in. No alarm sounded. She pointed to an alarm control panel just inside the door. It had a green light, indicating it was disarmed. "What does a disarmed alarm indicate to you, Trooper Britt?"

"Well, either Page left here thinking he'd be back soon, or someone else has been here to disarm it."

"Let's work together to clear the house, " he said. "Then we'll take a closer look at things."

Five minutes later they returned to the entrance; the house was empty. A spacious living room and large kitchen dominated the first floor. Floor-to-ceiling picture windows on the northwest side offered a commanding view of the majestic beach below and Lake Michigan. An ornate walnut buffet crowned with a gold embossed mirror rested against the wall adjacent to the windows. It held a variety of decanters and bottles of many colors. A massive sterling silver tray stood in the middle bearing half a dozen cut glass brandy snifters. Beside the buffet stood a wine rack holding twenty or thirty vintage wines. Above all this a painting of the New Buffalo marina at dusk, signed by a local artist

"Looks like he might throw a few parties," Markowski said. "I suppose it goes with the job." He looked for signs of recent activity and found none; there were no half-full beverage glasses that might yield a convenient set of fingerprints.

He watched with approval as Britt walked into the large open kitchen and inspected the cabinets—custom-made beauties with walnut-rimmed clear glass doors. She opened all the drawers and peeked into the high-end stainless steel appliances. She would make an excellent detective someday if she chose that career path.

"I don't see anything significant here," she said. "No dirty dishes in the sink. Clean dishes in the dishwasher. The refrigerator and freezer are tidy."

Markowski walked over to the door he had already opened during the sweep. "Let's try the garage."

Everything out there was neat and tidy. He reached into his pocket and pulled out a small evidence bag containing Page's car keys. He walked over to the Lincoln and tried the passenger door. It was unlocked. He handed the keys to Britt and said, "Why don't you check the trunk while I look inside?"

While inspecting the car's interior, Markowski speculated on how Page had gotten from here to wherever he had been murdered. This location was less than a mile north of Ruth Smith's house. He could have been out on a walk. Someone could have driven him. Or, could he have been murdered here and the body dumped a mile away? That seemed unlikely. He found nothing of help inside the car.

He found the lever to unlatch the hood and, after a brief look at the engine compartment, closed it.

"Nothing in the trunk but two snow tires," Trooper Britt said.

They went back into the house and up to the second floor. They saw nothing of interest in the first bedroom, which was on the east side of the house next to a bathroom. It was furnished and decorated in a style befitting a teen-aged boy but, judging by its neatness, hadn't been occupied recently. He made himself a note to find out where Page's son lived. Across the hall were an office and the master bedroom, both of which faced west and overlooked the lake. In the office, Trooper Britt made quick work of checking the drawers of a walnut roll-top desk but didn't seem to find anything useful. Two nicely-framed pictures stood on a side table. One showed Page and the mayor of Chicago. The other showed Page with President Jimmy Carter. There were no pictures of his family.

On a separate small table was a computer and keyboard with a printer on the lower shelf. Markowski didn't bother to boot up the computer; he made a note to send a tech guy out to explore the files on it. He stopped to admire another piece of local art, this one an oil painting depicting the sandy slopes of Warren Dunes on a blustery winter day. Britt had moved on to the master bedroom.

"Detective, you've got to see this!" Britt called to him.

He hurried over to find Britt standing at the foot of an ornate mahogany four-poster bed. Her back was to him; she was staring out a large picture window.

"Get a load of this view!" she said. "Imagine waking up to this every morning."

For a moment there, Markowski had thought she had found some important evidence but alas, her animated voice had been a reaction to the awesome view. He had to admit the shoreline and lake looked pretty spectacular from this second-story vantage point. With the sun unimpeded by clouds and low in the sky, its red reflections on the silver waves were hypnotic. The few puffy clouds hovering just above the sun had turned bright pink. He gave Britt a few more seconds to savor the picture.

"Wow," she said. "To think this is the view that he woke up to every morning and saw every night before bed. What a great room to observe the lake and its changing moods. I grew up on the shore just north of here, just outside of Bridgman, so I know the lake can be temperamental. Those waves, now lapping quietly against the beach, can change in a heartbeat from gentle caresses to angry roaring blows, attacking the sand, washing away big sections."

"That was pretty poetic," Markowski said, "and also a good analogy to the human behavior that keeps me in business. I've seen a lot of cases where gentle caresses changed into angry blows in a heartbeat."

"Are you thinking Page was killed during a lover's quarrel?"

"There's no evidence of that, but it wouldn't surprise me." He said, "Why don't you check out the closet and the bathroom while I look around in here?" As Britt disappeared into the large walk-in closet, he began pulling open the drawers of a dresser and found nothing but high-end clothes. Next was the bedside table. When he opened the top drawer and bent down to look inside, he said, "Finally!"

"Finally, what?" Britt said.

He jerked upright and looked back at her. She had padded up behind him on the soft carpet.

"Sorry, I didn't mean to startle you," she said.

He reached into the drawer and pulled out a thick stack of cash. "Finally, we might have our first clue." He handed the cash to Britt. "Bag that please." He reached back into the drawer, pulled out a small piece of paper, and examined it. "Not the cash so much, but this. It's a restaurant receipt from the Red Arrow Café, date-stamped October 13th at 12:45 p.m."

Markowski pulled out his notebook, copied down some details from the receipt and handed it to her. "Bag this too, please." While she did that, he resumed his search of the bedroom and found nothing else to help the investigation. He and Britt canvassed the rest of the house and the outside gardens. No more clues jumped out at them.

Once back at the post Markowski signed the evidence tags, with Trooper Britt as the witness, and had her put the cash and the restaurant receipt into the evidence locker. He got comfortable in his office and logged on to the State Police search network. While that was loading, he called the Red Arrow Café, identified himself and asked for the manager.

"Hello, this is Tina. How can I help you?"

He identified himself again and said, "Tina, before I continue, can you go to a room where you have privacy?"

"I'm in my office, alone. Just a minute . . . I've closed the door. Go ahead."

"I am investigating a crime which involves someone who may have dined at your restaurant on Friday. The server's name on the receipt is Maria. Would that person be there today and, if so, may I speak to her?"

"Wow! Does this have anything to do with the Edwin Page murder? He was here on Friday!"

It was a good thing this lady was in her office. If she had shouted that loud in the main restaurant, the news would have been all over town within minutes. "I'm not at liberty to say, ma'am."

"Oh, I see. Well, yes, Maria is here. Shall I go get her?"

"Yes, and Tina, please keep all this to yourself. Confidential police business, you know."

When Maria picked up the phone, Markowski repeated his introduction and the warning about secrecy. "Maria, I have a receipt from Friday at 12:45 p.m. You were the server. Would you by any chance remember who that was?"

"Friday was busy. What did they order? That's usually how I remember people."

Markowski looked at his notes. "One grilled sirloin steak with mashed potatoes and peas. One club sandwich with potato salad. Two white—"

"Got it! Two white wines, right? That's an easy one. It was Ed Page. He's one of our best customers and a really big tipper. He's some kind of big shot from Chicago, I think . . . oh my God! He's the one! The one that got murdered, right?"

"I can't comment on my investigation but, since it's been all over the news, it would be foolish to deny that he's been murdered. Please remember, it's really important to me that you tell no one about our conversation." He made her promise to do that.

"Now," he said, "there were two meals on the receipt. Can you describe the other person?"

"I can do better than that. It was Rhonda. I don't know her last name, but I see her around town. We played pool one night at The Rogue Wave; you know, that bar down near the marina in New Buffalo."

He made some notes. It was a piece of luck to get info on the other person, even if it was just a first name.

"Go ahead and describe her, please."

"She likes to think she is what you men—no offense—call 'hot.' About my age, mid-twenties. Blond. Big boobs—excuse my language. Great body. Dresses to kill . . . well that was a stupid thing to say, but you know what I mean."

"Do you know what kind of car she drives?"

"Yeah. It's a red Camaro. A magnet for guys. Again, no offense intended."

"Maria, do you remember anything about how they acted or what they talked about during lunch?"

"Lemme think. Only this one thing. They held hands for a while before I served the meal. I saw Rhonda kind of fondling his giant gold watch, gold neck chains and his big old ring. Oh, yeah, one more thing. He left before she did and when he stood up, he handed her two 100-dollar bills. I was close enough to see that and I almost bumped into someone with my tray while I was, er, staring at the cash."

"Thank you so much, Maria. I will have to get this all down in a written statement and bring it over for you to sign. Will you be there tomorrow, say about 4:00 p.m.?" When she said yes, he asked her to get Tina back on the line.

"Tina, do you guys have security cameras?"

"Yes, one overlooks the cashier's area and one's out in the parking lot."

Markowski thanked her, made her promise to preserve the tapes from Friday and said good bye. He swiveled his chair to face the computer monitor and searched for information on the people who occupied the two houses just south of Smith's. 5927 Water Street was owned by a Mark and Toni Harrington. The second house on that property, 5927 B, was owned by the Harringtons but rented to . . . hmm . . . a Mr. and Mrs. John and Rhonda Shain. That was too much of a coincidence. He tapped the keys fiercely to find out what kind of vehicles might be registered to the Shains. Bingo! A red Camaro.

What was it the waitress had said? Something about Rhonda fingering Page's watch, his gold chains and the ring? He'd have to get over to the Shain's tonight. The only question was, did he have enough probable cause to get a search warrant? Certainly not for suspicion of murder, which would require an in-person visit to the prosecutor. But what about the theft of the victim's wallet and watch? That could all be done by fax with the on-duty judge over in Niles. He decided to follow his instinct and call the judge. With any luck, it would be Judge Adams, with whom he had a good track record.

It was his lucky night. Judge Adams was home, had finished his dinner and agreed to issue a faxed warrant. Markowski dialed Britt's extension while praying she was still in the building. "Trooper Britt? Markowski here. I've got a late-breaking lead that can't wait and I need some help." He recruited her to wait for the fax while he rushed over to Rhonda Shain's address.

Chapter 10

Rhonda watched her fellow employees filter out of the office. God, was she glad Monday was over! Sheldun Sales Corporation was officially closed, but she needed some privacy before she could get out of there. Her boss Grady, the jerk, was still in his office. If he hit on her one more time, she would haul off and kick him in the nuts. She imagined what that would feel like. They would fire her, of course, but who cared? She now had $4,700, plus whatever she could get for the jewelry, to finance a move to the big city. A woman of her talents could do well in a big city like Chicago or Detroit.

Of course, she'd have to give a small cut to Bernie. What a useless, blubbering idiot he had been, standing over the body, paralyzed with fear. She decided she would take eighty percent and give him twenty. That was a generous offer, considering his wimpy refusal to touch anything.

She looked down into the footwell of her desk, where Page's $4,700, the diamond-studded Rolex, and two gold chains were stashed in her purse. It had taken her all afternoon to come up with a plan to hide them, and now was the time—if Grady would just stay in his office for a few more minutes.

She picked up her purse, stopped by the janitor's closet to get a screwdriver and went into the ladies' room. She entered the stall on her left and closed and locked the door behind her. Gritting her teeth, she knelt down on the not-so-clean floor, reached behind the toilet and unscrewed the cover plate on the wall. Thank God! There were a few pipes and valves in there, but the opening had plenty of room to stash the watch and gold chains. She removed the cash from the wallet, peeled off several bills and put those into her purse. After putting the big wad of remaining cash, the gold chains and the watch into the wall compartment, she screwed it back into place, stood up and stretched. The empty wallet went back into her purse. On the way home, she would toss that out the window somewhere. By the time she left the restroom, she was perspiring.

Grady was standing at her desk when she returned.

"My God, Rhonda, you really are sick! You look feverish. When you came in late today, to be honest, I had my doubts about your excuse. But now, I see it. You should've gone home long ago. What is it? The flu?

"No, sir," she said. "It just a case of . . . some female problems."

"Heh, heh," Grady said. "You can be my female problem anytime."

It was time to get out of here before she said or did something nasty to Grady. She smiled and said, "Goodnight, sir."

On the way back to Union Pier, Rhonda drove to a park about a mile from her home and pulled into a space as far as possible from the few other visitors. Even in the dim twilight, her candy apple red Camaro would attract unwanted attention. Late at night, this section was a hangout for young lovers; she and John had used it when they first dated. She got out of the car, walked down a footpath into the woods far enough to be hidden by a row of tall hedges and pulled Page's wallet out of her purse. She wiped it with a tissue, wrapped the tissue around the wallet and tossed it into the brush. ""Goodbye, Ed Page," she whispered.

Christ, he was really dead. It hadn't really hit her until now. Page hadn't been such a bad guy; he had treated her well. Okay, so he came across as an egotistical, adulterous, sleazy—but rich—politician. She wondered which of those character traits had gotten him killed. And now, who was going to pay for her divorce? She might have to forget Friday night's insult and invite PJ Conroy back into her life—and her bed.

Rhonda drove out of the park and, after a quick stop for some take-out Chinese food and a new bottle of white wine, she turned onto her street. A dark blue sedan was parked in front of the Harrington's' house. A man in a tweed coat was standing on their porch. She turned onto the gravel drive that led to her parking space in the back. The Harrington's house was dark and their station wagon wasn't here. They were typical Chicago people, here on weekends and holidays only.

It was too warm in the house; she had forgotten to turn the thermostat down. She stripped off her work outfit, changed into gym shorts and a t-shirt and sat down to enjoy her dinner. Just as she uncorked the wine, the doorbell rang. A glance through the peephole showed the man in the tweed coat. He raised a silver police badge up to her eye level. Of course. She should have seen this coming. Dark sedan, big searchlight on the side, ugly plain wheels with those dinky little hubcaps—unmarked cop car. She opened the door but kept the chain hooked up and looked out at the badge he was holding. The guy was mid-forties, just an inch or so taller than her five-five height. Messy brown hair, a five-o'clock shadow, average body, dark brown slacks and sturdy-looking brown Oxford shoes. He could be dating material if he'd comb his hair and shave.

"Mrs. Rhonda Shain?"

"Yes?"

"I'm Detective Sergeant Bruce Markowski, Michigan State Police." He looked over her shoulder into the house.

She turned to see what he was looking at; it must be the food and wine on her table.

"I'm sorry to bother you so late in the day," he said, "but there's been a crime in this area and we're trying to interview all the neighbors as soon as possible. Can you spare me a few minutes?"

"Sure," Rhonda said. She pushed the door closed enough to unhook the chain. When she tried to open it fully, it bumped into her penny loafers, which she had kicked off after work. She pushed them out of the way with one foot. The cop watched this with a little more interest than she had expected. Was it her long bare legs or . . . oh shit. She was bra-less under the thin white t-shirt! She considered putting on a robe or more clothes and decided against it. The more time he spent staring at her, the fewer questions he would ask.

"Why don't you take a seat on the couch? I'll put that food into the oven to keep it warm."

"I apologize for interrupting your dinner," the cop said.

"No problem." She sat down on a chair opposite him and crossed her legs. "Can I interest you in something to drink? Not the wine of course. I suppose that wouldn't be proper."

He smiled.

"Water? Coke? Orange juice?"

"No thank you, ma'am." He pulled out a notebook, thumbed through a few pages and studied something. He looked over at the table again and back at her. "May I assume that your husband John is not home right now?"

"That's correct." In fact, she had kicked John out several weeks ago after another one of his jealous rages. If she were lucky, she wouldn't be seeing him ever again. However, the cop didn't need to know all that. "He works nights."

He said, "I suppose you've heard about the, ah, crime reported at your neighbor's house over there." He pointed at Ruth Smith's.

"Yes. It was all over the radio news at work. When they mentioned the street address, I about had a cow. Haven't had time to see any TV reports yet. A man was found dead."

He asked her a string of questions and she rattled off answers. Where did she work? What time had she left for work this morning? Did she know the owner of that house? Had she noticed anything unusual Friday or over the weekend? She explained that she had been out partying late Friday night, came home and went right to bed.

"Everything seemed normal over there all weekend," she said. "Quiet. You know the place is vacant, right? Being remodeled."

"Yes, thanks. Did you know the victim, Edwin Page?"

"Not really. I mean, I know who he is, because he's a big shot from Chicago and he has a house in Union Pier, right up the beach from here, in fact. Oh, and I learned from a friend that Ed Page's brother owns the company that screwed up Ruth Smith's remodeling job."

The cop paged though his notes again. "You know, maybe I will take you up on that offer for a glass of water. No ice, please."

Rhonda was happy for the chance to distract him. She stood up, stretched and swayed her hips as she went to the kitchen. When she returned with the water glass, she bent over, closer to him than necessary, hoping he would get a look down inside her t-shirt. She sat down. "Will there be anything more, Officer, ah . . ."

"Sergeant, actually," he said. "Detective Sergeant Markowski. And, yes, I have just a couple more questions. Do you know a man named Bernard Smith?"

Christ! How much does this cop know? What did Bernie tell him? "Oh, Bernie. Sure. He's Mrs. Smith's—the owner's—nephew. I see him over there working on the house, trying to fix it up. We talk once in a while."

"Did you see him there this morning?"

"Today? Ah . . . no. Maybe Friday morning . . . I'm not sure. Sometime last week anyway."

Markowski leaned forward, put his elbows on his knees and crossed his arms. "Ma'am, I want you to think really hard about this. When was the last time you saw Edwin Page?"

But Offi . . . Detective, I just told you—"

"Before you go any further," he said, "you should know that I have a report from the Red Arrow Café that, on Friday, Councilman Page was seen in the company of a young, petite, blond-haired woman who fits your description."

"But . . . why, that could be any number of women. I am not the only—"

"Mrs. Shain, listen to me, please. Whom will I see with Page when I review the restaurant's security camera footage?"

All of a sudden, Rhonda felt cold and very underdressed. She had misjudged this guy. He wasn't drooling over her as she had hoped. Maybe she could still fool him with a story about sex. "Okay, okay . . . yes, I had lunch with Ed Page on Friday. And, I admit I was trying to hide that from you. I apologize. We're both married, you see. And, in the past Page and I have been, ah . . . intimate . . . on several occasions."

"I see." He sipped some water. "I have one more question. Over there by the door I saw a pair of shoes. Can you tell me when and where you last wore them?"

"I wore those to work today."

"Excuse me," he said. He stood up, walked over to the shoes and knelt down on one knee. "I see what looks like sawdust on the top of the sole—the welt, I believe it's called. Do you know where that came from?"

Rhonda jumped up and walked over to him. Shit! He hadn't been admiring her legs, he had been looking for some damn clues! "Sawdust? I have no idea." She reached down to pick one up, but Markowski held up his hand.

"Please don't touch those," he said.

That was it; he had pushed her to her limit. "What do you mean, don't touch? They are *my* shoes, in *my* house. I know my rights. Unless you have a search warrant, I'll—"

The doorbell rang. Rhonda didn't move.

"Don't you want to get that?" he said.

She opened the door to find a female state trooper with a small black bag in her left hand and a very large holstered pistol on her right hip.

"Mrs. Shain? I'm Trooper Britt, Michigan State Police. Is Sergeant Mar—"

"Come in, Trooper Britt.," the detective said. "Do you have something for me?"

The trooper, wearing light blue booties and rubber gloves, reached into a side pocket on the bag, pulled out a folded paper and handed it to the detective.

He said, "Now, Mrs. Shain, where were we? Oh, yes, you mentioned a search warrant." He unfolded the paper, looked it over and handed it to her. "Here it is. Please read it, then go over to the couch and wait there. Excuse me for a moment. Trooper Britt, do you have an extra set of gloves and booties in there? Good, thanks." He pointed at her shoes near the door. "Let's begin by bagging these."

Half an hour later, they had left. The female trooper had bagged her shoes and the clothes she had worn today. They had emptied her purse and confiscated the two $100 bills, despite her protestations that Page had given her those at lunch. They had also taken the screwdriver from work, which she had stupidly forgotten to return to the janitor closet. After searching everywhere, with special attention to her kitchen knives and her bedroom closet, Markowski and the lady trooper had left.

Rhonda closed the door, double-locked it and attached the security chain. None of those things made her feel any safer. She went into the kitchen, took the Chinese food out of the oven and put it in the fridge—who could eat at a time like this? Should she call Bernie? No. That cop might have her phone tapped. How had he learned so much so fast? She stared at the open bottle of wine, topped off her glass and took it over to the couch. A glass or two might help her think.

Chapter 11

Markowski met Britt in the post's back parking lot. They walked into the building together. He said, "Alice, can you check the evidence in?"

"Sure. I'll be back in a couple minutes." She turned left toward the evidence room.

Markowski went the opposite direction toward his office but stopped and turned around. "Trooper Britt, hold up for a second." He walked toward her, feeling a little silly using the conventional, more formal language when the station was almost empty. But that was the more professional way. She would understand.

"I need about twenty minutes to make some notes. After that, how'd you like to get a bite? It's 8:00 p.m. and, if we hurry, we could get to Norma's before they close. You could get one of those John Wayne Burgers and the Heart Attack Fries that I saw you coveting earlier."

"Sure. Dutch Treat, though. We must maintain appearances, you know."

Markowski switched on the light in his office, walked in and took off his jacket. The first thing he did was to check the message light on his desk phone. Nothing. He sat down, opened his notebook to a fresh page, and wrote "Day One" centered at the top, skipped a couple lines and made two columns. On the left he wrote "Suspects" and on the right "Motive."

Hell, all of the people he had interviewed today were suspects! And they all had pretty good motives. Ruth Smith had followed the victim's recommendation and hired his brother, with disastrous and costly results. Page had also voted against her programs in Chicago. Bernard knew this too and might hold a grudge against Page. Rhonda Shain was having sex with Page while both were married. In fact, speaking of marriage, that gave Rhonda's husband—and Page's wife—a motive for murder.

Markowski entered all their names into the suspects list, leaving plenty of space for notes. Under Ruth's name he wrote, "*Elderly. Not strong enough? Help from nephew?*" In Bernard's section, he put "*Skinny but strong. Has a record. Recruited by Ruth?*" He made similar notes in Rhonda and John Shain's sections and made a note to check on their respective alibis. Finally, he added a reminder to check out Page's wife.

It was time to sketch out an agenda for tomorrow. At the top of the list he put, "Interview John Shain and Page's wife." Then he added a reminder to put a rush on matching footprints and analyzing the suspected sawdust on Mrs. Shain's shoes. He should also try to determine who was the last person to see or talk to Page before his death.

He needed a break from all this. Maybe just an hour. It was time to introduce Alice Britt to the gastronomic delights of Norma's Burger Joint. He reached down to turn off his ancient computer but stopped before he hit the power button. There was one more thing he wanted to check.

Assuming for the moment that the last time anyone had seen Page was at lunch Friday, had there been any other suspicious events reported between then and Monday morning? He accessed the Chikaming Township Police records. There was nothing significant, at least involving human suspects. A couple of their officers had been called to corral an escaped horse on Friday evening. He read through that report just to see if it had a happy ending. Officers had blocked the public road in both directions and, under the watchful eyes of the entire the on-duty Chikaming police force—all two of them—the mare had returned home on her own recognizance. Saturday's and Sunday's reports showed nothing significant—one DUI on Saturday and one minor traffic collision on Sunday at the local Methodist church parking lot. Just to be thorough, Markowski printed out reports for all these and added them to his file.

What else should he check? He logged onto the New Buffalo Police database. Their jurisdiction began just south of Townline Road which was only a block or two south of Mrs. Smith's house. As the page was loading, Britt appeared in his doorway.

"Here's the receipt for the evidence," she said. "Are we ready to go? I am yearning for a high-cholesterol but tasty burger and fries. Maybe even a milkshake."

"You bet. I've got one last page to look at here, then I'll shut this . . . oh, oh, just a minute. Holy—" He swung the monitor around so she could see it. "You need to see this," he said. "But, please keep it to yourself for now."

Alice took several seconds to read the report. "I'm not the detective here, but I can surmise one thing. My John Wayne Burger will have to wait."

"Sorry, Alice. Some other time, I hope. I'll have to make a few calls. You might as well take off. Hey, you could still make it to Norma's before closing."

"We'll see," she said as she walked out the door.

He respected her for giving him privacy even though the new information was very tantalizing. This report about a pool of blood, from an address right next door to where Page's body had been found, could be—most likely was—a major break in the case. He dialed the New Buffalo Police Chief's home number. He wanted to go right to the top.

"Chief Wycoff, this is Detective Sergeant Bruce Markowski, Michigan State Police. Sorry to bother you at home but—"

"I remember you. You bluffed me out of a good hand at that poker game during last year's Law Enforcement Conference. It's nice of you to call me on my birthday."

"It's your birthday. Shoot! I mean, Happy Birthday, Chief. But that's not why I called. Have you heard about the corpse discovered in Union Pier today?"

"No. Just a minute. Let me go to another phone in the kitchen. Hey, you guys, hold it down! I'll be right back." After several seconds, the chief called out, "Okay Megan, you can hang up that phone." The noise level dropped to a tolerable level. "Sorry, Sarge. Family was just bringing out my *birthday cake*. I took the day off. This corpse in news to me."

"Again, Chief, I am so sorry for interrupting. I'll make this quick. Friday night, your officers investigated alleged blood in a bathtub. Are you aware of that?"

"Yes, not in our jurisdiction, but Chikaming was busy with a major road closure."

Markowski decided to leave out the details of the four-legged culprit in that case. "Yes. Well, today at 8:30 a.m., a murder victim was found in the house right next door to where the blood was reported. Chikaming responded to that one."

"Holy shit."

"I just need your permission to contact the New Buffalo officers involved and get copies of the lab results."

"You got it. In fact, I'll be happy to dump the whole bloody bathtub case into your in-basket if there's a proven connection. Tell dispatch you have my verbal permission. I'll make some calls, right after I have my cake and ice cream."

"Thanks, Chief. Go enjoy your party. Good night."

Markowski called the New Buffalo Police dispatcher, explained about the Chief's verbal permission and asked her to contact Officers Lechner and Baker. "Please have them call me ASAP," he said. While he waited, he consulted the report and found contact information for the property owners, a Mr. and Mrs. Mark and Toni Harrington. Damn. Their permanent address was in Chicago. Like many others along this shoreline, they must be part of the well-to-do Chicago crowd who buy up all the good places over here for their weekend getaways. Oops, that sounded a little snarky. He did a quick background check on each of them. The husband was an attorney; the wife had her own small business. They had two kids and multiple university degrees between them. They seemed to be unlikely suspects to have murdered someone in their own bathtub. Nevertheless, he'd have to get them over here tomorrow for interviews.

He dialed both their Chicago and Union Pier numbers and got answering machines each time. Well, he'd just have to keep trying every half hour. He stood up and, as he was wriggling into his sport coat, his phone rang.

It was Officer Lechner, calling while on a dinner break. He told him about the corpse and asked if he had noticed anything unusual at the Harrington's' house, other than the bloody tub. When he said no, Markowski asked if there was anything else that wasn't already in the report. Lechner said no.

"Is Officer Baker with you tonight?"

He was, and when called to the phone, had nothing to add. Markowski thanked him and said, "Be safe out there."

He used the intercom to buzz the State Police dispatcher down the hall. "Hi, Shari. Please call the trooper who's watching the house out on Water Street. You need the address? The murder site, yes. Ask that trooper to roll out some crime scene tape around the next house to the south." He gave her the address and thanked her. If anything comes up, please page me. I'm out of here."

As he approached the exit, he saw Alice sitting on a bench near the front desk. "You're still here? Norma's is closed by now."

She stood up. "Yeah, I know. I had an idea, though. Why don't I throw together a late dinner for us at my place?"

"Your place?" That was a stupid thing to say. It was a tell, just as revealing as those he had observed from criminals. She was smart; she would see his hesitation as a bad sign. First, she might think he was reluctant to fraternize with a fellow officer. This was not true; she was not in his direct chain of command. Worse yet, she might think he just wasn't attracted to her—which was definitely not the case. What healthy male wouldn't want to have dinner with a fair-skinned, long-legged, trim brunette who probably looked even better without body armor under her shirt?

"That's a great idea," he said. "I'll follow you."

Chapter 12

Toni set her evening tea on an end table and sat down next to Mark. She had just checked on the kids and set out their clothes for tomorrow.

"Monday Night Football's over. Shall we watch the late news?" Mark asked.

"Sure."

Mark picked up the TV remote control but before he could select their favorite news channel the phone rang. He handed the remote to Toni and reached for the telephone. "This is Mark Harrington." He listened for a few seconds, and then said, "Yes, we're the owners." His eyes widened and he sat up straight. "Hold on, please. I'm going to put you on speaker phone so my wife can hear this." While covering the mouthpiece with his hand, he said, "Toni, you are not going to believe this!"

"Okay," Mark said, "My wife Toni is on now. This is Detective . . . sorry, tell us your name again?"

"Detective Sergeant Bruce Markowski, Michigan State Police."

"Can you repeat what you just said to me?" Mark said.

"Yes. Mr. and Mrs. Harrington, there's no easy way to say this. An apparent murder victim has been found in your next-door neighbor's house. I think this might be related to the suspected blood found at your house Friday night."

"Oh God, I knew it!" Toni moaned. "Mark, remember my dream, my nightmare?"

Markowski said, "I'd like to hear more about that, but for now, I need to get access to your house early tomorrow. This will help me confirm, or rule out, a connection between these two events. Also, I will need to interview both of you as soon as possible. Can you both come over first thing tomorrow morning?"

"Give us a moment," Mark said. "I'm going to mute our speaker for a minute." He looked at her and said, "I don't see how we can refuse. They could get a warrant and break in there without us. I can get free tomorrow. What about you? Can we get a sitter on short notice?"

Toni said, "I've got an important staff meeting tomorrow at 9:00. It's already been delayed twice; once because of me and again when PJ called in sick today. Let's see, assuming we can get a sitter—my mom can probably do it—if you pick me up at 10:00, we could be there by 11:30. But you'd better say noon; that will give us time for a quick lunch."

Mark explained all this to the detective, who reminded them that Michigan time was one hour later than Chicago's so they agreed to meet at the house at 1:00 p.m. Michigan time. Meanwhile, according to Markowski, state troopers would seal off their property. Toni got on the phone and, after apologizing for the late night call, made arrangements with her mom.

"What are we going to tell the kids?" she said. "They don't even know about the bloody tub yet, let alone the murder."

"Let's figure that out tomorrow. Right now, let's turn on the news and see what we can learn."

They didn't have to wait long. The murder in Union Pier got top billing because the victim was a well-known Chicago City Councilman, Edwin I. Page.

"Never heard of him," Mark said.

Toni said, "Yes, you have; you just don't remember. When Jack and Jeri were driving us around Union Pier one day, remember the giant house they pointed out to us, the fancy waterfront place? Jack said that belonged to, and I quote, 'the allegedly corrupt Councilman Ed Page.'"

"Oh, yeah. Jack wrote a piece on him for the *Dispatch*."

The blurb on TV was very brief. The body had been discovered this morning and an investigation had been launched by Michigan State Police. No suspects had been named.

"Tomorrow promises to be an interesting day," Toni said. "I guess we'd better get some rest." She omitted the fact that, for her, sleep would not come easily tonight. She had a long menu of crises to worry about—the murder/bloody tub thing, the cash shortage at work, and when to tell the kids about all this.

*   *   *

"May I have your attention please?" Toni said. All the Simplified Data employees were present in the conference room. "Good morning, everyone. Happy Tuesday. So, we're having our Friday staff meeting on Tuesday. Sorry for the two postponements. A couple things came up beyond my control." She realized how big of an understatement that was. "Let's get started. First, PJ will give us a report on the

Detroit conference." She sat down. PJ stood up and walked over to the easel.

"Good morning, everyone," PJ said, looking each person in the eye and grinning broadly. "I think you're going to be pleased with my news." He pointed at the easel. "Can you all see this?" Everyone said "Yes." He flipped the cover sheet off to reveal some highlights of the conference and told them he had found some great opportunities for new business. He showed a list of promising new contacts from hospital and medical insurance agencies in six different states.

Toni watched his presentation with awe and, she admitted to herself, a little professional jealousy. He was such an enthusiastic guy! He used a fat marker to draw red circles around five of the ten nation-wide hospital corporations on his list.

"These five expressed great interest in our products. If only one or two of these companies buys our product, it will mean hundreds of thousands of dollars per year! And I have you guys to thank; you sent me over there with great promotional materials and great RFPs. We're on our way, folks!"

After PJ sat down, Toni led a discussion on how to manage the two new contracts that were likely to be signed with City of Chicago Department of Health. PJ restated his opinion that these were a "done deal." They only had to wait for the paperwork to arrive in the mail. Everyone left the meeting in high spirits. Toni allowed herself some optimism; maybe Simplified Data Systems's cash flow problems would soon fade away.

Toni caught PJ before he could slip away. "PJ, may I see you in my office for a moment?"

She had him shut the door and invited him to sit down.

"Uh, oh," he said, "am I about to get a lecture about spending too much money in Detroit?"

She smiled. On any other day, it would have turned into a good-natured laugh. "No, I haven't even seen your expense voucher for that one. This is something different. PJ, I've got to take the rest of the day off. Can you cover for me here?"

"Sure. What's up?"

Toni didn't feel much like answering that. She was too tired to make something up, so she said, "It's a personal matter that I'd rather not discuss right now. Maybe tomorrow. If you need me, call me at home, okay?"

"Right. I'm here for you, so don't hesitate . . . if you need anything."

After he left her office, she applied herself to the one-inch thick stack of unopened mail on her desk and found some good news. Here was a $6,000 check for one of the contracts they had completed weeks ago! Now she could meet this week's payroll, including her own paycheck, which she had deferred for two weeks.

The next envelope in the stack was the bank statement. She opened it, studied the summary and spread the cancelled checks out on her desk. The first two were easy to reconcile; one was for last month's rent and the other was their payment for a new computer monitor.

Toni said, "Oh, shit!" when she saw the next four cancelled checks, all signed by PJ. They were for $1,000 each! No wonder they have been having money troubles. She dialed his intercom number.

"Toni? I thought you had left."

"Not quite yet. Can I see you for another moment, please?"

"Sure, hon, I'll be right there."

She hated it when he called her, "hon." When he appeared at her door, she had him close it again and said, "PJ, have a seat. This is about some checks you wrote. But first, I want to ask you to stop using the word 'hon' when addressing me. I'm fine with first names, but the word 'hon' just sounds a little too familiar or perhaps even a little demeaning."

He grimaced and said, "I'm so sorry. I really didn't mean anything by it. But from now on, you will be either Toni or Mrs. Harrington. Now, you had a question on some checks?"

"Yes, these four. They are all made out to Edwin I. Page. I have learned he's a Chicago City Councilman. Each one is for a thousand dollars. That's a lot of money. Can you tell me what those are for?"

PJ smiled. "You bet. Councilman Page has fast-tracked our two latest RFPs for Chicago Health Department contracts. Those are, quote, campaign donations, unquote." He winked at her. "To help smooth the way . . . to grease the skids, whatever you want to call it. Totally legal, by the way. Besides, I think he actually listened to my pitch and sincerely believes our software will be good for the inner-city health care system."

"Are you sure about the legality issue?"

"Hon—oops, Toni—let's put it this way. There's no law against a private company making political donations. There was no quid pro quo, as lawyers like to say. It's the way business deals are made in the Windy City. Simplified Data Systems just happened to make those donations a week or so before the City Council voted to award us two contracts. Why are you so focused on this anyway?"

"Why do you think?" she said.

PJ cocked his head like a puppy dog trying to understand strange human language. Hadn't he heard the news yet?

She said, "Yesterday morning, Page was found dead over in Union Pier. Police are calling it a murder. It was all over the news last night."

"Oh, my God!" PJ's mouth opened but then closed. He leaned forward and rubbed his temple with both hands. "I just saw him last week! I didn't know. Haven't looked at TV or read a newspaper since Sunday."

"Well, now you can understand why those checks got my attention."

"Don't worry, Toni, those two contracts are signed, sealed and almost delivered. Page's death won't slow us down."

That, she supposed, was how a successful marketing man would see the situation. Toni made PJ promise to consult her before making any new "campaign contributions" and then said goodbye. He didn't need to know that Page's body had been found near her house, that her tub had probably been filled with Page's blood and that she was taking the afternoon off to be grilled by a homicide detective.

Chapter 13

They were halfway to Michigan before Toni worked up the courage to tell Mark about Page's connection to Simplified Data Systems. "Mark, there's something you should know about the murder victim, this Edwin Page."

"Please don't tell me you know him."

"No, I don't. But PJ Conroy does. And—brace yourself—my company has given Page $4,000 over the last three weeks in campaign contributions. Oh yeah, and PJ has wined and dined him with multiple, outrageously expensive business lunches."

Mark was quiet for a long time. They had traveled almost a half-mile down the Interstate before he inhaled and let the air out from one side of a puffed out cheek. He said, "Why didn't you tell me this last night?"

"I didn't know about it then! I only found out when I opened the mail today and saw the cancelled checks that PJ had written to Page. I called PJ back into my office to get the details."

Toni recounted her conversation with PJ, emphasizing his denial that this was a quid pro quo. "Mark, I think PJ is skirting the law when throwing around money like that, obviously trying to curry favor for Simplified Data. What do you think?"

Mark drove along for several seconds before chuckling and saying, "I'll try to visit you often at the state prison, especially if they allow conjugal visits."

She punched him on the shoulder.

After a quick stop for a sandwich on the outskirts of New Buffalo, they continued north to Union Pier. It was soon apparent they wouldn't be able to park anywhere near their own house. Three TV news vehicles, each with a satellite antenna raised high, blocked the curb. Well-dressed network reporters jockeyed for position to shove microphones in front of whomever approached the crime scene that, sadly, included their house.

They had to park a block-and-a half north of the house. Mark jumped out, jogged around to open her door and said, "Don't say anything. I'll handle this." He took her hand and they walked into the crowd of reporters, camera people and curious neighbors. He deflected all the questions with multiple "No comment" statements until one reporter stepped onto the sidewalk and said, "Mark?"

It was Jack O'Connor. Mark leaned into him and said, "Not now Jack! Our car's back there about a block, we'll meet you there in half an hour." Jack got out of the way and Mark hurried them along to the house.

Mark pulled her close and whispered, "So much for anonymity. Now Jack's blurted out my first name to all those news hounds and I've just told them where our car is parked and when we'll be back there." He led them up to some yellow crime scene tape that blocked access to the grounds. A state trooper noted their names and gestured to a man in civilian clothes standing on their front porch.

That man stepped down from the porch, walked over to them and said, "Mr. and Mrs. Harrington? I'm Sergeant Markowski."

He gave them what Toni judged to be a sincere, sympathetic smile and shook their hands. Maybe he was trained to do these things to gain their confidence. She guessed he was in his forties. He had light brown hair, wore a tweed sport coat with a silver badge clipped to the breast pocket, beige shirt, maroon tie and dark brown slacks. He was about her height, not too tall, and had an athletic build.

"Thank you for coming all this way on such short notice," Markowski said. "Let's get into the house and away from this media frenzy. Should we use the front door?"

Mark said, "It might be better if we use the back door, where the security system panel is." Mark led the way, disarmed the system and unlocked the back door.

"Before we go inside," Markowski said, "do I have your permission for me and my team to search your house for evidence in a possible homicide?"

Toni looked at Mark. Although he did not practice criminal law, he would certainly know enough to protect their rights. She trusted him to say the right thing. Mark hesitated for several awkward seconds.

"Sergeant Markowski," Mark said, "we have nothing to hide here. This is our dream vacation home, now tarnished by who-knows-what type of crime. I think I can speak for Toni when I say, we want this cleared up as much as you do. So, search all you like."

"Thank you," Markowski said. "Let me just get our forensics—"

"But," Mark added, "I do have one question before you begin."

"Yes, sir?"

"I am guessing that, if we had refused, you would have presented us with a properly executed search warrant. Am I correct?"

Markowski laughed. He opened his coat and pulled a folded paper halfway out of the inside pocket. "Of course. Guilty as charged, sir."

Mark grinned. "Go for it, Sergeant. Where do you want us to wait?"

When the detective walked off, they sat in the living room. Mark said, "I like this guy."

Toni watched as Markowski and other officers put on foot coverings, donned rubber gloves and canvassed one room after the other. The detective returned and sat down across from them.

"Thanks for your patience," Markowski said. "I've read through the report from the officers whom you saw Friday night. However, I find it helps if I can get each of you to tell the story in your own words, and this is best done with separate interviews. May I suggest that we use the kitchen for the interviews? The other person should wait here in the living room. Now, who'd like to go first?"

"I'll go first," Mark said.

Toni went into the living room and sat in an armchair as far away from the kitchen as possible.

Ten minutes later, Mark came in and said, "Okay, it's your turn."

Toni walked into the kitchen, where Markowski sat writing in a notebook. He stood up, smiled and said, "Thank you again, Mrs. Harrigan, for your cooperation. This won't take long. Please sit down."

It felt odd being asked to sit down in her own kitchen, as if she were a guest.

"Can you begin from the moment you arrived Friday night?"

Toni told the entire story, including the sordid details of the splattering blood and the spilled wine. She concluded with her admission to Mark that she hadn't been able to find her Union Pier key when they had departed.

"Oh?" Markowski said. "Mrs. Harrington, when is the last time you used your key?"

"The last time we were over here; I mean, before all this happened. About nine days ago."

She couldn't think of anything to add. The detective asked a few questions about their tenants, John and Rhonda Shain, for which she didn't have too many answers. Toni hadn't seen them in a while. She gave similar answers to questions about their neighbor Ruth Smith and her nephew Bernard. They were also Chicago residents but that's about all she knew.

"One last question," Markowski said. "Did you know the victim, Edwin Page?"

Toni said, "We've never met him. I know *of* him, of course, because he has a fancy house up here and he's often in the news back in Chicago, news about the City Council." She paused for a deep breath. "But, detective, there is one thing I need to tell you. My company, Simplified Data Systems in Chicago, has had dealings with Edwin Page." She couldn't quite bring herself to mention the large checks; maybe she could accomplish her goal some other way. "My partner, Peter J. Conroy, has taken Page to lunch several times in recent weeks. PJ—Conroy—is lobbying him for some city contracts."

"I see." Markowski seemed to pay special attention to the business name. "I assume you have receipts for these lunches?"

"Yes, of course."

"Please save them for me." After making more notes, he flipped his notebook closed and said, "That should do it. Thank you again. I may have more questions in the future. Is it okay to contact you at your home and your office back in Chicago?"

"Sure."

When she and Mark were back together, Markowski said, "Unfortunately, you won't be able to get back into your house for a day or two, especially if evidence shows a direct connection between the Page murder and your house. By the way, it would help me a lot if I could borrow a key to the front door. And, if you'd like us to set the security system, may we have the code?"

Mark's jaw tightened; he rubbed his chin. "Yeah, I suppose so." He reached into his pocket, pulled out a key on a leather fob and handed it to the detective. "Please take good care of it. It's the only one we have right now."

Toni said, "The code for the security is 3590."

"No, honey," Mark said, "it's 3950. You always get those middle two numbers transposed. That's why we have that sticky note on the refrigerator."

Markowski said, "Do I understand that you posted the security code on your refrigerator?"

"I'm afraid so," Toni said. "I'm the one who always forgets it."

*   *   *

Jack's car was parked in front of theirs. He pointed behind them. "Hurry up!" he said. "I see some other reporters heading this way. "Let's find someplace to talk."

Mark insisted they meet down in New Buffalo, which was on their way home to Chicago and far from the media frenzy in Union Pier. Jack said he was staying over in Union Pier; he'd take his own car and meet them at The Divine Drip, a small neighborhood coffee shop in New Buffalo just north of where Highway 12 intersects the Red Arrow Highway.

Mark chose a booth near the back of the coffee shop, far away from the two other customers. Toni asked for water only, saying she had already had lunch. Mark and Jack ordered coffee.

"So, someone finally got Page," Jack said. "If it was you two, I'll put you up for a humanitarian award."

"Jack, that's not funny!" Toni said. "Can you please stop with the jokes? By now, that detective probably thinks we did it. God knows, I gave him a good reason to suspect us."

She was immediately sorry for saying that. It caused a Pavlovian response in Jack as he pulled out a note pad and a pen.

"Tell me all about it," he said.

Mark said, "Now, wait a minute. Is this off the record, just between us friends, or are we going to read about this in tomorrow's *Chicago Dispatch*?"

Jack ruffled his curly red hair. "Look guys . . . seriously, I know neither of you did this. But I can see how a detective might be suspicious. Blood in your tub. A dead body found in your neighbor's house. And now Toni hints that you might have a motive? I can't help it; that just whets my reporter's appetite."

Toni said, "Sorry, Jack, I don't feel comfortable sharing any of this for publication right now. Maybe later."

"Okay, Toni, I respect that." He took a sip of coffee. "How about off the record then? Try to see it from my perspective. This is a juicy story. If I get a jump on the other papers or TV networks, it could mean a lot for my career. Also, I have sources in the two local police departments. Maybe we can work out a trade. You tell me what you know—off the record for now—and I'll tell you what I've learned so far."

Mark looked at her; she nodded. "We agree. You go first. Tell us what you've learned so far."

"One thing, what I just said. My sources tell me the body was dragged into the vacant house. He was apparently killed somewhere else."

"Yeah," Toni said, "Guess where?"

"A couple other things," Jack said. "The same sources say your neighbor Ruth Smith and her nephew Bernie—whom I actually know, by the way—discovered the body Monday morning. They were seen at the Michigan State Police post in New Buffalo Monday afternoon, presumably to be interviewed. Finally, an observant neighbor of yours told me that she saw two State Police vehicles, one patrol car and one unmarked car, outside your tenant's house Monday night. The State Police walked out with a big black bag, which I can only guess is evidence of some kind or another."

"Wow, you really know how to root out the news, don't you?" Toni said.

"And, that's not all. This morning, State Police visited the Red Arrow Café and confiscated their security camera tapes from Friday night, when—according to my sources—Page had dinner in the company of a cute young thing who is not his wife." Jack picked up his pen. "Now, it's your turn. Tell me, Toni, why the detective might suspect you had a hand in this murder."

Toni explained about the "coincidence" of Simplified Data Systems's contributions to Page, the lavish lunches and the City Council's decision to award contracts to them.

When the conversation began to dwindle, Mark said, "Jack, we've got to get going back to Chicago so we can miss rush hour. I wish you could find us some news that would clear all this up. I really don't know what more we can do. How do we extricate ourselves from this?"

"Don't worry, my friends. Twenty-five or thirty years from now, you'll laugh about all this trouble. You should be out of prison by then."

Toni wadded up her napkin and threw it at him.

Jack easily dodged the flying napkin and said, "I promise to be serious from this moment forward."

Mark glanced up at the ceiling. "Please, God, make it come true!"

"No, really. Toni and Mark, I promise you I'll try to interview Markowski first thing tomorrow. If I learn anything new, I'll call you."

"Hey," Toni said, "how'd you know his name? We haven't told you yet."

"It takes a great reporter like me to figure that out. Also, there is this: They've only got one detective in the New Buffalo office. I've interviewed him before." Jack stood up and grabbed the check. "My treat. Have a safe trip home."

They said goodbye to Jack and sat for a few minutes while Mark finished his second cup of coffee.

Toni said, "I know what you're thinking—again."

"So, tell me."

"You are thinking, 'Jack was sure eager to pick up the tab for two cups of coffee, but he didn't lift a finger on Saturday night, when the dinner tab was over a hundred dollars.'"

"You know me all too well. Is it that obvious that I'm a cheapskate?"

They sat for several minutes, trading ideas and guesses about the killer's identity. Finally, Mark said, "Well, it's all in the hands of the Michigan State Police now. Sergeant Markowski's got his hands full; it seems everyone in town has a motive to murder Page."

"Including us . . . or, really, just me," Toni said. If Simplified Data's $4,000 of political contributions—aka kickbacks, bribes or whatever—became public knowledge, her reputation and that of her company would be tarnished forever. She was not going to let that happen. The quickest way out of this mess might be to solve this herself. But how?

"Hello, hello?" Mark said. "You seemed in a trance there for a moment. What's on your mind?"

"Oh, sorry. Just thinking about the kids." Damn! Toni scolded herself. I mean, darn! Two more sins, a lie and a curse word. But wouldn't God agree with her in this situation? Mark didn't need to know she was about to get involved in a murder investigation.

Chapter 14

"Oh, my God," Toni cried as they pulled up to their apartment building. Two TV trucks were parked directly in front of the main entrance. "They must have gotten our names and address by checking our car registration after you—"

"Yeah, don't rub it in, "Mark said. "I'm already kicking myself for announcing to Jack where our car was parked." He turned into the alley leading to the parking lot.

"There they are!" someone shouted when they approached the entrance. Vehicle doors opened and news people poured out.

Mark hustled her inside and told the security guard, "Don't let them in!" He pushed the elevator call button and the doors slid open. They stepped in and Mark pushed the button for their floor. As the doors closed, she could hear the security guard fending off reporters with stern warnings about this being private property for residents and invited guests only.

Toni rang the bell. Her mom would have to let them in because, if she had followed Toni's mandate, she would have latched the security chain. Several seconds later, the chain rattled and the door opened.

"Thank God you're back! The phone's been ringing constantly. All from news people. I finally had to take it off the hook."

They both stepped inside, gave her mom hugs and thanked her for the short-notice kid-sitting. "I hope they behaved well," Toni said.

"Of course," her mom said, "but I'm afraid I—"

"Mom! Dad!" It was Allen, with an excited Emily close behind him. "Why didn't you tell us? This is so cool! Wait 'till the kids at school hear that our tub was filled with—"

"Hold on, honey," her mom said. "Grandma needs to tell your parents something first. Can you both wait for us in the living room, please?"

"Oh . . . okay. C'mon, Emily," Allen said.

When the kids were out of sight, her mom said, "Sorry, so sorry. I was trying to tell you before Allen ran out. I had the TV news on and went out to fix an after-school snack. The kids both saw a news report about that terrible murder and saw video of the crime scene, which included your house. Emily doesn't quite understand, but as you saw, Allen thinks this is the greatest thing since the circus came to town."

Toni gave her a big hug. "It's okay, Mom. You just saved us the trouble of figuring out how to tell the kids about this."

Mark said, "Why don't we all sit down and we'll explain everything we know so far to you and—" He pointed down the hall. "—those two little kids peeking around the corner and spying on us."

"Allen! Emily!" Toni said in what she hoped was a stern voice. "Go sit down and wait for us." After they had disappeared, she looked at Mark and her mom and whispered, "That was so cute!"

Mark gave a summary to her mom and the kids, leaving out the more graphic details.

Allen's first comment was, "Did the body stink? On TV, the dead bodies that lay around—"

"Allen, honey," Toni said, "We don't know anything about that. See, the, ah, victim was found in our neighbor's house, not ours."

"But," Emily said, "I'll bet it was his blood in our tub." She paused, frowned and gave them an accusing stare. "And we didn't even get to see it!"

Toni leaned over to her mom and said, "So much for Emily not quite understanding."

"That's enough for now," Mark said. "Mom will fix your dinner and I'll drive Grandma home. I'll be back in time for dinner."

"No need," her mom said. "I'll just take the 'L.' That's how I came over this morning."

"I insist, Sadie. It's getting dark now; driving will be much quicker and safer."

After giving Mark a 20-minute head start, Toni heated some frozen home-made lasagna left-overs, microwaved some peas and put salad greens onto four plates. Red wine would be appropriate for this meal, but she wasn't quite ready for it. After apologizing to the wine gods, she opened a bottle of Chardonnay and poured it into a decanter. When Mark returned, they had a nice family meal that was blessedly, and surprisingly, free of talk about blood or murder. She wondered how Mark had convinced the kids to avoid that topic.

While she washed and he dried the dinner dishes, she asked him about that.

"Oh, it was easy. I bribed them."

"And what, may I ask, did you promise them?"

"Sorry," he said, "that's going to be my little secret. For now, at least. Hey, may I be excused? Allen asked for a little help on his arithmetic homework and I want to do that before the World Series game begins."

Mark went off to the study while she finished up in the kitchen. When she left the kitchen, she decided to look in on the homework session.

"Okay, Allen," Mark said, "Here's some arithmetic word problems. Let's say you are a police detective and you are called to a murder scene. There are five rooms in the house. You've already searched two of them and found no bodies. How many rooms do you have left to search?"

"That's easy. Five minus two? That equals three. Three more rooms to search."

"Great! Now here's one where you could use either addition or multiplication. Same scenario . . ."

Toni kept herself out of sight. Scenario? Since when did a second-grader know what a scenario is?

Mark continued, "Detective Harrington, when you search the last three rooms, you find *two* dead bodies in each of the rooms. So how many bodies is that?"

"Uh . . . two in each room. Three rooms . . ." Allen's face lit up. "I get it! Three times two is six. Six dead bodies!"

"Correct! See how easy math is?"

Toni stepped into the room. "Mark, honey, may I see you for a moment in the kitchen, please?"

"Sure. Allen, while I'm gone, why don't you write down the addition and multiplication problems we just did? Not the dead body part; just the numbers."

Toni took Mark's hand, pulled him down the hall to the kitchen and turned to face him. She was breathing hard.

"What?" Mark asked.

"So. This is how you got him to keep murder talk off the dinner menu?"

"Well, yes, I thought it was a brilliant idea at the time. Why not appeal to what's on his mind at this moment? Show him how to incorporate book learning into the real world? But, ah, I sense you do not share my enthusiasm for this approach."

"I wish we had a dog," she said.

"Dog? What's a dog got to do with it?"

"Because, if we had a dog, we'd have a doghouse. And that's where you would be sleeping tonight!" She folded her arms across her chest and said, "Really, Mark? Do you really think counting dead bodies, or multiplying them or whatever, is appropriate for second-graders? And where's Emily during all this anyway?

Mark said, "The last I saw of her, she was trying to drain imaginary red blood out of the bathtub in her Barbie house."

He backed away and ran down the hall, thus dodging the wet dish towel she threw at him.

"Just kidding," he said as he retreated to the study. "She's reading to herself in her room."

"Coward!" she called out to him. She went to see Emily before Mark could afflict her with any more of his bad ideas. Bless her little heart, she had already changed into pajamas and brushed her teeth. Toni sat on the bed next to her and selected a book about a cute mother raccoon. "Let's read a story," she said.

It wasn't yet official bedtime so after the story, she and Emily joined the boys in the living room. The kids played with non-murder-related toys or read books while Mark found the TV channel for the World Series game. After he had taken her aside and apologized for his arithmetic teaching technique, she had let him out of the doghouse, figuratively speaking. Her forgiveness was made easier because he presented her with a second glass of Chardonnay.

"I'm surprised you even want to watch this," she said. "Especially after the Cubs were eliminated—again."

"Yeah, but it's the World Series, after all, and kind of an unusual one. It's the first cross-town series since 1956. Both teams are from the Bay Area, the Oakland Athletics and the San Francisco Giants. Tonight's game is in San Francisco. Oh, here we go. They're doing the pre-game show. That's Al Michaels, the announcer and Tim McGraw, who's a retired pitcher, now also an announcer. Wait . . . look at that! "

The whole stadium was shaking, undulating up, down, left and right. The very tall light poles swayed through ridiculously large arcs. Toni wondered why the heavy light arrays didn't break off. Then the picture got fuzzy and disappeared. They could still hear Al Michaels saying, "I'll tell you what, we've having an earth—" The audio stopped.

"Holy Moley!" Mark said.

After ten seconds of fuzzy white, a green screen appeared with the words, "Technical Difficulties."

The audio came back on with Michaels's unmistakable nasal voice saying, "Well, that's the greatest opening in history, bar none!" Screams from the panicked crowd came through clearly until the network shut off live coverage and switched to re-runs of the Roseanne sitcom.

They let the kids stay up past bedtime while they waited for news updates. Mark switched between the three major networks; all of them had somber-looking new anchors, broadcasting from New York or Washington, D.C., passing on telephone reports of collapsed buildings and fires in downtown San Francisco. One station showed video from the Goodyear Blimp, originally in place to show the game, now hovering over a collapsed section of the Oakland Bay Bridge.

Toni said, "We'd better get the kids to bed."

After good-night hugs, kisses and reassurances to Allen that Game Three would be rescheduled, they closed the kids' bedroom doors and returned to the living room. San Francisco's local stations were beginning to come back on-line using backup power sources and car phones when necessary. It had been a 6.9 magnitude quake with the epicenter 60 miles south of San Francisco. Multiple fatalities had been reported.

Their phone rang. Toni was closest to it and she answered.

"It's Jack. Have you been watching the news?"

"Yes, it's terrible, just unbelievably terrible."

"San Fran, one of my favorite cities," Jack said, "now up in flames. And that freeway collapse? At 5:00 p.m. on a weekday? Hell, that would've been packed with commuters. God help them. Say, can you put Mark on the line?"

Toni said, "Sure, hold on." She stretched out enough cord and handed the phone to Mark.

Toni concentrated on the awful earthquake news while Mark talked with Jack. After a minute or so, he hung up the phone and handed it back to her.

"What's the latest on the TV?" he asked.

"Oh, Mark it's just awful. There are squashed cars on that bridge with people trapped inside them. Unofficial death count rising past twenty. Fires are raging out of control in San Francisco. I feel so sorry for those people."

"Believe it or not," Mark said, "the earthquake is not the main reason that Jack called. He's got news about the murder investigation." He put his hand over hers and squeezed. "And, it's not good."

Toni looked at her untouched glass of Chardonnay on the coffee table. "Will I need a sip of this to fortify myself?"

"Maybe. Jack's sources report that the murder weapon has been found."

"Okay. And . . .?"

"This is where you might need the wine. State Police have reportedly found the murder weapon in our house."

"No way! What weapon?"

"Jack doesn't know. He'll try to follow up tomorrow. Of course, this is all off the record. But he says to be prepared for a visit by Markowski."

Toni finally took a sip of the wine. She looked at Mark, who picked up his own glass, then put it back down.

"Toni, give me your hand. Let's say a prayer for the earthquake victims in San Francisco. Their problems make ours look insignificant."

"That was sweet, Mark," she said when they finished the prayer.

They watched the earthquake news until they couldn't stay awake any longer. That night, they held each other tighter than normal and they whispered, "I love you" to each other—multiple times. Soon, she felt Mark's body relax and his breathing fall into a regular rhythm. With this kind of love, they could overcome anything. Her last thought before drifting off to sleep was, "Does 'anything' include being charged with murder?"

Chapter 15

At 8:15 a.m. the next morning, just after sitting down in her office chair, Toni got the call she had been expecting.

"Mrs. Harrington? It's Sergeant Markowski. There have been some new developments in the case. I'm sorry for the short notice, but I need to interview you again, preferably at your office. Will you be available at 11:00 a.m.—wait, make it 10:00 a.m. Chicago time?"

She said yes and gave him the address and suite number.

"Can your husband be there also?" he asked.

She put him on hold and used a different line to call Mark, who agreed to come over. After getting Markowski back on the line, she said, "Yes, Sergeant, Mark will be here too."

Toni stood up and stretched. There would be no time this morning for a stress-relieving workout at the gym downstairs. She satisfied herself with a walk down the hall to the boardroom, where she refilled her coffee cup and stirred in some raw sugar. She walked over to the window and glanced down at Chicago's lakefront. It was a blessedly clear day; the sun was now about ten degrees above the horizon. She had come in early today and had seen it rise, but not from directly east as one would expect. Mark had tried to explain this characteristic of the sun's azimuth in fall and winter but Toni just took it on faith. In fall, the days got shorter and the sun poked its head up over the horizon from significantly south of due east.

The flag flying over the Art Institute was limp. A few brave joggers were out on the paths of Grant Park. Michigan Avenue and Lakeshore Drive were now clogged with cars, buses and trucks moving at a snail's pace in both directions. Toni was happy she was high enough to not hear the blaring of horns that only Chicago drivers could create. Frost had not yet intruded on the lake front, so Chicago's gateway was vivid with marigolds, geraniums, impatiens and mums. Leaves were changing color each day. She wondered if Mark was looking out his own office window at this same awesome multicolored collage that could have been painted by a rampaging Van Gogh.

PJ walked into the conference room. "Good morning! Hey, did you ever see anything like that quake? It looked like World War III right on the television set."

"I'm still in shock," Toni said. "There's been such a terrible loss of life."

"Yeah, but they say it could have been a lot worse. People had left work early to attend the World Series game or watch it on TV. Many of those would have been in rush-hour traffic on the Oakland Bay Bridge when it collapsed." He paused. "So . . . what's on the agenda for today?"

Toni shut her eyes and took a deep breath. It was time to tell PJ the ugly news. "Well, until a couple minutes ago, I was looking forward to a nice morning adding up the dollar value of our new contracts. But something has come up. At ten o'clock this morning, we're getting a visit from a Michigan State homicide detective."

"Huh?"

"It's about Edwin Page's murder. PJ, I'm sorry, but yesterday when I left early, I just couldn't bring myself to tell you the whole story. So here it is. Friday night, when we arrived in Union Pier, we found our tub was full of blood. Police were called, but they found nothing else. Then Monday, Page's body was discovered in the vacant house next to ours."

"No way!"

"Unfortunately, it's true and that's why I was called away yesterday. Mark and I were summoned to Union Pier by the State Police. They had connected the report of our bloody tub with the corpse next door. I presume they now have proof that it was Page's blood in our tub. A detective interviewed us and I had to tell him about your expensive lunches for Page. I haven't yet told him about the thousand-dollar payments.

"That's ridiculous!" PJ said. "Impossible!"

"To make matters worse, last night we got a call from a reporter friend of ours, Jack O'Connor—you've met him. He has learned that police found the murder weapon in our house."

"Weapon? What kind of weapon?"

"Jack doesn't know. I think it is safe to say that Mark and I are now suspects in the murder and the detective is coming over to learn more about our connection to Page. He hinted that there were some new developments. God, he might even arrest us for murder! Would they do that? What would happen to the kids?"

"Toni, I know you and you're not a murderer. Neither is Mark. I'm sure all this will get cleared up in no time."

"I hope you're right."

PJ said, "Of course I'm right." He grinned. "I'm always right! By the way, did you say you went to Union Pier Friday night? I thought you and Mark had a date for the symphony here in Chicago."

"Mark's flight came in too late," she said. "We went Friday night."

"Toni, do you want me to be with you for the police visit? I could postpone my visit to the County Hospital."

"Thanks, PJ, but Mark's coming over any minute, so I'm good. But I do have a favor to ask. Those four thousand-dollar checks you made out to Page? Are those listed on your expense account sheets?"

"Sure. Why not? The sheets are in order. Anyway, they hardly constitute murder evidence."

"I would appreciate it if you would bring me the expense file. I'd like to go over those sheets before the police get here."

"Toni, a beautiful and gifted girl like you shouldn't be troubled about money. Frowns don't go well with your new chic coiffure."

"Thanks for noticing that," she said, even though she had had the new, shorter length hair for several days now. "Nonetheless, I would like to have them, PJ. Please get them for me."

"Well, Toni, I thought we were partners. When did you become my boss?"

"I'm sorry PJ; I didn't mean to be rude. These detectives showing up here have me quite upset. Please humor me, just this once. I promise I won't be bossy again. But I really would like to check that file before the police do."

PJ went back to his office, returned with the expense file and put it on her desk.

"Thanks, PJ, for being so understanding. Again, forgive me for being pushy." She took the file and sat down at her desk.

On the way out of her office, PJ said, "I'll be back for those in a few minutes."

Toni opened the file, extracted the applicable sheets and locked them and the four cancelled checks in the bottom drawer of her desk. She placed the file folder in her outbox for PJ to retrieve. The intercom buzzed.

It was Margaret, the receptionist. "There's a Detective Markowski here. And some other guys. The detective says he has a ten o'clock appointment."

"Yes, I'll be right there." Toni said. She wished she had briefed Margaret on all this; now rumors would fly.

She directed Markowski and three other men down the hall to the conference room, but she stayed back and said to Margaret, "You've seen all the news, right? I mean, besides the earthquake. The Michigan murder case. Our house is next door to all that. These gentlemen are investigating. When my husband gets here, please send him to the conference room."

Toni caught up to the four men just as they entered the room. They all filed in and stood on one side of the long conference table. She closed the double doors and sat opposite the men. "I'm Toni Harrington." She pointed at the buffet. "There's coffee and tea over there if you'd like some." They all declined.

Markowski said, "Mrs. Harrington, on my left is John Barron. He's a Michigan State Police detective and an accountant. "On my right are Detectives Sullivan and Andreotti from the Chicago Police."

They shook hands all around. At that moment, the door opened and Mark walked into the room. Right behind him was a surprise—Jack O'Connor.

Markowski said, "Nice try, Jack, but you need to wait outside."

"Oh, c'mon, Bruce, even if I'm their personal friend?

"I don't care if you're a personal friend of God himself. This is police business."

Jack departed, mumbling, "Well you can't blame a guy for trying."

Mark stood with his arms folded. "So, Sergeant, you're on a first-name basis with Jack O'Connor?"

Markowski shrugged. "I guess. He's worked a story or two about previous crimes in our county. I try to stay clear of him if possible. He's like a fish hook. Once he gets into you, he's difficult to get out."

Toni snickered. So did the other State Police detective.

Markowski repeated the introductions for Mark's benefit and they all sat down.

"Detective Sullivan," Markowski said, "May I have the warrant please?" Sullivan reached into his coat pocket, pulled out a paper and handed it to Markowski, who gave it to Toni.

She scanned it; the language almost caused her heart to stop. It authorized the search and seizure of any "pertinent" documents or digital records at Simplified Data Systems *and* their Chicago apartment. Pertinent was defined as anything related to City of Chicago contracts, company finances and/or anything mentioning Edwin I. Page. She handed it to Mark, who read it and slid it back to her. She left it on the table; if she tried to pick it up, everyone would notice her hands were shaking.

Markowski said, "These three gentlemen would like to inspect your records. Where should they work?"

"Right here," Toni said. "This room has the most space. Hold on a second." She buzzed Margaret. "Margaret, it's me. I'm sending three detectives out to see you. Their names are Sullivan, Andreotti and, ah . . ."

"Barron, ma'am," said the accountant.

"And Barron. They will want to inspect some of our files. They'll use the conference room. Please give them all the help they need. If you have any questions, just come get me. Thanks." She turned to the detectives and said, "Okay, gentlemen, Margaret will find the files and help you bring them in here."

The three stood up and left the room.

Markowski remained seated and said, "Mr. and Mrs. Harrington, the Chicago police have kindly allowed me to interview you about some further developments in the Union Pier murder. We'll need a private place to do that."

"My office will work," Toni said.

Once they were settled in her office, Markowski said, "Before I say anything more, I would like you to know that you are under no obligation to speak to me. If you do so, it will be totally of your own choice. Is that clear?"

They both nodded. Mark said, "Yes. We'll talk to you, but we reserve the right to stop anytime."

"Okay. Now, one more thing, please. I'd like to interview each of you separately, like we did over in Union Pier, but this time with Mrs. Harrington first. Is there someplace Mr. Harrington could wait.?"

Mark stood up and said, "I'll be out by the reception desk."

Once they were alone, Markowski produced his notebook and flipped it open. "Do you own a tent?" he asked.

"No, we don't," Toni replied. "In fact, we had to borrow a tent to go camping."

"How long ago did you do that?"

"No more than two weeks ago. And, it wasn't really camping; we just set it up in the back yard for the kids to sleep in."

"Do you remember the color of the tent?"

"Uh, wait. It was dark when we set it up. But the next morning I went out and . . . it was a faded green. I'm pretty sure."

"From whom did you borrow the tent and when did you return it?"

Toni said, "We borrowed it from the Barclays, our neighbors here in Chicago. As for returning it, you'd have to ask Mark." She was dying to ask him why so many questions about a tent but sensed that would be unwise. She wanted this to be over as soon as possible.

Markowski wrote some notes and said, "I suppose you've seen the news reports—some from your friend Jack out there, no doubt—that we've found what might be a murder weapon in your house."

"Yes."

"Aren't you curious about what we found?"

"Yes."

Markowski chuckled and broke into a smile. "Mrs. Harrington—may I call you Toni?

She nodded.

"Toni, I admire your brevity, and I totally understand. I really do. You don't want to say too much, don't want to volunteer anything that will get you into trouble. But here's the thing. A possible murder weapon was found in your house. One of your kitchen knives had traces of blood on it. The victim was found partially wrapped in a green tent that most likely came from your house. Lab results on the bloody tub and the knife are not in yet, but you can see how—"

"My God, a kitchen knife? Ugh. One of ours? And that tent, I wonder if Mark ever returned it? I can totally see how this looks bad for us. But I swear to you, I do not know anything about any of this. For the life of me, I still can't figure out why Page would have been in my house or how he might have gotten in. This is all a nightmare!"

"I appreciate that, Toni. Now, I need to ask some questions about your business. Tell me about Simplified Data Systems, who owns it, how many employees it has, products or services you provide, annual income, who writes the checks, that sort of thing."

"That's kind of a tall order," Toni said, "but I'll do my best. It's an LLC—you know what that means, right?"

He nodded.

"Simplified Data Systems, SDS for short, grew out of my old company, Borelli's Data Processing. Borelli is my maiden name, you see. I had a small office on the south end of the loop near Roosevelt University. I developed a pretty good following in the health field, but I needed more visibility, more growth. That's why, about six months ago, I merged with PJ—that's Peter J. Conroy—to take advantage of his experience in marketing. We're co-owners.

"As our name implies, we design data systems which would work for any large corporation. All of our business so far has been with health care systems, hospital chains and HMOs, primarily ones located in underserved minority communities."

Markowski asked, "Why just health care?"

"Well, you could say that's my passion, maybe because of what I saw growing up here in Chicago and then doing graduate research on how to improve health care for low-income communities. I've done some consulting with the state on fighting infant mortality among that population. In fact, my research is mentioned in a recently published book, *The Great Health Care Divide.* But I'm getting way off track here."

Toni focused on what Markowski had asked for. She named the three employees she had brought to the merger—an accountant, a receptionist and one other programmer besides herself—and PJ's two marketing experts. She explained to him how they worked. Once PJ had been educated on what SDS could offer, he went out to advertise it. Once he brought in a sales lead, Toni's side would work up a plan, which PJ's staff would turn into a professional RFP. She had to explain what that was to the detective. PJ's job was to present the RFP and make the sale.

"Oh yeah," she said. "You wanted to know who writes the checks. That would be PJ and me." That reminded her of the four cancelled checks in a locked desk drawer just inches from her knee. Did Markowski really need to know about those? For now, they would stay locked up. "Dealing with corporate executives and politicians is PJ's area of expertise. He's got the connections, and God knows everything in Chicago has a political tie-in. PJ's father was formerly the Commissioner of Streets. He grew up in the shadow of City Hall and learned all the ins and outs—whom to see, what to ask, how to deal with the city budget system. That's why

PJ is such an asset for our business. He told me he's known Page for a long time, but exactly how well I don't know."

"Is Mr. Conroy here right now?" Markowski asked.

"No. He was in earlier but is out at meetings for the rest of the day."

"I see. Well, I think that's all I need from you. Please wait here while I go get your husband." He closed his notepad, picked it up and walked out.

Once Mark was back in her office with the detective, Toni wandered out to the reception desk and sat down next to Jack. Margaret was not at her desk; she had left a note. *On break. Downstairs in coffee shop. Back in 15 min.*

"Jack, something's a little strange here."

Jack, always starved for news, was all ears.

She said, "Why did the detective go out to get Mark? Why didn't he send me out to tell him it was his turn?"

"That's easy, my love," Jack said. "Markowski is just following procedure. He doesn't want his two suspects—oops, I mean witnesses, or whatever—to compare notes about the interview."

"I think you were right the first time," she said. "I am definitely beginning to feel like a suspect."

The conference room doors opened. One of the Chicago detectives emerged and approached her. "We'll need your secretary to make just a few more copies and then we'll be done. I'm not sure if Sergeant Markowski has told you, but he and Detective Barron will be taking a box of documents, originals, for which we'll give you a receipt. The copies are for you to use until we return the originals."

"All right," Toni said. "It'll be just a minute. Margaret's on a short—" The office door opened. "Oh, here she is now."

Toni sent her to the conference room to get the documents and sat down again.

Jack had his notepad out. "Okay! Tell me all about it! What did he ask you?"

Before she could tell him, "Not now," her office door opened and Mark and Markowski walked into the reception area. The phone rang; Toni answered it from Margaret's desk.

"Simplified Data Systems, Toni speaking."

"This is Trooper Serra, Michigan State Police. I have an urgent message for Sergeant Bruce Markowski. He left this number as a contact point. Is he still there?"

Toni handed the phone to Markowski. "A Trooper Serra for you."

Markowski listened for several seconds and then said, "When? Okay, I'm leaving now." He replaced the phone in the cradle and said, "Sorry folks, we've got to leave in a hurry. There's been a . . . ah . . . rather interesting development back in Union Pier. Thank you, Mr. and Mrs. Harrington, for your cooperation. Let's go, John."

Detective Barron picked up the box of documents and followed Markowski and the other two detectives out the door.

"Wait!" Jack called out. "Aren't you going to tell us what this quote, unquote, interesting development is? Hell, Bruce, you know I'll find out soon enough anyway."

Markowski stopped, turned around and chewed his lower lip for a second or two. "Jack, you're probably right. I guess it won't do any harm to tell you. Someone just walked into the post and confessed to killing Page." He turned and walked to the elevator, where Barron was holding the door for him.

Jack raced after him, shouting, "Who? Who confessed?" He tried unsuccessfully to stop the elevator, then rushed back into the office.

"Toni! I need to use your phone. Gotta call in a story!"

Chapter 16

Markowski thanked the Chicago officers for their cooperation and promised to keep them updated on the case. He opened the driver's side door, unlocked the other side for Barron and pulled away from the Peoples' Gas Building into heavy lunch-hour traffic. Pedestrians, a mixture of shoppers and office workers on break, clogged the crosswalks, slowing vehicle traffic. Evidently the flashing "Don't Walk" signs were optional for Chicagoans. Hordes of school children poured out of the Art Institute and into school buses stationed along the east side of Michigan Avenue waiting to take them back to their schools. Once they hit the Dan Ryan Expressway, the congestion eased; he used the light and siren and made it to New Buffalo in record time.

Only a handful of press people lingered in the parking lot outside the post. The news from San Francisco had taken over the media and Markowski felt a little ashamed to be happy about this. The tragedy in California had snuffed out many lives and demolished acres of property. But he was relieved that his case was off the front page, at least for the time being.

Alice Britt met him in his office and told him Trooper Serra had briefed her on the individual who had confessed.

After listening to Alice's description of this new development, he asked her, "What's your opinion?"

"Well, he confessed, right? But . . . I don't know. He hasn't said much, but something seems out of place. I've seen this guy; he looks too meek to be a killer."

"Interesting," Markowski said. "Give me a few minutes to read his statement, then let's get him into an interview room." He walked downstairs to the interview room, sat down and read the statement from George Wilkens. Where had he seen that name before? He opened his notebook and flipped through the first several pages. Ah, there it was. Wilkens's wife had been the one killed by Page's car last year. That would qualify as motive. Another memory popped up. This was *Doctor* George Wilkens, Ph.D., author of a book on Chicago's inner-city infant mortality problem. In an ironic coincidence, this book was the very same one that Mrs. Harrington had mentioned, *The Great Health Care Divide*. Even stranger was the fact that he had read it himself, years ago.

Wilkens turned out to be a thin elderly black man about five-five, with short greying hair. He was dressed in a well-worn grey sweater with leather patches on the elbows, a white shirt, brown slacks not unlike his own and dark brown Oxford shoes. He walked very slowly into the room with Trooper Britt close behind. The man's eyes were lowered, focused on the floor. His shoulders slumped forward. He did not speak.

Markowski stood up. "Thank you, Trooper Britt." When she had backed out of the room and closed the door, he offered a handshake and said, "It's a privilege to meet you, sir. I've read your book." That got Wilkens's attention.

"You have? It's kind of you to say so."

"I know what you're thinking," Markowski said. "Why would a homicide detective read my book?" But my undergraduate degree is in English. I started out as an elementary school teacher in Detroit. I got kind of a rude introduction to inner city youth, their families and problems. Your book was actually in a bookcase in the teachers' lounge; I learned a lot from it."

Wilkens gave him a brief smile and said, "That's nice to hear."

"Please sit down," Markowski said. When they were both seated, he said, "So, Dr. Wilkens, let's take it from the top. What brings you here?"

"I killed Edwin Page!" The old man's hands trembled; he tried to conceal that by placing them one on top of the other.

"Tell me about it. How did it happen?" This gentle human being did not look capable of hurting a flea but then, many killers didn't look the part.

"I walked by the Harrington's house, not too far down from mine. I have a friend that lives next door. That's Ruth Smith, whom I know from Chicago. I saw Page through the window; that is, the Harrington's window. I . . . I just lost it. I went in there and . . . well, you know. I killed Page."

"Why?"

"I have my reasons. Reasons, plural."

"How did you get in?"

"The door was unlocked. I have no idea what he was doing in there. He was just standing by the window."

"Okay. What happened next?"

"There's not much to tell. I grabbed a kitchen knife and stabbed him. Page was a villain, an evil person. He had ruined my life. I had no use for him."

"Where did you get the knife?"

"It was in a kitchen drawer."

Markowski made a note of that. He seemed to remember a big maple knife block on the kitchen countertop, full of knives. There had been none in any of the drawers he had inspected. "Where exactly where did you stab him? And how many times?

So far Wilkens had been looking down at the tabletop, but when he heard this latest question, his eyes flickered up to the ceiling.

"Ah, I was in a great rage. I don't remember. I just lunged at him."

"Page was a pretty big man. Didn't he try to fight you off?"

Wilkens looked up at the ceiling again. "I think I surprised him. Yes, caught him by surprise."

"So, you must have stabbed him in the back, then?"

The old man took a deep breath, exhaled with a long wheeze and closed his eyes for a moment. "It's all a blur in my memory. I suppose so. I suppose I stabbed him in the back. I just don't remember."

"Did you use any other weapons?"

"I stabbed him to death! Why would I need more?"

"Okay, okay," Markowski said. "You stabbed him. Then what?"

"He fell onto the living room floor."

"The floor. Okay." Markowski made a note.

Wilkens said, "Wait. It's all pretty unclear. I seem to remember he fell backwards into a tub. Not onto the floor."

Markowski almost called off the interrogation right there. He already had three or four glaring inconsistencies between the evidence and Wilkens's story. Everything he had mentioned so far were facts he could have read in the newspaper. Markowski had intentionally omitted the head wound or the fireplace poker from media releases. And what about that latest statement that his victim, a mortally wounded guy, having been stabbed in the living room, somehow falls up a flight of stairs and into a tub? Really? But, in the unlikely event that Wilkens was the murderer and just had some kind of amnesia, he pressed on with more questions.

"What did you do next?"

"I got him out of there. I dragged him by the feet."

"You don't look strong enough."

"I'm stronger than I look." Wilkens gave him a defiant glare.

"So, you dragged him out of the house. What did you do then?"

"I pulled Page across the yard and through the bushes to Ruth's house. I knew it was vacant during the remodeling. I pulled him in there, intending to return Saturday and then bury him someplace. I figured Bernard wouldn't be back until Monday."

"It must have been a mess to clean up afterwards."

"Yes, sure."

"What did you do with the knife?"

"Threw it away. I threw it away in a pile of construction trash in Ruth's back yard."

"Dr. Wilkens, why did you choose to kill Page?"

"Because he ruined my life." Wilkens sagged forward, covered his face with his hands and began to sob.

Markowski stood up, went around the table and patted him on the back. "It's all right, sir. You'll be okay."

"It was Page's car that killed my wife, you see. Even though Page himself wasn't driving, I blame him for allowing his reckless, irresponsible kid—or a kid's friend, maybe—to drive it around. You see, about a year ago—"

"No need to tell me, sir, I've read the report, and I'm very sorry for your loss."

"Thank you."

"How long have you known Edwin Page?"

"Oh, fourteen, fifteen years. He bought that place shortly after Martha and I found our cottage. I'd see him on the beach. He was a pretty social chap, but we had nothing in common except our skin color. There were wild parties at his house and down on the beach. It was always a pain when he was down here, which really wasn't that often. He hated my dog."

"Why was that?"

"Chowder used to bark a lot. I could tell that bothered Page. Not long after Martha died, Page took him and beat him. I could never prove he did it, but I'm sure of it. Chowder was gone four days before I found him in Bridgman. The dog was in such agony, I had to put him to sleep."

Markowski weighed his options. Charging Wilkens with murder didn't seem to be a wise choice. Sure, there was a motive, or motives if you counted the dog story. But why now, a year after these events? Wouldn't he have done something sooner? Anyway, there were just too many holes in his story. For some reason, Wilkens was confessing to a murder he didn't commit. Why?

"How about a glass of water?" Markowski said. Wilkens accepted and he poured a cup from the metal pitcher on the table. His suspect used both hands to raise it to his lips. He could see beads of sweat on Wilkens's forehead. He might be close to a nervous breakdown. Was this a murderer or a man evolving into serious depression? Or both?

Markowski made a decision based on evidence, instinct and—although it was a little unprofessional—some empathy for this old professor. "Look, Dr. Wilkens, I suggest you go back to your cottage. You're close by and I know you're not going anywhere. Go on back. Get some rest. Watch a movie or something."

"But, I should be charged with murder! I told you I killed Edwin Page. I have a motive. I had every reason to kill him. He ruined my life." He covered his face again, trembled and sobbed heavily.

This was a man who needed professional help. Markowski would never forgive himself if this guy went home to an empty house and committed suicide. "Dr. Wilkens, I am very concerned about you. I believe the best thing is to get you admitted into the hospital in Michigan City for some rest. This has been a terrible ordeal for you. I want to make sure you're okay."

"I'm just fine. I don't need a hospital. Just charge me with murder."

"Not just yet, sir. I want to make sure you are well enough before I make a move."

"Do you think I'm crazy?"

"Oh, no, Dr. Wilkens. I don't think any such thing. I just want to be sure you are going to be healthy enough to stand all the ins and outs of being charged with murder. Just a couple of days will make a difference. Do you agree to this?"

"I guess so."

"Wait here for a moment, please." Markowski went out of the room, called the hospital's psychiatry department and asked for Dr. Paul Solomon. When Solomon came on the line, he said, "Paul, it's Bruce Markowski. I need a favor. It's important to a case I'm working." He related Wilkens's story and they both agreed this would be the best course of action.

It was totally against procedure, but he arranged for a trooper to follow Wilkens home so he could pack a bag and then drive him down to Michigan City. "This is sort of like protective custody," he told the trooper, "but the paperwork is not quite done yet."

Sadly, the paperwork would be enormous for this, if only because the Michigan City was not in Michigan but just over the line into Indiana. It was, however, the closest city to New Buffalo with an adequate psychiatric care facility. Markowski promised himself to file authentic protective custody papers tomorrow, after he had a chance to think about why an innocent man would confess to murder. Who was he trying to protect?

Chapter 17

PJ Conroy wound up his final sales meeting of the day. While the elevator took him down to the ground floor of Northwestern University Medical School, he considered his options. It was too late to return to the office but maybe a little too early to go home. He needed some relief from a stressful week. Perhaps he should stop in for a drink at that trendy Irish pub down by Navy Pier; it wasn't that far out of his way. The only question was, should he drink alone or invite the redhead? Or, maybe the brunette he had met last week? He stopped at a phone booth in the lobby and mentally flipped a coin. The redhead won. He dropped a quarter into the phone and dialed her number.

She gave him the good news and the bad news. She couldn't make it today but she was available *next* Wednesday during the late evening. He decided she was worth a one-week wait so he made a date. He reached into his pocket for more change and came up empty. He could get change for a dollar over at the newsstand and call his backup plan, the brunette. But, was he really that desperate? It was a matter of pride; his ego might be severely damaged if she turned him down too. He walked out and headed for the pub. A few drinks alone would do him no harm.

At 5:00 p.m., he walked out of the pub into a windy and wet Chicago afternoon. He decided to skip the standing-room-only 'L' ride and hailed a taxi. Would Heather be home yet? She had yoga on Wednesday afternoons, but he couldn't remember the class time. As the taxi drove up to his house, he noticed a silver Cadillac pulling out of his driveway. He didn't recognize the car or the driver.

The cabbie pulled into the driveway and said, "Nice house! I like the style. What is it, Old English?"

"Tudor Revival, actually," PJ said. "We were lucky to find it about fifteen years ago. Probably couldn't afford it today." He handed the cabbie his fare and a modest tip.

The front door opened when he was halfway up the brick walkway. "PJ," Heather said without her usual smile, "you're home early."

She didn't sound too happy to see him, which made him all that more curious about who had just driven away. He walked up to Heather and gave her a hug. She responded with little enthusiasm. When he tried to kiss her on the lips, she turned and presented him with her cheek.

"No yoga today?" he asked.

"PJ, we have to talk." She walked away toward the kitchen, leaving him to close the front door.

He put down his briefcase, took off his raincoat and hat and followed her into the kitchen, where she was seated at the big butcher-block center island. On the island was a two-inch thick stack of documents. He sat on a stool across from her and took a quick glance down at the one on top. Uh, oh. It was their bank statement.

"Roger Morton just left. He called earlier and wanted to discuss some irregularities in our savings accounts, specifically the trust for our kids." She slapped her hand down on the papers with such force that he flinched. "PJ, how could you? How could you—why did you—take money out of the kids' trust? It's for their college expenses, for God's sake!"

PJ took off his suit coat and loosened his tie. That wasn't enough to keep him from perspiring so he unbuttoned the collar of his dress shirt. Morton had been Heather's dad's accountant; she had kept him on after her parents' tragic death in a chartered plane crash in Colorado. Had the trust company showed Morton the withdrawal forms? If so, had Morton noticed that Heather's signatures on those forms were forgeries? And, had he told Heather?

"Look, honey, this is just a temporary thing," he said. "Do you remember a couple weeks ago, when I said the merger and start-up costs with Toni Harrington would be expensive? And that, to make that happen, I'd have to borrow a little from our savings?"

"A little? Do you call *eighty thousand dollars* a little?" she shouted. "All that trust money came from my parents! Roger tells me there are big penalties for early withdrawal." Tears welled up in her eyes. "Why not use our own savings?"

This would not be a good time to tell her he had already withdrawn $15,000 from their personal savings to cover his gambling debts. Evidently Morton hadn't caught that one—yet. Heather's hand was still on the papers. He reached out to touch her but she drew her hand back and folded her arms across her chest.

"Answer me!" she said.

"Honey, you have told me many times in the past you don't want to be bothered with money issues, so I have tried to honor that by—"

"Honor? Is going behind my back and robbing our kids' savings your way of honoring my wishes?"

"All right, look," he said. "If you want to know the truth, Toni needed more money than we have in our personal savings. The business might have failed if I hadn't been able to invest that $80,000."

"It's wrong, PJ; it just plain wrong!"

He leaned forward and did his best to look confident. "We'll get it back, with interest, in a couple months, honey. There will be enough to cover those early withdrawal fees. Contracts are beginning to roll in. Why, just yesterday, we got $165,000 of new city contracts. You've got to trust me on this. I'd never do anything to risk our kids' futures; you know that, don't you?" He hoped she wouldn't read too far down in that stack and discover more evidence of his borrowing from their savings.

Heather reached for a paper napkin and dabbed her eyes with it. "I . . . I suppose so. It's just . . . I wish Dad were still around. He would know what to do. If you had needed money, he would have loaned it to you. But that trust fund? When Dad and Mom gave that to us, I know they intended that we would pass it down to their granddaughters for their college tuition, a down payment on a house or a condo or something."

"It will be okay, Heather, I promise you."

"Oh, PJ, I miss Mom and Dad so much!" Her mouth quivered and then she dissolved into more tears and moans.

PJ stood up, walked over behind her stool and put his arms around her. He was pleased that she didn't pull away. "I know you do, honey, and that's okay. You are going to have these attacks of grief from time to time. Remember what the counselor said? They can hit you when you least expect it, even after a year. Even after ten years."

"I try, PJ, I really try. But I can't erase that memory. I try to scrub it out of my brain, but it keeps coming back. The TV footage of the crash site, the graphic photos in the newspaper and the endless stream of reporters crowding our porch. And, all that grief counseling? It didn't really help. I just couldn't get comfort from listening to other mourners' problems. The neighbors helped at first, but after a while they went their own way, worried about their own problems."

PJ said, "But Heather, even our own daughters have urged you to put that crash behind you and get on with your life."

"I know, I know. But no one understands how devastating it was to lose Mom and Dad. One day they were here, alive and vibrant and well, and the next day they were gone. Gone! I was not ready for that. I never got to say good bye." She teared up again.

PJ waited while she buried her face in her hands. When the sobbing diminished, she reached for a fresh napkin to wipe her cheeks.

"Sometimes I just wish things would have been different," she said. "Between you and them, I mean. I know it's not fair, but I often wish you and Dad had been closer. You both have the same passion for marketing. I wish you hadn't left Beacon and Beacon. You had a great future there, especially with dad on the board of directors."

PJ was tempted to snap at her but knew that would not be productive. The goal was to calm her down and get her off the subject of money troubles. "Now honey, you know that your dad understood my decision. He recognized my need to branch out on my own. Once I explained the partnership with Toni and Simplified Data's potential, do you remember what he said?

Between sniffles, Heather laughed. "Yeah. He said, 'Damn, son, I'm only sorry my firm didn't get in on that deal.'"

"That's right. Your dad had faith in my judgement. You should too." He unwrapped his arms from her shoulders and swiveled her stool around so she faced him. "Now, I've got an idea," PJ said. "There's about an hour of daylight left. Let's go for a walk down on the lake and watch the sailboats. I know that always cheers you up. After that, I'll take you out to dinner at that Italian place you've wanted to try. When we get home, we'll call the girls and catch up on all their news. It will be like old times. Happier times."

Chapter 18

It had been four days since the San Francisco earthquake, but Toni couldn't get the tragedy out of her mind. Sixty-seven people had died, three thousand had been injured and property damage was estimated at over five billion dollars.

Tonight she had her own problem. Well, problems—plural—if you counted the fact that she and Mark were back on the list of murder suspects. Jack had called earlier. According to Jack's "usually reliable source," the police had serious doubts about the validity of Wednesday's confession. The source had cited several discrepancies in the details of the murder as told by the suspect, Dr. George Wilkens. George was a neighbor in Union Pier and someone with whom she had collaborated on a book long ago. Why he confessed was a mystery. Even though this put Mark and her back under suspicion, Toni couldn't help but be happy for George. She couldn't imagine that frail old grey-haired widower as a killer.

Right now, however, at almost midnight on Saturday, she had her arms wrapped around her most immediate concern. Her son Allen was having bad nightmares.

"Mom! Mom!" he had shrieked. "The blood! It's every-where! There's a dead guy!"

Toni sat on the side of his bed. She had wiped perspiration from his forehead and whispered to him, "It's okay honey. I'm right here with you." She sang his favorite song from infant days. *"Hush, little baby. Don't you cry . . ."*

Mark, also jolted awake by Allen's screams, brought in a glass of warm milk for their son and a cup of tea for her.

She rearranged some pillows, propped Allen up in bed and gave him the glass of milk. Mark gave her a hug and, since there wasn't enough room on the bed, he knelt on one knee and patted Allen on the leg.

"Are we going to church tomorrow?" Allen asked. "It's Sunday."

"Sure," Mark said. "Let's make it special. We'll go to the Cathedral."

"Good," Allen said. After a second sip of milk, he said, "I'll pray very hard for God to solve this."

"That would be a very nice prayer," Toni said.

"God won't let them take you guys to jail, will he?"

Toni had to turn away so Allen wouldn't see her tear up.

Mark saved the day by telling Allen, "No, son, God knows we are innocent. He will help the police find the guilty person very soon. Now, take another sip of milk, then maybe a bathroom break, and I'll read you a story until you get sleepy."

Mark walked down the hall with Allen; he turned on the hallway light, presumably to make it a less fearsome journey. The moment they left the bedroom, Toni couldn't help herself. Tears cascaded down her face; she sobbed and her chest heaved. What kind of a life am I giving my children, where they have to lay awake at night worrying that their parents might be arrested? She looked around for a tissue. Finding none, she wiped her eyes and nose with the sleeve of her shirt. Resisting the urge to scream or shout, she just growled like a wild animal whose babies had been threatened.

"Shit!" Toni spat out another whisper-shouted epithet or two, which served to free her from fear and a sense of helplessness. The murderer had unknowingly crossed a line and was now her mortal enemy. The crime itself was bad enough, but now her son was threatened—probably Emily too—with fear that Mom and Dad might be locked away in jail for murder. Watch out, Mister Murderer, I am not waiting for the police to find you. I am coming after you myself! Tomorrow morning!

"What did you say, honey?"

Oh, no! She must have said that last part out loud. "Ah, I was mumbling, 'When are you guys coming back? It's almost morning.'"

Mark gave her a strange look as he tucked Allen in and opened a book. Toni leaned over to kiss Allen, picked up her teacup and went to the kitchen. She took one last sip, rinsed the cup and put it and the saucer into the dishwasher. She climbed back in bed and set the alarm early enough to cook a leisurely breakfast before church. Oh yeah, and then there was that small item she had just added to her agenda—go catch a murderer.

*   *   *

"We're in luck," Mark said while they were getting dressed. "The radio says we will have bright blue skies all day today. It's a perfect day to dress up and enjoy a crisp sunny walk to Holy Name Cathedral."

"Uh, exactly how crisp will it be?" Toni asked. "How many layers of clothes will we need?"

"More good news. High today will be sixty-five, which they say is about five degrees above average for—what is it—the 22nd of October?"

Toni went over to Emily's room and gathered her blonde curls into a ponytail. She clipped a bright red bow to her hair to match the cheerful red plaid jumper Emily had pulled out of her closet. Allen and his father buttoned their sport coats and waited at the elevator. Toni caught a last glimpse of her own designer suit in the hall mirror. Everything was in order.

They set off south on Rush Street at a lively pace. The children jumped and skipped past the string of night spots that only a few hours earlier had vibrated with revelers celebrating Octoberfest. In the bright sunlight the locked-up bars had a shabby look. Allen did not mention his bad dreams during the night. Mark was trying his best to keep the kids focused on today's expedition to the cathedral.

"Kids," he said, "did you know that Holy Name Cathedral is a hundred and fifteen years old?"

"That's old," Emily said. "Maybe even older than Grandpa."

Toni opened her mouth to defend her father's honor but Mark had leaned over close to her and cupped his hand over her ear.

He whispered, "Should I tell them to look for the bullet holes still visible in the cathedral's cornerstone? They're supposed to be from Thompson .45 caliber machine gun slugs fired during a 1926 mob assassins—"

"Stop!" Toni hissed back at him. "Haven't we had enough about murder lately?"

Toni stole a glance at the cornerstone as she walked by but couldn't see anything. She held Emily's hand as they climbed the eight steps to the Gothic-style cathedral's tall center entrance. The heavy bronze doors were already open, of course. A deacon once told her that each of the two doors weighs over half a ton. Emily tugged at her coat sleeve. She bent down to listen.

"Mommy, there's so many people!"

"Yes there are," Toni said while leading the family over to the right, where it was less crowded. "That's because this is a special Mass, called a High Mass. The Cardinal himself will celebrate. Look over there." She pointed to the center aisle. "There's about thirty priests in fancy vestments making a big procession."

"I can't see," Emily said.

Of course! She's only three feet tall. Toni stopped and picked her up.

"Wow! That's pretty. I like the colors. And, look up there!"

Emily gawked at the choir loft where the robed singers were filing into their seats and the first notes were reverberating from the massive organ pipes. Mark's gentle prod reminded her that they were causing a traffic jam in the aisle, so she put Emily back down. Mark and Allen took the lead as they hurried up the aisle and squeezed into the front pew, where Allen loved to sit. Fall flowers, yellow, bronze and red, decorated the altar. As they seated themselves, choir voices rang out, jubilantly praising God. Allen was staring at the magnificent altar but Emily twisted around, distracted by two of her favorite things—music and singing.

She didn't see the procession coming down the aisle toward them and was surprised when the Cardinal sprinkled them with holy water. When this ceremony ended, the Cardinal mounted the steps to the altar and the Mass began.

Allen watched every part of the Mass with delight. However, Emily soon became distracted and looked up at the high ornate ceiling. She tugged on Toni's sleeve, pointed up and said, in an embarrassingly loud voice, "Who put those hats up there, Mommy?"

Toni looked up at the group of red ceremonial sombrero-like Cardinal's hats hanging high above. "Sshh," Toni whispered to her. "It's a long story. I'll tell you later."

"How did they get up there?" Emily whispered.

Toni said, "That I don't know, but I'll find out and tell you. Later. Now, pay attention to the Mass."

The Cardinal's homily addressed a very real and very modern problem—homelessness. When he quoted a biblical phrase from Isaiah about bringing the homeless poor into your house, Toni saw Allen whisper something into Mark's ear. Mark patted him on the shoulder and said something in return, but she couldn't hear it.

Toni's curiosity got the better of her and she leaned over to Mark and said, "What did Allen say?"

"He asked, 'Where do the homeless live, Dad?' I answered, 'That's the problem son; they don't have anywhere to live.' Do you know what he said next? He said, 'I'll have to fix that.'"

Toni reached over, squeezed both their hands and said to Mark, "We have a great son!"

Allen tapped her on the shoulder and whispered, "We can't bring any homeless to Michigan now. There's too much blood down there."

Toni patted him on the shoulder and said, "It'll be okay, honey." Then she turned away and dabbed her eyes with a tissue.

"Mom?" Allen said.

She put the tissue into her pocket and turned toward him. "Yes?"

"We have lots to pray about."

Emily didn't last through the entire ninety-minute High Mass. When her fidgeting became a distraction, Mark took her out to the bathroom and then had stayed in the vestibule where she could at least walk around a little. When the final blessing had been given, she and Allen joined them outside on the steps.

Allen said, "I'm glad we came. Now I know everything will be all right. I prayed a lot."

Mark smiled at Allen and patted him on the back. "That's great, son." He turned to her and whispered, "Honey, thank God we have him. We may need all his prayers. It's been a strange week."

On the way home, Allen jumped off the curb and out into the street at State Street and Chicago Avenue. Toni grabbed him and pulled him back. "Allen! You have to look for traffic first!"

"Okay, Mom. I'm just excited. I can't wait to get home. Can I go down to the playground? Wait 'till the guys hear about my weekend. "Blood, a dead body next door and now I saw a real Cardinal at church! They'll think it's awesome."

Mark said, "Toni, I've got this." He led them across the street and stopped under the awning of a department store. He squatted down to get on Allen's level. "Look, son, I've got to ask you a favor. You shouldn't talk about all that crime stuff right now. Maybe later. But, you see, the police are still investigating and they don't want us, or you, doing any talking right now. It might give away some secret police stuff." He looked at Emily, who was listening with rapt attention. "So, let's keep it quiet for now, okay? Both of you."

"Sure Dad, you can count on me." Allen said. He nudged Emily.

"Yes, Dad, me too." Emily mimed zipping her mouth closed, locking it and throwing away the key.

"Emily, where on earth did you learn that?" Toni asked.

"Oh, Allen taught me. He makes me do it whenever I see him do something bad."

"Em!" Allen shouted. "You promised!"

Mark laughed and grabbed both kids' hands. "Let's go home and have lunch."

After a lunch of cold ham and cheese sandwiches, chips and a section of orange, they spent a few hours of quiet family time reading and helping the kids with their homework. Mark packed a bag for his evening flight back to Houston. Tomorrow morning, opening arguments were scheduled in his court case; he'd be gone until Friday. He'd get a late dinner down there with his colleagues.

When it was time to leave, Mark hugged the kids and told them to be good. He said, "Kids, Mommy and Daddy are now going to be doing a lot of kissing and hugging and saying good byes."

"Eewww," Allen said. He turned and ran for his room. Emily followed.

"Great technique," Toni said. "Now, please follow through with the kissing and hugging part." She put her arms around him. After an especially long kiss she said, "Mmm. I'll miss you."

After they separated, Mark reached down for the handle of his roll-aboard case. "Oh, one more thing, my love. I heard what you were saying to yourself last night."

"When?"

"When Allen couldn't sleep and he and I went to the bathroom. On the way back to his room, I distinctly heard the words, 'police' and 'coming after you myself.' You haven't done anything stupid—ah, let me rephrase—anything irresponsible or dangerous, have you?"

"No, Mark, really. I haven't."

They kissed again before she closed and locked the door. She was proud of herself; she hadn't lied. She hadn't done anything dangerous—yet.

Chapter 19

Rhonda locked up the Camaro and walked across the parking lot, dreading another boring Monday sorting mail and typing letters at Sheldon Sales. She had zero interest in paperwork or taking dictation from her sexist boss. All she wanted was a private moment to use the company phone. She and Bernie had to meet, had to figure out a plan.

Just before opening the door, she noticed the workmen next door ogling her. She turned to them, swishing her long blonde hair, waved and said, "Hi there." It was nice to be noticed, even while wearing an overcoat in chilly weather. That meant she still had "it," the sexy stride accentuated by the click of her high heels on the asphalt. She cinched the belt of her overcoat to accentuate her trim waist and the rise of her breasts.

Why bother, though? These guys weren't in her league. They were common laborers. "It's your fault, Dad," Rhonda said out loud, but not loud enough for the laborers to hear. Her dad was the one who had built up her ego and even encouraged a healthy form of exhibitionism. As a child, dad used to dress her as like a doll. He would cart her over to the bar in Three Oaks and set her on the counter. All the local guys admired her. At seventeen, dad had encouraged her to compete in the Miss Southwest Michigan beauty pageant and she almost had won—the First Runner-Up trophy was in her bookcase at home.

Rhonda hung her coat on a rack and sat down at her desk. She couldn't get her mind off her dad. He had been a good guy, never a mean drunk but a drunk nevertheless, which is what eventually killed him. He had never quite gotten over her mother's abandoning them both, only a week after she had been born. Damn him, why did he have to die so early? Her coping mechanism had been to attach herself to the first man who came along. That had turned out to be John, a.k.a. the loser husband. Within a six-month period, John had married her, flunked out of college and gotten fired from two separate jobs. After their latest flare-up, she had kicked him out for good. He seemed to have gotten the message; he had moved to Detroit and gotten his own apartment. When she had asked him how he could afford that with no job, he had told her he was now a long-haul truck driver with a modest income. More importantly, he had told her he wouldn't contest a divorce filing as long as she paid for the whole thing.

Mr. Grady was in a staff meeting, which gave Rhonda the time and privacy to place a call to Bernie. She'd try his Aunt's house; the police must have released it by now.

"Bernie, it's me, Rhonda."

"What do you want?" He sounded surly. "You've got me in plenty of hot water. I don't really want to talk to you."

"Bernie, I have to talk to you. It's important. Meet me for lunch. You name the place."

She waited several seconds, hearing only Bernie's breathing.

"Okay," he said. "Noon at Townline Station. I really like their hot dogs. Bring some cash."

He hung up before she could answer.

*   *   *

Rhonda walked into Townline Station, saw Bernie already at a table and walked over to him. She sat across from him in the booth.

"Well, I'm here," he said. "What's up?"

"I have all the stuff. We need to figure out how to hock the gold."

"Shut up, woman. Here comes the waitress."

The waitress stepped up to their table and gave each of them an enormous menu sealed in clear plastic pages. The entire first page was covered with pictures of the old days, when this building had been the actual train depot for Townline.

Bernard studied the pictures and flipped the menu over to read the back. "I been here a dozen times and I never paid attention to this. Man! This place is a historic building. It dates back to 1870, when the train stopped every five miles to serve the farmers. And I never knew that Townline was the original name of this area. This was the next-to-last stop on the route. Shoot, now AMTRAK roars right through town without even slowing down. But they've done a great job converting this into a little café and—"

"Bernie, stop! We've got to talk about that jewelry and how to hock it."

"I'm not going to the chair for any gold."

"Who said anything about the electric chair? Are you a suspect?"

"I sure am," he answered. "That detective . . . hold on; here she comes again."

Bernie ordered two hot dogs, fries and a soda pop. Rhonda requested a hot dog and a cup of coffee. The waitress was familiar to her; she must have served them on one of their previous visits. Thank God the girl didn't ask them any questions about the Page murder. The California earthquake was still monopolizing the news and gossip around town. Over sixty deaths and almost 4,000 people injured.

When the waitress had moved on to another table, Bernie said, "Yes, Rhonda, I am definitely a suspect. That detective is out to get me. All he needs is a motive and stealing qualifies."

She slid her hand across the table and lifted it, exposing three hundred-dollar bills "This will make you feel better," she said with a smile.

He glared at the money for several seconds before sweeping it off the table and into his pocket.

"Bernie," Rhonda whispered, "we have to sell that gold. Where do we do that?"

"How would I know? You think I'm some sort of fence? I'm a pretty straight guy whether you know it or not."

Rhonda leaned across the table and touched his hand. "Bernie, baby, this is me, Rhonda. I thought we were pretty good friends. Now you're acting like you can't stand me. Could that be true?"

Bernie looked at her as if he were seeing her for the first time. "Woman, think about it. You are a cute, innocent-looking little white girl. Now—" He tapped his own chest. "You see what this is? This is a black man with a record who is now on that cop's radar. So, I got to be extra careful. I can't just go around asking people to buy a murdered man's jewelry."

"So, don't do it around here. Find somebody back in Chicago."

"Rhonda, for as steel-hearted as you are, you don't think straight. You tell me I am supposed to go back to my 'hood, which is also Page's neighborhood, and try to hock the Alderman's own gold and his fancy watch? Everybody on Chicago's West Side would recognize that stuff in a heartbeat."

She could see that he was rattled, and for good reason. He was right. They couldn't hock the jewelry here or in Chicago. She would need a little time to come up with a plan. She could send him on a train or bus to St. Louis or Detroit. That might cost a few bucks but would be a lot safer. Before she could offer that idea, their food arrived.

Bernie was right about the hot dogs; they were special. Devin's Meat Market over in Three Oaks provided the fat, juicy dogs and the tangy mustard. She watched in amazement as Bernie doctored up the dogs with relish and extra mustard. He had finished both of his before she was halfway through hers and went to work on his fries. Good old Bernie; he could always be diverted by food. As skinny as he was, he ate a ton.

Rhonda told him about her plan to hock the jewelry in either St. Louis or Detroit. He promised to ask his Chicago buddies, very discretely, of course for the names of some "cooperative" pawn shops down in St. Louis.

As he swallowed the last of his French fries, he said, "Where's the stuff?"

"It's in a safe place. No way could anybody find it."

"Good. Just so it ain't at your house. They're bound to search."

Bernie didn't need to know the cop had already paid her a visit. She said, "I don't think your sweet detective would want to search my house, but—" She giggled. "Perhaps he wouldn't mind searching me."

"Well, if you don't beat all!"

Rhonda said, "Hah. You just take everything the wrong way. Sex isn't all I ever think about."

"That's true. Money first." Bernie laughed.

She sensed his worries had dissipated. Now they could make some plans. "Find out what you can about hocking the watch and the chains. Meanwhile, I'll keep the stuff in a safe place. If you're called in just tell them you only know what you told them already."

"Yeah. I told that guy, 'Why would I kill somebody and put him in my aunt's house and then call the police? Does that make any sense?"

"No, it doesn't. Somewhere out there is someone who really hated Ed Page. Could be anybody. They'll find him and we'll be home free. You know that whoever it is will be stuck with theft as well as murder."

"I s'pose so," said Bernie. "I just wish that cop would forget about me and Aunt Ruth."

"Well, my friend," Rhonda stood up as she spoke, "I'm out of here. Back to work."

"Hey, I'm still eating. What about dessert?"

"Get what you want. You handle the check. Talk to you soon." She laid a ten dollar bill on the table and walked out.

"Good morning, cousin!"

Toni looked up from the stack of papers on her desk. "Oh, my gosh! Tuesday morning! I'm sorry Fred, I totally forgot you wanted to meet today."

"No problem. With all the commotion about the Union Pier stuff, I'm surprised you're even at work. If it was me, I'd be too stressed. Speaking of stressed, as Simplified Data's accountant, I am sorry to have missed the police raid the other day. I might have—"

"It was not a raid!" Toni said, with a little too much emphasis. "Yes, they took some of our records because they see a connection between us and the murder victim. It's all a mess. Too many coincidences make the police curious. We—meaning PJ—take Alderman Page out to several lavish lunches at high-end restaurants. A few days later, the City Council awards us lucrative contracts. Then the Alderman gets murdered. Not just murdered, but murdered in *my* house!"

"My God, Toni, the way you describe it, you're the prime suspect."

"Well, that may not be far from the truth, although several people in Union Pier and at least a few in Chicago had grudges against Alderman Page. Mark and I are cooperating with the detective to get this solved."

"Wow. What do your mom and dad think about all this?"

"I knew they'd hear about it on the news, so I called them and told them we know nothing about the murder. Dad, of course, wants frequent updates."

"Look, Toni, do you want to skip this week's financial update? You seem to have a lot on your mind right now."

"No, let's do it. I need a little bit of normal business to take my mind off the murder."

"Okay." Fred opened a file folder and pushed it across the desk so she could read it. "This is a lot of good news. We've finally got some good cash flow. Business seems to be picking up. That makes my job a lot easier."

He spent the next ten minutes going into the details of recent invoices, payments, liabilities and assets. She was glad to have Fred, a trusted cousin whom she had known since childhood, here to explain all this in plain language. Balancing the books was not on her list of favorite things to do.

"I have only one concern," he said. "I can't make our income-versus-expense sheet balance. There are four $1,000 checks that have been cashed but I do not see any expense sheets to document them. I should have the cancelled checks by now but they seem to be missing."

Toni picked up her key ring and then put it back down. She couldn't open that locked drawer and show Fred the checks PJ had written. That would implicate him in a coverup.

She said, "Give me the dates of the checks and I'll look in my records and also ask PJ."

Her phone rang. "Anything else?" she asked Fred. He said no, patted her on the shoulder and left the room. She picked up the phone on the third ring.

"Toni, it's Jack. Mark's office told me he's unavailable so I've got an update for you."

She got out a note pad and picked up a pen. "Yeah, Mark's out of town on a court case until Friday. Go ahead."

"Well, my earlier scoop about George Wilkens's bogus confession has proven correct. Bruce—Markowski, that is—told me, in so many words and off the record, that old Wilkens just doesn't have his facts straight. Bruce thinks he's trying to protect someone."

"But who?"

"No idea. Bruce also told me that, in addition to being neighbors in Union Pier, you have a professional relationship with Wilkens?"

"Yes," Toni said. "A year or so ago, George interviewed me for a book he was writing." She explained the book and Wilkens's interest in her system for improving health care for low-income neighborhoods. She said, "As much as I'd love for him to be the murderer, he is just too nice a man. Based on what I've seen of him at social gatherings in Union Pier, he's not a killer. Oh . . .wait . . . I get it now. You are thinking that Markowski suspects Wilkens is trying to protect *me*!"

"Ah, well, that thought crossed my mind," Jack said, "Here's one more tantalizing tidbit, and this one is public information, as I just got it off the police scanner. There is an APB out for Bernard Smith. 'Wanted for questioning' is what I heard."

"Ruth's nephew?"

"Yeah. I'm trying unsuccessfully to pump Markowski for more details on that. "

"Do you think Bernard's the murderer?" Toni asked.

"It would be convenient, wouldn't it? I sat down with Markowski and speculated about that, off the record, of course. God, wouldn't I love to print all this day-by-day? It would be like a real life murder mystery, published clue-by-clue in the newspaper. I am making good notes, though, and hope to publish—"

"Jack, please. Answer my question."

"Oh, sorry. I wish I could say. But if you press me for an opinion, I would say no, I do not think Bernard did it. Number one, it's illogical. Kill a guy and dump the body in your own aunt's crawlspace, thereby making you both prime suspects? No way. Number two, my gut feeling is, Bernard is too nice a guy to be a murderer. I've spoken with him a few times over the hedges while visiting you. I sense Markowski feels the same."

"Great," Toni said. "Hmm. Everyone's too nice to be a killer. What you're saying is, the State Police don't have a likely suspect yet, except Mark and me. What does Markowski say about us?"

There was a long pause. "I asked, Toni, several times. All I got was a lot of 'No comments.'"

Toni hung up after thanking Jack and asking him to keep her informed. She ran her hand through her hair and got a brush out of her desk drawer to brush it back into place. She ought to visit the ladies' room to do this right. On her way down the hall, she saw Margaret push back from her desk, stand up and walk over to see her.

"Toni, while you were on the phone, a Ruth Smith called. She said it was urgent. Here's the note."

So much for a few moments of relaxing, peaceful hair brushing. She thanked Margaret, did an about-face and returned to her office, where she opened the note. Ruth wanted her to call immediately; it was about Union Pier.

"Mrs. Smith, it's Toni Harrington."

"Oh, Mrs. Harrington, thank you for calling back. My, this is awkward. I don't know where to begin. I know we're neighbors and such but I hardly know you. I am beginning to think . . . you see . . ."

"Mrs. Smith—may I call you Ruth? And please call me Toni. Please just tell me what's on your mind. Don't be worried; we're all under a lot of stress due to the murder."

"Thank you, Toni. It's about George Wilkens. I just got off the phone with him. I'm worried about him. Did you know that the police put him in a psychiatric ward? He tells me he confessed to the killing but the police don't believe him. Neither do I. But what I really wanted to talk about is something George said. Look, it would be better if we could talk face-to-face. Are you free to meet me for coffee or an early lunch?"

Half an hour later, Toni walked into the Art Institute café. Ruth had suggested it because it was close to both of their offices. She was at the counter stirring sugar into a coffee. There was no one in line behind her, so Toni walked up and said hello.

Ruth said, "Thanks for coming on such short notice. What can I get for you? My treat."

"Thanks. How about an herbal tea? I've had too much coffee already."

Ruth led the way to a small table and they sat down.

Toni had a sip of her tea and smiled at Ruth. "That's a very pretty necklace you're wearing."

"Thank you. It was my mother's. Pearls set in silver. She told me it had been an anniversary gift from my dad."

Ruth's eyes had a warm, friendly glint and her smile was that of a person who had fond memories of her parents. Toni found it easy to like this woman; her body language said, "I'm sincere, friendly and approachable." It wasn't long before the smile left her, replaced by a frown.

"God, what a terrible week it's been," Ruth said. "Toni, he didn't do it. George, I mean. I've known him for years. He would not kill a man. But, why would he say he did?"

Toni said, "I like George. I watched him interact with our kids at last summer's party. And, I agree; he does not strike me as a killer." She reached for her cup. "Have you considered that he might be trying to protect someone?"

"Protect someone? Who? Oh, I see, You think he's trying to protect me."

Toni couldn't help it. She laughed, but then reached out and put her hand over Ruth's. "No, no, Ruth. Not you. I was thinking he was trying to protect *me*!"

"You?" Ruth closed her eyes and shook her head.

Had Ruth been offended at her laugh?

Ruth began a slow chuckle herself, which soon became a more robust laugh. "What a fine pair we are." She squeezed Toni's hand. "Neighbors and now murder suspects, at least in our own minds!" She laughed even harder. It was contagious. For about ten seconds, they both dissolved into fits of uncontrolled giggling.

"My gracious!" Ruth patted her chest. She looked at the customers at nearby tables. "That laugh felt really good! A great stress reliever. But, people are staring. They must think we're drinking something stronger than tea or coffee. If they only knew we were in a serious discussion about being—" She leaned across the table and whispered, "—murder suspects."

Toni made a decision to trust this lady whom she didn't really know but could not imagine as a killer. "At least in my case, it's not just in my own mind. That detective has been over to my office with a search warrant." She went on to explain the connections between her business, Edwin Page and Chicago city contracts.

"Toni, that's another thing I wanted to talk about. This chain of coincidences is ridiculous. Do you know what I do for a living?"

"Well, I just know you're a nurse."

"That's true," Ruth said, "but, my God, there's much more to it. I work for the city. I'm the Director of Public Health Nurses and my budget for new nurses has been sucked away by some new consulting company, promoted by Ed Page, by the way. It's called "Simplified—"

"Data Systems." Toni said the last two words with her. "Uh, oh. But wait, I can—"

"Hold on. So I've been hating your company for the last several weeks . . . until I spoke with George yesterday. After we got done talking about all the murder news and his silly confession, he mentioned your name. He said you two had worked together before and he trusts you and your product. He says you have always been dedicated to the same thing I am—providing care to low income people."

"That's what I was trying to say," Toni said. "I can explain how we can—"

"Girl, let me finish! I am trying to apologize here for hating your company. And, can you imagine how hot I got when I found out that you, my next door neighbor, are the owner!"

They both had another good laugh.

Toni said, "Ruth, why don't you come over to my office sometime and I'll show you how we can work together to make it better for your patients?"

"I'd love that, but only if you come with me on some clinic visits in the projects, where the rubber meets the road."

They shook hands, vowing to make all that happen.

Ruth stood up. "Well, I'm glad we talked. Now I've got a staff meeting to run."

Toni pushed her chair back and got to her feet. She walked around the table to Ruth, wrapped her arms around her ample girth and gave her a big hug. "Ruth, all this murder stuff . . . we'll get through it. I know we will. And George will be cleared—he'll be all right."

"Yeah," Ruth said. "I've got a good feeling about that detective. I pray that he'll solve this soon."

Toni nodded and, for a moment, considered telling Ruth that she was not going to wait for Markowski to do the solving. She decided it was a little too early in their relationship for that level of trust.

Chapter 21

Toni didn't sit down right away after returning to her office. She paced back and forth in front of the window, ignoring the stack of papers and notes on her desk and casting occasional glances down at the lakefront. On-shore winds had angered Lake Michigan. Surf pounded relentlessly against the breakwater, sending cascades of white foam into the air. Near the shore, the lake was grey and gloomy but further out she noticed patches of bright blue sky and sunlight on the water.

Who was she kidding? Murder-solving was not a skill listed on her resumé. Maybe she should leave it to the police after all. She stopped pacing and gave that some thought. Markowski seemed competent enough and—no, the hell with it! This was personal now. The blood in her tub and the dead body next door were both threats to her family. She was going to go after the—careful, no bad words!—the perpetrator.

There wasn't time to visit the public library and check out a book on how to solve murders; she'd have to follow her instincts. She resumed pacing, four steps in each direction, which covered the width of her office. Clues! Look for clues. Okay, the blood in the tub and the bloody knife, assuming the blood matches Page's, are big clues. She shuddered to think about it. Page was stabbed in her house and presumably died in her bathtub. Yuck! How and why did he get in? And, speaking of getting in, why was the murderer in her house? One of those two must have had the security code.

Toni congratulated herself on her first "a ha!" moment as an amateur private investigator. The killer must be the one with the code, since a dead man didn't set the code on the way out. Three people knew the code for sure: Mark, Jack and herself. Could Jack be a murderer? Was that possible? Not really; she and Mark had figured out he was in Chicago on Friday night. Unfortunately, since she had cleverly pasted the code on her refrigerator door and even labeled the note, "Security Code," anyone who had been in her house since then could have seen it.

So, who had been in her house since she had posted that note back in July? Darn. A whole cast of characters came to mind. At their Fourth of July party, everyone had been in the kitchen at one time or another. George Wilkens, Ruth Smith, their tenant Rhonda, PJ—.

"Whoa, Toni, you're making me dizzy! Is that a new form of workout?"

"Oh, hi PJ. I'm pacing aimlessly, worrying about how and why Page came to be murdered in our house."

PJ, leaning against her door frame and wearing a perfectly pressed grey suit, sparkling white shirt and a narrow dark blue tie, said, "Didn't I hear that someone confessed to Page's murder?"

"Our friend Jack O'Connor told us that Dr. George Wilkens confessed. He's got a weekend place in Union Pier. You met him last summer at our Fourth of July party. But

Jack also tells us that the detective doesn't believe George's story. He's got some of the details all wrong. So, in my opinion, Mark and I are still prime suspects." Toni sat down; it was more of a collapse into her chair rather than a graceful maneuver. "I guess I'd better try to do some work. How's your day going?"

PJ said, "I've just returned from Page's memorial service over at the City Council chambers."

"Why would you go?"

He smiled. "I like to keep my shining face before the city fathers. As you might guess, it is good for business."

"I can't see how going to a memorial service will do anything for business, but that's not my call. Anyway, how was it?"

"I've never heard so many nice things expressed about Page," he reported. "I wondered if I accidentally went to a memorial for somebody else. All those superlatives about how kind and generous he was . . . fighting for his people and all that. I'm sure they mixed up some words. They could have said fleecing his people instead. The council is just one big brotherhood, like Knights of the Round Table. The Mayor is King Arthur."

"Do they really go that far?" Toni asked.

"They went further," he answered. "They said Page helped make this city great. Everyone knows Al Capone did that." PJ laughed at his own joke.

"It couldn't have been that bad," Toni said.

"Believe me, it was worse. I couldn't believe all those wolves dressed up in their best sheep's clothing prancing around in front of TV cameras from every station. They had a giant portrait of Page sitting in front of the podium. The galleries were packed, like an opening night at the theater."

"Maybe that closes the book on Edwin Page," Toni said.

"We can only hope," PJ said. "Say, did you know that, before the memorial service, the City Council voted to give a $25,000 reward for information leading to Page's killer?

"Oh, maybe I can claim that," Toni quipped.

"Really?" PJ narrowed his eyes, stared at her for a second or two, and then his expression softened. "Toni, I need a favor. Actually two. First, please sign a blank letterhead for me. I have to get a letter out today which would look a lot better over your signature. You're better known than I in the health care business."

"Sure," she answered, reaching into her desk for stationery. I'll sign two in case you make a mistake. What's it for?" she asked as she signed the two sheets.

"It's for those idiots at the City. They require a ton of paperwork. I'll handle it later. And the second thing. Later this afternoon, do you mind if I use your computer? Mine is giving me some trouble."

"Okay, go ahead. At two o'clock, you'll have my office to yourself. I'll be down in the gym for an hour. But, you should get yours fixed. Fred knows a good computer repair service; check with him."

"That'll be great. I've got an errand to run between now and 2:00. And yes, I'll check with Fred about computer repair." PJ turned to leave but hesitated. "Oh, one more thing. I'd like to get those expense sheets from you. You know, the ones that show how many times I took Page to lunch. And the ones showing our campaign contributions. You must have forgotten to put them back in my file folder. I'd like to change some of those expense sheets to show the money went to other people.

"Sorry, PJ. Those are out of sight until this is over."

"But why?" he asked.

"The police don't yet know about the campaign contribution checks or the expense sheets for those. I'm not letting them out until this is over. They already have the receipts and expense sheets for the pricy lunches you had with Page. So, we have enough problems without adding any doctored-up sheets."

"You are really getting paranoid, Toni," said PJ. "Jeez." He came over to her desk, scooped up the two signed letterheads and stalked out.

Toni spent the next hour reading a proposal from Jim Davies, their junior programmer. He had included a diskette with prototype software that, according to him, would make their system even more user-friendly. She inserted the diskette, opened the program and ran some sample entries. It looked promising but had some rough edges in one section. Jim was not in today; he only worked three days per week. On the other days he handled childcare for his three kids. She wrote a note thanking him and suggested a time they could meet to discuss it further.

After a 45-minute workout in the gym and a quick shower, she walked back into the office, where Margaret said, "Mrs. Conroy called; here's the note. She asked for you specifically and made me promise to tell you it's urgent. Her number's on there."

"Thanks, Margaret." PJ's wife, Heather? It was highly unusual for Heather to call for anyone but PJ. Toni closed the door to her office, sat down and dialed Heather's number.

"Oh, Toni, thank you for getting back to me so quickly. I . . . I don't know what to do. Something's going on and . . . and . . . I think something's wrong. Is PJ there?"

"No, he's been in and out all day, but I think he's got a 3:00 p.m. meeting at Loretto Hospital, out on the West Side."

"Good," Heather said. "Toni . . . can I trust you to keep a secret?"

Toni considered how to answer that. "Heather, is there something going on, some kind of dispute, between you and PJ? If so, I don't want to get caught in the middle."

"It's about money, some money that PJ has invested in your company. I am not good with money. I admit that. That's why I asked my accountant, Roger Morton, to come over and ask you a couple questions. He's actually on the way over there right now. Will you at least listen to what he has to say?"

"I'll listen, as long as he gets here before 4:30. But that's all I'm promising. I can't guarantee I will have answers or if I will even feel comfortable answering."

*   *   *

Twenty minutes later, Toni was sitting at her desk across from Roger Morton, holding his business card in her hand. He was in his sixties, white-haired, and thin. He wore a conservative grey suit. Morton had explained his history with Heather's family finances. He had made a point of saying he was not really PJ's accountant; Heather's parents had been his clients until their untimely death in a plane crash. Heather had continued the relationship since much of their wealth had been inherited from her parents.

"Mrs. Harrington—"

"Please call me Toni."

"Right. Toni, as you know, Mrs. Conroy asked me to see you. I am very much aware that you may have privacy or confidentiality issues with answering my questions. I will not be offended if you choose not to answer." He stopped and took a deep breath. "Toni, I'll get right to the point. Within the last thirty days, has PJ given this company a check for $80,000?"

Toni's eyes widened. "$80,000? Did you say *eighty*?"

"I'll take that as a 'no.' Now what I am about to say is confidential and I ask for your discretion. I have Mrs. Conroy's permission to tell you that, in her opinion—and mine—Mr. Conroy has drained a trust account intended for their children's education, and done so fraudulently. He claims he deposited it all into Simplified Data Systems."

Toni tried to maintain a poker face but failed. "Hell, no, he didn't!" It was the robbing of a trust fund intended for children that swayed her to volunteer more information. "Just a minute." She punched the intercom button for Fred and put the call on speaker phone.

"Fred, can you get me the amounts and dates of all cash that PJ has put into the company?"

While Fred was looking for the data, Toni said to Morton, "Fred is our company accountant."

Fred came back on the line and said, "There's been only one check from PJ. It was for $5,000 and it was dated October 13th."

She thanked Fred, looked at Morton and shrugged. "What can I say?"

Morton rubbed one finger inside the collar of his shirt, as if it had suddenly gotten too tight. He said, "I hesitate to use the word, but this smacks of embezzlement. I must report it as such to Mrs. Conroy and let her confront her husband. Further, I might be legally bound to report it to the police."

"Can you keep my name and that of my company out of it?"

Morton rubbed his chin for a moment and said, "Yes, at least for now. I have access to the Conroy's bank information. I think I can 'find' that $5,000 cancelled check on my own. Later, of course, if the police get involved, they will probably come knocking on your door."

Morton stood and offered a handshake. "Thank you, Toni. I hope the rest of your day brings happier news."

She escorted him out to the lobby and said good bye. Chicago police knocking on her door? They might have to wait in line behind the Michigan State Police.

Chapter 22

Bruce Markowski sat alone in the station's break room. He had just finished a bottle of root beer, a plate of macaroni and cheese leftovers and an apple. While rinsing out the plastic food container and the bottle (might as well get that nickel deposit back), he mulled over the recent developments. Today was Wednesday, almost exactly twelve days to the minute since he had been called away from another lunch for his introduction to Edwin Page. The suspect board in his office was a mess; there were too many names on it! He had almost run out of room for the three-by-five-inch notecards listing suspects. Most of them had both motive and opportunity to kill Page. That thought inspired him to go back to his office and rearrange the list.

He lifted the cloth privacy cover up and over the easel, pulled the tripod holding the cork board closer to his chair and stared at it. Just before lunch, his investigation had come to a screeching halt due to a shortage of the little plastic push-pins used to stick cards onto the cork. With ten suspects in the left-hand column, each requiring its own row of two more cards—one for motive and one for opportunity—he had run short of pins. A fresh box of pins now rested on his desk, thanks to Linda.

"There's got to be a better way," he said out loud.

"A better way for what?"

Markowski looked up to find Alice standing in his doorway. She seemed to have a talent for sneaking up on him. "Oh, sorry. Didn't know you were there. Come in. I was just thinking of this mess of a suspect, motive and opportunity list. Three cards for each suspect. And, if I want to move a suspect up or down the list based on priority, I've got to move all three cards for each one I move."

"Why don't you use the blackboard side?" Alice asked.

"Tried that; it got to be a pain when I needed to shuffle the names all around."

"Hmm," she said. "Let me think about that. I'll bet there's an easier way."

He leaned forward and pulled George Wilkens's cards off the board and moved them near the bottom of the list. He moved John Shain's cards down to the very bottom. Alice raised her eyebrows.

"I know, I know," he said. "It would be so convenient if the jealous husband had done it, but he has an alibi. John Shain hasn't lived with Rhonda for several months. They're separated. He was a little difficult to track down, since he's now a long-haul moving van driver based in Detroit. When I called his motel in Flagstaff, Arizona, Shain said he had been somewhere between Oklahoma and New Mexico at the time of the murder. Company records confirm this. Of course, he could have hired someone to make the hit, but that is very unlikely."

"Who's Conroy?" Alice asked.

"He's a colleague of Toni Harrington and had some business lunches with Page. I got interested in him right away, but during a phone interview, Conroy pointed out he had every reason to keep Page alive and happy since Page had paved the way for Simplified Data's large city contracts. In any case, Conroy was in Detroit on Friday the 13th. He promised to mail hotel receipts and other documentation to prove it." Markowski made a note to follow up on those.

"I see Jack O'Connor is on the list. Is that the reporter for the *Dispatch*? Haven't I seen him around here before?"

"Yeah, I left him on there only because he's a friend of the Harringtons and he knows the code for their security system. Plus, he's been a little too pushy for details on the Page murder, even for a newsman. But I verified he was in Chicago on the night of the murder. Plus, he's about the only person on that list who doesn't have a motive, at least not one that I can see."

Alice said, "So, those at the top—it looks like there's five with check marks—those are your top suspects right now?

"Yes. The Harringtons are not above suspicion, but my instinct is to concentrate on the Bernard-Ruth-Rhonda scenario. Both Bernard and Rhonda seem to be hiding something. As for Ruth, she comes across as matronly and harmless, but is she really?"

Markowski's intercom line buzzed.

"Sergeant," the desk clerk said, "You'd better come out here. A man has found your murder victim's wallet."

Markowski grabbed some gloves and an evidence bag and hurried out to the front desk. Alice followed.

"This is Mr. Franklin Jones," the clerk said.

Franklin Jones was a tall, elderly black man, fit looking, with salt and pepper short hair. He wore what looked like a chauffeur's cap, a thick grey Eisenhower-style jacket, matching pants and sturdy black lace-up chukka boots.

Pointing to a shiny black billfold on the desk, the sergeant said, "Mr. Jones found this today. He says Edwin Page's I.D.'s inside. I haven't touched it yet. Wanted you to see it first."

"Thank you," he said to the desk clerk. "And thank you, Mr. Jones, for bringing it in. I'm Detective Sergeant Bruce Markowski. I'd like to get some details from you but give me just a moment." He put on gloves and inspected the wallet. I.D. and credit cards were there but he found no cash. He closed it up and noticed some gouges on the exterior. He put the wallet into an evidence bag and asked Alice to log it in and get forensics to check for fingerprints. "Now, Mr. Jones, do you have a moment to answer some questions?"

He got Jones seated in his office and asked for identification.

"My I.D. says Franklin but everybody, even Hilda—that's my wife—calls me Mailman. You see, I'm a retired mail carrier. Thirty-five years. Walked about a million miles, most of it in New Buffalo and Union Pier. After retirement, I still walk a lot, but it's for my own self and my dog, Crackers. It was Crackers who found the wallet."

Jones went on to say Crackers had chased two birds into some bushes and had come out with something between his teeth, which had turned out to be a wallet. Jones had trouble getting it away from the dog. That explained the gouges—teeth marks from a small dog. Jones had opened it, recognized the name from recent news stories and contacted the Chickaming Police, who had referred him here.

Markowski had Jones identify the park on his large wall map of the township. He put a yellow pin into the map at that location and asked, "Would you be willing to go out there with one of our troopers and point out the exact location?" After Jones agreed, he said, "Mr. Jones—Mail-man—would it be okay if we got fingerprints from you just so we can eliminate yours from any others on the wallet?"

Markowski thanked Jones again and asked him to pass on his thanks to Crackers. He sent him off be fingerprinted. After finishing off his notes, he stood up and looked at the new pin on his map. The wallet had been dumped about a mile north of Rhonda Shain's house.

A volunteer staffer appeared in his doorway, holding a large envelope.

"Hi, Julie," he said.

"Hello, Sergeant. This just came by messenger service."

He pushed back his chair and almost ran across the room to take the envelope. "Yes!" he said. "Thanks, Julie; this is just what I need. Would you please close the door on the way out?"

Maybe today would be the day—the day where every-thing came together for this case. He opened the envelope a little too vigorously, ripping the outside label, and extracted the lab report and the coroner's findings.

The knife wound to the chest had been the primary cause of death. Damage done by the fireplace poker had caused a skull fracture but not a fatal one. All the blood samples matched. Page's blood type had been in the tub, on the murder weapons, Ruth's porch and her kitchen floor. The sawdust on Rhonda's shoes matched what was on Ruth's floor. One set of footprints had exactly matched Rhonda's shoes. He stopped reading and picked up the phone.

Twenty minutes later, troopers were on the way to bring in Bernard Smith and Rhonda Shain. He felt confident that warrantless arrests were justified and made the proper notations in his records. He'd worry about Ruth Smith later. He rotated the big cork board over to the blackboard side and grabbed a piece of chalk. His mind was racing ahead to which questions, and in which order, to throw at . . . whom? Who should be first? He decided on Bernard. If he could break down Bernard, he might find out if Rhonda had been in on it. He jotted down a list of questions for both suspects and sat down to stare at his suspect list and develop a game plan for the afternoon's interrogations.

*　　*　　*

Bernard Smith was located at his aunt's house, where he had been hard at work on a new sub-floor. He had come in voluntarily, been read his rights and was waiting downstairs in an interview room. After giving Bernard a few minutes to sit and worry, Markowski walked in carrying a brown leather briefcase, sat down and said, "Hello, Bernard. Are you sure you don't want a lawyer?"

"Naw. I got nothin' to hide. I got nothin' to tell you that I ain't already told you."

"Okay." He opened the briefcase and pulled out a mini-cassette tape recorder. He set it on the table, turned it on and spoke to the recorder. He identified himself, stated the date, time and whom he was interviewing.

"Bernard, I respect you; I think you are basically a good person. Why? Well, one reason is all that work you are doing for your aunt. I think you are a good nephew to her. If you were my son, I'd be very proud of you for that."

"I try to be a good nephew."

"So," Markowski said, "here's the thing. I think you have been caught up in something very bad here. I'm not sure what exactly that is, but—"

"I didn't do nothing. How many times do I got to tell you that?"

"Did you like Edwin Page?"

"Hell, no! You've seen my aunt's house, that remodeling job all screwed up? It was Page that convinced Aunt Ruth to hire his brother. They stole from her, tried to scam her! But that don't mean I killed the guy."

"Can you explain where you got these?" He reached into the briefcase and pulled out three hundred-dollar bills found in Bernard's wallet.

"I got those to buy some pipes for the house."

"Who gave you the money?"

"Aunt Ruth. She wants the house ready for winter."

"If I call her and ask her," Markowski said, "do you think she'd tell me the same thing?"

"Sure, she would," Bernard said. "Do you think I'm lying?"

"Sadly, yes I do."

"You just want to hang me because I'm black."

"Oh, please. I don't care what color your skin is. What I care about is the truth. Are you being truthful, Bernard? Are you guilty of murder? Who helped you?"

"Nobody. I didn't do it! How could I need help if I didn't do it?"

"Did your aunt set you up? Would you really do it for $300 or have you got more coming?"

"Aunt Ruth? Set up a murder?" Bernard laughed. "You gotta be kidding me, man. She is the nicest, most peaceful lady on earth. She gave me that money for pipes."

"Then where were you going to buy them?"

Bernard pulled a tissue from a box on the table and wiped beads of perspiration from his forehead. He rocked back and forth in his seat. "I don't know. I hadn't got that far."

"Come on, Bernard," Markowski insisted. "You and I know that you got the money from Page's body. If you'd tell me the whole truth, I might be able to help you when it comes to trial. But I need all the information. I'd hate to see you get stuck with a murder wrap if you didn't do it. Lying won't get you out of it."

"How do you know it's Page's money?"

"I don't, but it's pretty strong circumstantial evidence. You can't explain where you got it. I'll get a statement from your Aunt Ruth and see if it matches. If it doesn't, you're in big trouble."

"It will."

Markowski made a show of looking at his wristwatch. "Good, it's 1:30. The receptionist at your aunt's office told me she'd be back from a meeting by now." He pushed back his chair and stood up. "I'll let you wait here while I go call her."

"Uh, hold up a minute . . . I might be wrong about that cash. You see, my gramps—my grandfather—I think he gave me that money, not Aunt Ruth. I'm just not sure."

"Okay, I'll call him too. How do I reach him?"

Bernard said, "He lives with Aunt Ruth, like I do."

Markowski returned to the table and sat down. "Well, that's convenient. I've got her home number." He stared at Bernard. "You and I both know what they are going to say." He waited for a denial or other reaction from the kid but his eyes were focused on the table. "Let's move on to more questions." He pointed down at Bernard's sneakers.

"Are those the same shoes you were wearing when you discovered Page's body?"

"Yes."

"We'll need to borrow those to match them against footprints in the house." Markowski opened the briefcase again. He removed Page's wallet and slapped it down onto the table.

Bernard's eyes bulged. "Where'd you get that?"

"What? This? You recognize it, don't you? Come on, Bernard, you know whose this is. Tell me."

"No, no," said Bernard, "I . . . I just got surprised when you slammed it down on the table. I've never seen it before."

"Did you take Page's wallet?"

"No. I would not touch a dead body!" Bernard shouted in a voice half an octave higher. "I'd be too scared."

"If you didn't take it, tell me who did and where you got the money we found on you."

"It's not Page's money," Bernard said. "I don't know anything about a wallet."

"Listen to me for a moment, Bernard. Your future and your freedom may depend on it."

Bernard nodded. "Okay."

"I am going to share some information with you on this case. I got some lab results back today. First, there are three sets of fresh footprints in your aunt's kitchen, all made after the body was dumped into the crawlspace. There should be only two sets, yours and your Aunt Ruth's. Who else went in there with you?"

"Nobody! Nobody! Just me and Aunt Ruth."

Markowski said, "Can you tell me where you were between noon on Friday the 13th and noon on Saturday, the 14th?"

Bernard closed his eyes, rubbed them with both hands and said, "Shit. Sorry. Look officer . . . officer . . .—"

"You can call me Detective or Sergeant or you can call me by my first name, Bruce. It's a lot easier than Markowski."

"Detective, I got a problem with that night, Friday night. This is no bullsh—this is no lie. After working on the house—I left there about five—I went to the bowling alley and drank some beers at the bar with two guys. We got to talking about Mike Ditka and the Bears. We rehashed the old Super Bowl. I guess we just kept drinkin'. They were buyin' and I was drinkin' with them. I'm not really a drinker. Never have any money to begin with and it affects me pretty quick. I suppose I got really smashed. I woke up about noon on Saturday in the van over near that fancy new inn up north.

"Give me some names."

"I didn't know them. Just guys in a bar. White guys. Somebody was Bob or Bill or something. Seemed like nice guys. They probably wouldn't help me anyway."

"Why not?"

Bernard shrugged again. "They're white. I'm black."

Markowski considered saying "That's too bad," but decided this was not the time to discuss race relations in Michigan. He made a note about the alleged unnamed drinking buddies. "Do you remember what time you left?"

"No, sir, like I said, I was pretty drunk."

Markowski ran his hand through his hair and frowned. "Great. Can you see how bad this looks for you? You have no alibi. You seem to recognize Page's wallet. You have $300 that almost certainly came from that wallet. Who knows? Page's DNA may be on one of those bills. And, you've already told me you don't like Page. Added to all that, you've lied to me at least twice." He leaned closer to Bernard.

"Bernard, I advise you to think really hard. Think about telling me the truth when I come back. Only the truth will get you out of this jam." He stood up.

"Where you going?" Bernard asked.

"I'm going to get Rhonda to sign her statement. She's been arrested too."

Bernard sat straight up; his eyes were even wider than when he had seen Page's wallet. "Rhonda? Why Rhonda?" The beads of sweat were back on his forehead.

Markowski saw an opening, a chance to make some real headway, with only a small exaggeration of the facts. He wasn't entirely sure that Rhonda had been arrested yet. "My gut tells me you know exactly why she's here. In fact, she's already told us some very interesting facts about this case." That was technically correct; she had done that several days ago. He opened the door and stepped out, moving slower than he normally would.

"Wait!" Bernard shouted. "Come back! I'll tell you the real story—how it really happened."

Chapter 23

Toni clicked off the slide projector and turned up the lights. "So, that's our system," she said. "One simple program that manages patient appointments, records, billing, employee pay and benefits, and Federal and State income tax obligations. Even for a department as large as yours, two people could handle all the work."

"Two?" Ruth said. "My God, the city's got two or three people for each of those tasks you just mentioned. And, some of that's not even my department. What's the City going to do with those extra people?"

Toni leaned forward and said, "It's not my place to say, Ruth, but if I were you, I'd get rid of them and use the money you save to hire more nurses."

Ruth smiled. "I like the way you think, girl! Speaking of nurses, are you still up for a trip out to East Garfield Park today?"

"Sure." Toni removed the slide carousel from the projector and turned it off. The cooling fan remained on. It would have to stay on the conference table for several minutes. She put the carousel back into its box and set it aside. "Margaret will take care of all this. Shall I drive?"

"No need to drive," Ruth said. "You'd be crazy to do that anyway with all the traffic. Marillac House is only about two blocks south of the Green Line 'L' station at California Avenue. It's less than thirty minutes from downtown, including the walk. Are you okay with that?"

"Yes, sure. I'm free for the rest of the afternoon. Let's get a little lunch in the café downstairs; you can tell me all about Marillac House."

Over soup, sandwiches and iced tea, Ruth gave her a quick history of Marillac House. Toni was surprised to learn that the program had been around since 1947, when it was founded by a group of Catholic nuns, the Daughters of Charity.

"I've bragged about Marillac so many times that I can recite their blurb from memory," Ruth told her. "Marillac House—officially Marillac St. Vincent Family Services—is a social service agency offering accredited early childhood education, programs for youth, services to isolated seniors, access to food and outreach to adults and families."

"That sounds wonderful," Toni said.

"Yeah, but that one long sentence is too impersonal. It doesn't capture the real soul of the place, the essence of it."

"So," Toni said, "tell me in your own words. What is Marillac to you?"

"You know, it's just not that easy to describe to someone who doesn't live in the projects, or is trying to raise kids out there. Or . . . sorry; give me a moment." She got a tissue out of her purse, dabbed some tears away and sniffled. "Sorry." She took a deep breath and said, "Imagine this: You're a kid living out there. Mom might be working two jobs. No dad around. Who makes your breakfast? Where do you go to play? There's too much crime on the streets, too many bullies, too many gangs. And drugs? God! Who keeps you safe? Who helps you with your homework?" She wadded up the first tissue and tried to blink away more tears while digging unsuccessfully in her purse for a second tissue.

Toni got a small package of tissues from her own purse and gave it to Ruth.

"Thanks." She wiped her eyes again. "Heck, I just gave you an autobiography. Didn't mean to, but I get emotional about Marillac House. You see, as a teen, that's where I went every day after school, and on weekends, even holidays. My mom, bless her heart, tried her best but she had to work all the time. You know how we always harp about today's youth? Well, back in my youth, the exact same problems existed—drugs, violence, teen pregnancy and all that. Especially in the projects like Rockwell Gardens, poverty and crime are everywhere.

"Marillac House was my safe harbor from all that bad stuff. The best thing Mom ever did for me and my little brother was to get us into programs at Marillac. We got snacks, a safe place to play—but only after we did homework, and they had tutors to help with that too. The opportunities I got there probably saved me. Not just me but by now, literally thousands of inner-city youth. They have a program now called Project Hope to address teen pregnancy. Even more important, in my opinion, is a spin-off called Hope Junior, which teaches younger girls how to avoid going down that path. It has saved many kids from disaster."

"Thanks for sharing that, Ruth. I didn't mean for it to get so personal, but thanks."

Ruth said, "I suppose you're not so much interested in all that. You just want to see a community nurse at work out there, so let's go!"

Toni reached out with both hands and squeezed Ruth's. "You're wrong, Ruth. I *am* interested in all that. As a mother, I'd want my kids to have a safe haven like Marillac. And, look, if their programs helped produce a woman like you, well . . . it must be a hell of a place."

Twenty-five minutes later they emerged from the 'L' station onto California Street and walked south to Jackson Boulevard. Ruth stopped at the corner and said, "Marillac is right around the corner, just past this old dime store." She pointed at an old brick building with graffiti-covered plywood sheets over the windows. Any window that hadn't been boarded up was broken.

Toni noticed the faded and peeling name painted above the main door. *F.W. Woolworth.* She had a flashback to walking hand-in hand with her mom down the aisles of another Woolworth's—one in her neighborhood, now also closed—gawking at the amazing collection of toys, pretty dresses, shoes, and much more, all packed into shelves separated by narrow aisles. She wasn't sure if any of the Woolworth's were still in business; the appeal of more spacious big-box stores had made them obsolete. That was sad.

Ruth said, "Here we are. This is Marillac House"

The three-story brick building was of equal age and style to the Woolworth's but it was in much better shape. Each floor had tall, white-framed windows that contrasted nicely with the bright red brick exterior. A fenced, well-maintained playground and basketball court was off to one side.

"The first two floors house a day care center, food pantry, kitchen, small gym and offices," Ruth said. "The nuns who run this place, the Daughters of Charity, live on the third floor. Bless their hearts, they are a wonderful influence on this community." She paused and laughed.

"What?" Toni said.

"Well, you know that common perception that nuns are quiet, unassuming, soft-spoken people? At least that was my idea when I first started coming here."

"Hah," Toni replied. "You wouldn't say that if you had attended a Catholic grammar school."

"Okay, point taken. But why I laughed is, I remembered a story. It's kind of a legend around here, a true story about Sister Mary William, who was Marillac Director back in the Sixties." Ruth paused, trying unsuccessfully to stifle another laugh. "Sister Mary William was anything but meek. I knew her and—excuse my language—she had balls. She talked Rockwell Gardens into renting her an apartment for one dollar per year. That's those high rises over there." She pointed to a cluster of tall buildings a few blocks to the west. "Sister Mary William stocked that apartment with food, diapers, and other stuff and gave it away to the residents. She also offered programs for youth right there at Rockwell. They called it 'The Outpost.'"

Ruth had started up the steps to Marillac's door but stopped. They both had to move aside while a very pregnant young woman waddled up the steps. Toni waited, sensing there was more to the story.

"The gangs didn't like The Outpost. They broke in, stole all the stuff and sold it on the streets. Sister Mary William put up stronger metal bars on the windows but they just broke those too. Did that nun back down? No, ma'am! She demanded a meeting with the gang leader—got right up in his face, I am told—and asked him, 'How can I make you stop?' He told her they just wanted jobs and a basketball court to play on. Within a week, Sister Mary William had found jobs for any gang member who wanted one. Within two weeks, they had a basketball court."

"Did that work?" Toni asked.

"You bet. The Outpost thrived, and so did Marillac House. In fact, during the tragic riots after Dr. Martin Luther King's assassination, almost everything you see around here was burned. But this building . . ." She patted the stone railing. "This building was untouched. Come on. Let's go in."

Once inside, the first thing Toni noticed was the noise; there was evidently a big party happening down the hall to the right.

"Oh, dear," Ruth said, "I forgot. Today's Wednesday the 25th. Edwin Page's funeral was this morning and his sister May scheduled a luncheon in his honor afterwards—here, down in the gym. This was his district; he was popular here."

"You didn't want to attend the funeral?" Toni asked.

"I attended the memorial service a couple days ago; that was a city-sponsored event. But, the funeral? I was invited, but I was uncomfortable with it, being as how Page's body ended up under the floor of my house."

Toni noticed a woman approaching them from the opposite hallway. She leaned over and whispered to Ruth, "Don't you dare introduce me as the woman in whose bathtub Page was killed! I'm just a lady whose software will help nurses, okay?"

Ruth rolled her eyes and nodded. "Hi, Gracie! You're just the person I need to see." When the woman got close enough, Ruth gave her a hug and said, "Nurse Grace Roberts, this is Toni Harrington, my new associate. She writes software for medical care in the projects. She's here to see a real nurse at work."

Grace was a short, trim young black woman in her late twenties, with a white lab coat over pink blouse and brown, knee-length skirt. Her smile was bright and her handshake was firm. "Welcome to Marillac House, Toni," she said. "I'm afraid I don't have any patients at the moment, unless someone gets indigestion from all the food they're serving over there." She tilted her head toward the gym. "By the way, are you hungry? They're just about to close down the serving line but there's bound to be lots of extra sand-wiches, cookies and so forth."

"No thank you; we had lunch before coming out." Toni said. Ruth nodded.

"Well," Grace said, "at least I can show you my little of-fice. Follow me, please." She walked off down the corridor opposite from where the gym was.

Grace hadn't been kidding when she said, "little office." It was only slightly larger than a walk-in closet. It held a small desk, two chairs and an examining table. Next to the desk was the combined scale/height measurement de-vice common to medical offices. One wall was covered with posters of human anatomy and the opposite wall had infor-mation on the benefits of healthy eating and exercise.

Grace offered the two chairs to her visitors and hopped up onto the examining table. "What would you like to know about my work here?" she said.

"First," Toni said, "and this is just on a personal level, what type of patients do you see here?"

"Everything from little kids' scraped knees and elbows to teens coming down off drugs or needing advice on preg-nancy tests. Sadly, as you may know, teen pregnancy is a big problem out here. Marillac is one of the few places with a support system for these poor girls. We have the girls make a promise, in writing, to stay in school and not get pregnant. We feel it is a very effective program.

"Anything that requires a prescription, a nurse practitioner or an M.D., I send them to either a local doctor or Cook County Hospital. We also have some programs for senior citizens, who are not immune to some of the aforementioned problems. Except, ha, ha, perhaps the pregnancy issues?"

Her smile disappeared. "Sometimes, there's, uh, a little more to it. Thank God it doesn't happen too often, but if I see evidence of physical or even mental abuse, I'm obligated to report it."

Toni spent the next few minutes explaining to both Ruth and Grace how her software could help even an office as small as this and how records here could be interfaced with higher levels of care. Ruth asked a question about privacy and security against computer hackers and seemed reassured that Simplified Data had designed a secure platform.

"Well," Ruth said, "Thank you Grace, for your time."

Toni added, "Yes, thanks, and you have my great respect for what you do for this community. I know it's not easy, and I know the pay's not the best."

Grace's eyes widened. She said to Ruth, "You didn't tell her?"

"What?" Toni asked, looking at them both.

Ruth said, "Grace is here only two days per week, Wednesdays and Thursdays, as an unpaid volunteer. The other five days she works full time at Loretto."

"My God!" Toni said. "If I could, I'd nominate you for sainthood."

"Now, if Toni still has time?" Ruth said.

"Sure."

"I wouldn't object if someone dragged me into the gym to see if there's any cake left." Ruth stood up and walked out.

"Psst!" Toni whispered to Grace as they both hurried down the hall to catch up to Ruth. "You should talk to her about her diet. I think she could stand to lose—"

"I heard that!" Ruth said without breaking her stride toward the cake.

Grace grinned and made a hands-off gesture.

Once inside the gym, with about thirty people still enjoying refreshments, Ruth said, "I'd better go say hello to the family. Grace, why don't you get us all some cake and I'll take Toni over to meet May." She led Toni to the opposite side of the gym, where two women stood, apparently deep in conversation. Halfway there, she stopped and said, "The tall one is May Brown, Edwin Page's older sister."

When an opportunity presented itself, Ruth stepped closer and said, "Hello, May."

May was dressed in a dark green dress with a narrow white collar, a matching small green hat, light brown hose and brown flats. She was grey-haired, taller and much more rotund than Ruth, but she moved quickly to give Ruth a tight hug and then stepped back to look at her. "I'm so glad you could make it. Did you get anything to eat?"

"Thank you, although I'm not sure I deserve it. Grace's over there getting us some cake. You see, I didn't make it to the church for the funeral. I'm actually here to introduce Grace to my new associate, Toni."

Toni reached out for a handshake but was soon enveloped in a warm hug. It felt good. "That's a nice outfit, May," she said.

May's face brightened. "Why, thank you honey! It's new. As, uh, the Chief Mourner, I needed something nice but subdued. Welcome to Marillac House. I'm sure Ruth and Grace have told you all about it. My granddaughters love it here. Let me get them over here and introduce you." She called out to a teenaged boy sitting alone about twenty feet away. "Justin? Justin! Please find the girls and bring them over here."

The boy stood up and walked off toward a play area for younger kids.

May exhaled deeply. "Toni, Justin is Edwin's son—oh, wait. Do you know about Edwin Page, my brother? He's—he was—a city councilman. He's the one who was murdered over in Michigan. His funeral was today and this brunch was in his honor."

"Yes, I heard about it," Toni said. Boy, had she ever heard about it! "I am very sorry for your loss."

"Thank you, dear. Anyway, back to Justin; he's staying with me for the day. He lives with his mom down in St. Louis and goes to some kind of fancy military-style boarding school down there. The poor kid. He hasn't said more than three words to me since he arrived and those were, 'Where's the food?'" She looked at the woman to whom she had been talking and said, "Oh my, where are my manners? Toni, this is Mrs. Amanda Billings. We live in the same building over at Rockwell Gardens and her son Charles—we all call him Chuckie—and Justin have been friends for a long time."

Toni noticed that Mrs. Billings flinched at the word "friends." However, she smiled and extended her hand. Toni shook her hand and said, "Pleased to meet you, Mrs. Billings,"

"Likewise. And, please, call me Amanda."

Ruth took one of May's hands and said, "May how are you doing—really? Is there anything I can do to help?"

"Thank you, Ruth, but you know these people in Rockwell Gardens. Edwin used to say, 'We're all family here.' Well, that's the truth. Rockwell might not look that good to some, but in time of trouble, neighbors become your family. I can't hardly count the number of casseroles and salads that have been left at my door. Families on three floors offered to house our Mississippi relatives, some who even came up by Greyhound bus. Aunts, uncles and cousins down there are very proud of Edwin.

"The Church of the Spirit, of course, has been wonderful. The choir sang and about a dozen little girls in white dresses scattered rose petals down the aisle." May swept her hand around the gym. "This whole reception was planned by my best friend Amy. The Mayor was even here earlier! And, you know what else? I hope this doesn't sound disrespectful, but it seems my brother has done more for Rockwell by his death than he did in real life. Ruth, you've seen our building and been to my apartment, right? When's the last time you saw the elevator work? Or the stairwell cleaned? Or the garbage not overflowing and attracting rats?" She shuddered.

"With all the dignitaries coming to pay respects and the reporters to cover events, guess what? They fixed the elevator, pressure washed the sidewalks and cleaned up the stairwell."

Amanda said, "Don't forget, the garbage has been picked up three times in a week. I've lived here my whole life and never seen that!"

Justin returned with two girls, both under ten years of age and about a year apart, by Toni's estimate.

"Marcella, Jennifer and Justin," May said, "you remember Miss Ruth the nurse, right? This is her friend, Miss Toni."

There was an awkward pause.

May said, "Well?"

The older of the two girls actually curtsied and said, "Pleased to meet you, ma'am." This was followed by a chorus of "Pleased to meet you" by the second girl and Justin.

"I am very pleased to meet you too," Toni said.

The younger of the two girls said, "I'm Jennifer. We got a ride in a big black car. A lemur."

"No, honey," May said. "That was a limo, not a lemur. A lemur is what you saw at the zoo last week."

Toni leaned down and said, "Wow! Was that fun?"

Jennifer nodded. "The zoo was great! My favorites are the polar bears and the monkeys. Oh, and the. . . um . . . limo was fancy."

"Okay, girls, you may go back and play. We'll be leaving soon." May put her hands together in a praying gesture and said, "Please, God, keep them from ripping up those nice church clothes."

Justin asked to be excused and said he was going back for another sandwich.

The four of them talked for a few more minutes. Toni was relieved when Ruth gently diverted the topic from Page's death to their new alliance and joint ideas on improving medical care for low income patients. She repeated most of what she had said in Grace's office but used less technical language. She finished with, "The bottom line is, Simplified Data Systems can help people like Ruth and her nurses serve the public better. The mission is to get people the care they deserve."

"Amen to that," said May.

Ruth said to May and Amanda, "Well, we'll let you two get back to your conversation and we'll go have a bite of cake."

As soon as they had joined Grace, the young nurse stood up and said, "I hate to run off, but I have a patient to see in about five minutes. Toni, it was nice to meet you. Miss Ruth, take care."

As they ate cake, Ruth pointed her fork at May and Amanda, who were still standing and talking. "Take a look at them and tell me what you see."

Even from a distance, Toni could tell that Amanda's body language showed worry or anger, or both. She said so.

"Well, there's a little history you should know about. It involves Ed Page, or at least his son. Do you remember the accident over in Union Pier that killed George's wife?"

"I read about it in the newspaper," Toni said, "but we were pretty new to Union Pier then."

Ruth looked at the nearby tables, which were vacant. "This is just gossip, but I've heard it from more than one reliable source. Those two boys, Justin and Chuckie, were in Page's big car when it hit Martha. Poor Martha. She had stayed behind in Chicago to help some patients—she was a nurse too—and was just trying to get to the cottage to join George. By the way, George will never forgive himself for agreeing to let her stay behind. He told me if he had been driving, maybe he could've done something, seen the accident coming and avoided it or whatever.

"Anyway, back to the boys. Chuckie took the blame as the underage driver and Justin got off with just a slap on the wrist. But, in the story I heard, Justin was the driver and, in addition to not having a license, he was drunk at the time. Ed Page allegedly bribed the boy into taking the blame, thus saving his own son's ass, pardon my language."

"But why would the other boy agree to that?"

"Page offered—allegedly offered, I should say—free college tuition and who knows what else. So now Chuckie is serving two years in juvenile detention."

"Wow." It took several seconds for her brain to connect that story with the conversation she was witnessing. "Oh, I get it. No wonder Mrs. Billings looks so upset. Now that Page is dead—"

"You got it. There's no one to honor Page's promise to Chuckie. Nora, Page's estranged wife, certainly won't want to help Chuckie. I understand she hates Page's cheating ways, both with women and the city's money. I think she knows the truth about the car accident, too. She left him and moved back to St. Louis right after that."

"Gosh, that's all terrible. If it's true, of course. But . . ."

"What?"

Toni said, "I feel bad saying this, but I think this gives us two more people with a motive to kill Ed Page—Nora Page and Amanda Billings."

Ruth opened her mouth to speak but stopped when she saw Grace approaching their table.

"Ruth, a call came in for you on my office phone. It's your nephew Bernard."

Ruth excused herself, leaving Toni to battle with her conscience about having a second piece of cake. She compromised and settled for a cup of coffee. Before she could finish stirring in the sugar, she saw Ruth at the door to the gym, waving at her and looking very stressed. She hurried over to see her.

"Bernie's been arrested over in Union Pier," Ruth said. "I've got to go over there and try to bail him out."

"Oh my God! Is it—"

"He says they think he did it. The murder, that is. I've got to go now. My car's over at my building just a few blocks from here. Do you want me to give you a ride back to your office?"

"No, that'd take too much time. You go. I'll take the 'L'."

Ruth gave her a hug. "He didn't do it, Toni. I just feel it in my heart." She hurried out the door.

After a moment of reflection on what Ruth had just said about another person who "didn't do it," Toni walked over to where May was sitting with Justin. She said, "May, Justin, I'm on my way out now. Again, I am very sorry for your loss. It was nice to meet you both. And the girls are really cute. Please tell them I said so."

"Thank you," May said. "Where's Ruth?"

"She just left. Got called away to an emergency . . . down at her office." God would forgive her for this lie. The truth was sometimes too painful to mention.

Chapter 24

Toni pushed open the door to Simplified Data Systems just after 5:00 p.m. Margaret already had her coat on and was putting the cover on her typewriter.

"Oh, hi, Toni. I didn't think you'd be back today. Everyone else is gone."

"I hadn't planned on it, but I remembered that I had some work to do on a couple RFPs before tomorrow's meeting. Is there anything else that I need to know about?"

"Nope," Margaret said. "Do you want me to stay on a little bit?"

"Thanks, but no, you go on home and I'll see you tomorrow."

Toni turned on the hallway lights, went down to her office and flicked on the light switch. She rebooted her computer. While waiting for it to perform all the clicks and beeps and other mysterious things it did to get going, she replayed two events from earlier today. Both involved PJ. First, if PJ really believed that his payments to Edwin Page were legal, why would he want to forge expense reports to hide those payments? He was supposed to be the expert on Chicago politics and how to pave the way toward lucrative city contracts. But, he had acted like a spoiled child when she had refused his request for the reports. Perhaps he was not as confident as he previously stated about the legality of it all. Second, and even more troubling, why would he tell his wife that he had loaned $80,000 to the company? She could find no answer that cast a good light on PJ's character.

The computer monitor announced that it was ready for work. Toni forced herself to concentrate on two draft proposals for hospitals up in Wisconsin. She read through the first one and noted several paragraphs that could benefit from small revisions. The illustrations were bar graphs but she thought the message would be clearer if these were displayed as pie charts. She wrote this suggestion in the margin. The only change she recommended for the second RFP was changing the bar graphs to pie charts. To make these changes would delay the project for a day or two but would enhance their chances for acceptance.

When she had made all the appropriate notes, she saved the files and copied them to a floppy disk. After removing the disk, she shut down her computer, turned off her office lights and headed down the hall toward Margaret's desk. As she passed PJ's office, she noticed his computer monitor was still on. He must have gotten it fixed.

Toni stepped into PJ's office and debated the wisdom of turning off PJ's computer. She was all for saving energy, but what if there were an unsaved document there? No, she'd leave it on. As she turned to leave, she noticed the "message waiting" light blinking on his answering machine. On any other day, she would have ignored it. Not today, not with all these crazy allegations against PJ and his suspicious behavior. She walked over and, after a short debate with herself on office ethics and privacy, pushed the "play" button.

What she heard caused her to pick up the phone and ask the long distance operator for the New Buffalo office of Michigan State Police. A few minutes later, she was told that Sergeant Markowski was unavailable but he could be paged.

"Please page him! I have urgent news about the Page murder case. Tell him to call Toni Harrington. He has my numbers."

She hung up. What should she do next? A reasonable, mature person would go home, play with her kids and wait patiently for a call from Markowski. Could she do that? Just sit back and wait and wait for the police to do their work? No way! She picked up the phone again and called her mother.

"Mom, it's me. I'm still at work, but I need a big favor. Would you be able to stay with the kids for about, ah, four more hours? I've got to dash over to Union Pier." She told her where she was going. "Thank you, Mom. Yes, it's related to the murder investigation. I'll tell you all about it when I get back. Give the kids hugs and kisses from me."

Chapter 25

Markowski looked through the one-way glass at Bernard. The young man had just finished a sandwich, some chips and a pop. He had been escorted down the hall for a bathroom break and was now back in the interrogation room.

He opened the door, sat down across from Bernard and restarted the tape recorder. "Go ahead, Bernard."

"Last Monday I got up early to get a start on the house. When I got to the house I saw this guy—I knew right away he was Page. He was dead . . . dead . . . and he was turned an ugly kind of green. He was starting to smell. I panicked. Didn't know what to do. I'm not ashamed to tell you I was scared and needed some company. So I ran over to Rhonda's house to tell her. She was about ready to go to work."

"What time was that?" Markowski asked.

"About seven-thirty."

"She was going to work at seven-thirty? How far does she have to go?" Bruce asked.

"Not far; maybe six miles. She has to be at work at nine."

"That's an awful lot of time to go six miles. Are you sure about that time? She does drive there, right? Not ride a bike or jog or something?"

"Rhonda, ride a bike or jog? I ain't ever seen her do that." Bernard said. "No, she drives. But wait a minute. My watch is on Chicago time; so it was 8:30 here in Michigan."

"Okay, go on," Markowski said.

"I told her Ed Page's dead in Ruth's house."

"I guess you were pretty sure he was dead?"

"Well, I ain't never seen a dead person up that close, but, I mean, he was turning all different shades of green and his skin was kind of shriveled. And, the smell! I knew. I said, 'Rhonda come look at him.' She did; she just stood there for a long time. Then she changed. She got all excited and anxious and said, 'Bernard, that watch cost $10,000. He don't need it. Slip it off.' I tell her I won't touch no dead body. I wouldn't do it. She's a tough little white girl; she did it. Took it right off his arm. Then she took the two gold chains around his neck. She said, 'Page's got a lot of hun- dred-dollar bills in that billfold. Slip it out of his pocket.' Not me, Rhonda, I say. No way. She kept trying to get me to do it, but I wouldn't." He paused a moment; he was a little short of breath.

"'All right, I'll do it,' Rhonda says. 'You gotta lift him up.' I wouldn't touch him. So I got me a two-by-four about this long—" Bernard stretched out his arms. "—and raised him up. She took it out of his pocket and we got out of there. We went back to Rhonda's house and she counted the money. There were forty-seven hundred-dollar-bills, two gold chains and the fancy watch. She had to go to work. She took 'em with her and left me alone. Like I told you, I was scared; I didn't know what to do. I called Aunt Ruth and waited un- til she came. I stayed out in the van and waited. When she came, she called the police."

"Where did those three hundred-dollar bills come from?" Bruce asked.

"Rhonda called me this morning and wanted to go to lunch today at the Townline Station in Union Pier. She said it was important. We had to make plans. She gave me the three bills and I went back to work. What's gonna happen to me sir? You said you'd help me if I told you the truth. You still gonna help me now?"

"I will, Bernard. I'll do my best. Did you kill Page? Did Rhonda kill Page?"

"I didn't. I just found the body. I don't think Rhonda did it. I don't know."

"All right," Markowski said. "When I get all this written up, will you sign it?"

"Sure. It can't make things much worse," Bernard said. He was fighting back tears.

Markowski left the room and was pleased to see that Rhonda occupied one of the two holding cells. He looked at her but did not speak. He whispered to the trooper on duty to take Bernard out of the interview room and put him in the cell next to Rhonda. Then, before they had a chance to talk, he asked for Rhonda to be brought to him. While all this was happening, Markowski went upstairs for a drink of cool water. He drank it slowly and waited another ten minutes, which he hoped would seem like hours to Rhonda.

"Hello again, Mrs. Shain,"

"You can't hold me here without charging me," she said.

"I'm sorry, Mrs. Shain, but that's not entirely correct. I have forty-eight hours before I am obligated by law to profer any charges, so you might as well get comfortable. Did they give you any lunch?"

"Ha. Yeah, if you can call a cold cheese sandwich, some pretzels and an apple lunch."

He picked up a paper from the arresting officer. "Mrs. Shain, you are a suspect in the robbery and murder of Edwin Page. I see here you have already been read your rights. Did you fully understand them and, if so, do you agree to answer a few questions?"

"Sure. I've got nothing to hide."

"Mrs. Shain, Bernard has implicated you in the theft. He tells us that you are actually the one who did the taking."

"Me? Are you kidding? I panic at the sight of a paper cut. How on earth could I touch my dear friend, Edwin, lying there dead?"

"I see. So, does that mean you did see Page lying there dead?"

"Oh no. Oh no. Let's see. Was that Monday morning? I left for work at about 8:30. Stayed all day; what a drag. I was not feeling well, but I stayed until the boss sent me home about 6:00 p.m. When I got home, police were running around everywhere."

"Yes, I know. But Bernard claims that your involvement occurred before you went to work."

"Well, for heaven's sake. Imagine Bernie saying that. It's just not true!"

"Mrs. Shain, you must tell me the truth. I have to know what your part is in this whole affair. I don't want to charge Bernard with murder if he didn't do it."

"I don't know what Bernie did. He certainly could have killed Page." She pulled a tissue from the same box Bernard had used and wiped her eyes. "Poor Ed. He was such a good friend. I thought the world of him."

"You are the first person to speak well of the man since he was killed."

Once again Rhonda wiped her eyes. "You couldn't ask for a better friend. I loved him like a father." After sobbing for several seconds, she said, "Why me? I can't believe Bernard would accuse me of anything like this. He knows how dear Ed is to me . . . or was." Her voice trailed off.

Markowski had to repress the urge to laugh at Rhonda's description of her relationship with Page. The witness at the restaurant had described something very different than a father-daughter affection. "Bernard tells me that you actually took the Rolex watch off the body and then slid the wallet out of his pocket."

"I can't believe I'm hearing this!" she said.

Markowski opened his briefcase and took out the two hundred-dollar bills confiscated from Rhonda on the 16th. "Now, you told me that Page gave you these two bills on Friday at lunch. Tell me about that lunch. Was Page wearing a Rolex watch?"

"Yes; it glittered with diamonds. He said it was worth $10,000."

"Did he have any other jewelry?"

"He had a couple gold chains around his neck. Oh, and a fancy gold pinky ring with a big diamond, maybe more than one carat."

"Did he carry a billfold?"

"Sure, in his back pocket. It was black and stuffed with cash."

Markowski reached into the briefcase, pulled out Page's wallet and put it on the table.

Rhonda gasped. She swallowed and said, "How did you find it?"

"How did you know it was missing?"

"Didn't it say that in the newspaper?"

"No, ma'am. The missing billfold was not one of the facts we gave out to the press. Only someone involved would know that we did not have it. The fact is, however, now we do. It was found earlier today. I don't know where the watch and the jewelry are, but I believe you do."

Rhonda's tears seemed real this time. She muttered, "Shit, shit, shit!" and banged her fists on the table. Her makeup had dissolved into dark streaks dripping down her cheeks.

"Let's control this, Mrs. Shain. All we want is some cooperation and the truth." He handed her another tissue. "You might want to dab under your eyes; your eyeliner is running."

She took the tissue and looked around. "I need to stand up for a second and use that mirror."

"Sure," he said, "help yourself." Of course, the mirror was really a one-way mirror so Alice Britt, on the other side of it, would get a close-up of the makeup repairs.

Rhonda sat back down and said, "Okay, I've told you the truth. Why do you believe Bernie and not me?"

Markowski thought about that for a few seconds. He said it was important to match their stories. "Wait here please." He got up, opened the door and whispered to Alice. He remained at the door and, in a few moments, answered a knock. Alice brought Bernard in, seated him at the table opposite Rhonda and handed Markowski a single typewritten page.

"Thank you," he said. He put the paper in front of Bernard and said, "Read this silently please and, if is correct, sign it." He put a pen on the table and sat down at the narrow end of the table. Bernard's lips moved while he read the statement. Rhonda was breathing so rapidly he feared she would pass out. Bernard picked up the pen and signed it.

"Thanks, Bernard. Now, read it out loud."

When Bernard reached the point at which Rhonda had asked him to remove Page's watch, Rhonda screamed, "Lies, lies, lies!"

"Not lies, Rhonda," Bernard said. "You know I'm tellin' it just the way it happened. We have to tell it like it is. They know everything."

"Bernard Smith . . . you know I went to work Monday. You know I had no part in this."

"Rhonda, we didn't kill Page, but if we don't tell the truth, we're both going to take the rap for it. I don't want to be called a murderer and neither do you."

Rhonda slumped forward, put her elbows on the table and closed her eyes. She rubbed her forehead with both palms. The only sound was her rapid breathing. She slapped her hands down on the table, pushed herself back into an upright posture and inhaled deeply. "Okay, he's telling the truth. We didn't kill Page. We found him in his aunt's house Monday morning. Well, Bernie found him first and called me over. We did take the money and the stuff. It seemed like a good idea at the time." She stopped and asked for a glass of water.

Markowski poured it for her. As he slid it across the table to her, he said, "I'm sorry, Mrs. Shain, but the truth is the best way out of all this."

When she put down the water cup, he said, "Mrs. Shain, where have you hidden the rest of the money and the jewelry?"

"There's a little access door in the ladies' washroom at Sheldun's, where I work, out on the Red Arrow Highway. The money and stuff are in a manila envelope behind that door. I put it there on Monday when I got to work. I took five hundred out yesterday. I couldn't get to it today. The two hundred I had, Ed actually gave me at lunch Friday. You already know about that, right? I told you the other day that I had asked him to help me get a divorce. He wouldn't give me a straight answer. He said to take the two hundred and buy something, as if that was going to solve my divorce problem." Her voice ran down like a record on an old hand-crank Victrola record player. She dabbed at the makeup stains on her cheeks.

"Bernard and Rhonda," Markowski said, "Thank you for being honest. I believe you."

"What's going to happen to us?" Bernard asked.

Markowski drew a few breaths before he spoke. It wouldn't be wise to give them any false hopes. "Well, to be perfectly honest, I don't know. You obviously committed multiple crimes. You stole from a dead man and then lied about it. The fact that you eventually told me the truth tonight—it is the truth, right?"

They both nodded enthusiastically.

"That could work in your favor. I can put in a good word for you, even if I had to, shall we say, coax it out of you. It might help that you can return most if not all of the items stolen. The decision to prosecute you for theft will be up to the State of Michigan Attorney's Office."

They both sat silently.

"Now, two more questions for both of you," Markowski said. "Does either of you have any idea who might have killed Edwin Page? We think he was killed between Friday night and Sunday morning. Did you see or hear anything unusual Friday night or anytime on Saturday?"

Rhonda shook her head and Bernard said, "No, sir."

"All right, then," Markowski said. "This interview is over." He pushed the "Off" button on the tape recorder, stood up, and opened the door. "This trooper will show you back to your cells."

Bernard said, "I got one more thing to say, detective."

"Yes?"

"Thank you. For what you said, earlier, about how you'd be proud of me if I was your son. That meant a lot. Now, I suppose you ain't too proud of—"

"No, Bernard, I'm still proud of you. It takes a lot of courage to tell the truth."

After they left, Markowski sat down and opened his notebook. He jotted down the word *Believable????* The four question marks were a reminder for him to think this through later, after the euphoria of getting the confessions—for theft, not murder—had subsided. Could he answer the "Are they believable?" question right now or should he listen to the tape a few more times? Could Bernard and/or Rhonda do something that seemed stupid but could actually be fiendishly clever? Would Bernard kill a man and dump the body in his own aunt's house with the expectation that the police would think that so illogical as to judge him innocent? Could Ruth have convinced him to do it using similar logic? Or was Ruth innocent and Rhonda the one who lured Bernard into this scheme? Markowski had trouble believing any of them was that devious.

When he finished the notes and his thinking, he looked at his watch. Crap. He had missed a 9:00 p.m. dinner date with Alice Britt. To make matters worse, he had spent a

twelve-hour day, including a two hours of intense questioning, and was no closer to solving the murder than on day
one. He'd had it for the day. He was going to rush straight
over to Alice's house and decompress. If she would have
him this late.

Chapter 26

Traffic had been terrible on the Dan Ryan; I-90 and I-94 had been no better. Once she got off I-94 onto Union Pier Road, things improved; she almost had the road to herself. However, she stayed a few miles per hour under the speed limit. It would be a bad evening to get a speeding ticket and, anyway, she hated driving in the dark. There was a little sliver of moon up there somewhere—she had seen it on the way out of Chicago—but it was no longer visible. She could sure use some company. Ruth was over here, probably at the Michigan State Police post trying to bail out her nephew, but she had no way to contact her. Her house was still torn up and vacant, so she certainly couldn't be reached there.

Her dashboard clock said 7:15 p.m. when she pulled into the parking lot. Of course, here in Michigan, it was 8:15. Toni locked the car and rehearsed her speech on the way to the lobby. She had only seen it from the beach side but had admired the building, painted in bright turquoise with white trim around each sash window. It had been written up in the local newspaper as an elegant, well-preserved example of the 1920s-era Queen Anne-style architecture that had once been common for southwestern Michigan beachfront homes. Evidently, not many had survived. From the street side, it was even more impressive. A brightly lit wraparound porch with ornate white spindle wood columns, matching porch rail and highly polished oak flooring led to double entry doors with panels of beveled glass.

She had to wait while a couple at the reception desk received their key and signed a large, ornate guest book. "Welcome to the Nine Cranes Inn!" the clerk said to her. "Please wait here a moment while I show these folks to their room. I'll be back in a jiffy."

"Sure," Toni said. She gave him her best smile.

Alone now at the front desk, she saw an opportunity. She walked up to the counter and flipped the guest book pages back to Friday the 13th. And there it was. The sight made her knees shake and her hands tremble; she had to hold on to the countertop for support. PJ Conroy's signature was there! He had checked in at 9:40 p.m. on the 13th—a night when he should have been in Detroit! At the sound of footsteps on the polished wood floor, Toni flipped the guest book pages back to today's list just as the clerk returned.

"Good evening," he said. "How may I help you?"

She said, "Hi, I'm Toni Harrington. I am hoping that my colleague Peter J. Conroy has called you about this, but . . ." She reached into her purse, opened her wallet and showed the clerk her driver's license and her business card. "Your inn left a message on our office answering machine over in Chicago. It's about a sport coat Mr. Conroy accidentally left in his room when he checked out the other day. He's in Chicago, where we both work, but I have a cottage here in Union Pier so he asked me to drop by and pick it up for him."

The clerk looked a little lost for a moment and then said, "What day did you say that was?"

"He checked in on Friday the 13th and must have checked out on the 14th."

After flipping through his own ledger, the clerk said, "Yes, here he is. The Lake Suite." He turned around and looked at a cork bulletin board on the wall. "Ah, I don't see any notes from the day shift about a call from Mr. Conroy."

"Oh, my," Toni said. She chuckled. "That doesn't surprise me. PJ—Mr. Connor—probably forgot to coordinate this. Just like he forgot his coat."

"Well, I don't know if I should . . . I'm not even sure if the coat is here."

"Could you at least check your lost and found? You see, this is the last night I'll be up here in Michigan for quite some time."

The clerk disappeared into a back office and returned less than a minute later with a navy blue sport coat on a wire hanger. "Here it is." He looked at the handwritten tag on the hanger and said, "The Lake Suite. October 14." He picked up the business card and studied it. "Well, I guess it's okay. I see both your names on this card. Let me just write down some information from this card."

"Thank you! Thank you!" Toni reached into her wallet and pulled out two $5 bills. She slid one toward the clerk. "I'm sure Mr. Conroy would like you to have this. And please give this one to housekeeping or whomever found the coat. Good night."

She forced herself to walk calmly out the door and down the steps. Once there, she ran to her car, unlocked it and tossed the jacket onto the back seat. She shivered. She told herself to think this through. Think, think, think! Why would PJ have gone to Union Pier when he should have been in Detroit? Had he even been in Detroit? Yes, she had seen the receipts; he had checked into a hotel on the 13th and checked out on the 15[th.] Okay, could he have made a round trip from Detroit to Union Pier and returned to the conference? Yes, he had a rental car. She wondered how many miles he had put on that car. She shivered again, and not because of the fall temperatures.

Toni put the key into the ignition switch but didn't start the engine. She removed the key, reached back for the jacket and got out of the car. My God, she was a nervous wreck, trembling in fear at the sight of a blue sport coat! Well, not the coat itself, really, but the man it represented—a man whom she didn't know or trust any more. A man who might be a murderer. There might be some innocent reason for PJ's trip over here, but she had trouble imagining what that might be. She opened the trunk lid, tossed the jacket in, and slammed the trunk shut. That silly act made her feel a little safer. She backed out of her parking space and drove south, looking for a pay phone. This was now a job for the police.

Toni found a convenience store with a pay phone outside and got some change from the clerk. She pulled out the note she had made earlier with Sergeant Markowski's number. Her hand trembled as she dialed. Of course, he was still unavailable. She left another message: *Please, please call me at home sometime after 10:30 p.m. Chicago time tonight!* After that call, she considered her options. Calling Mark from a pay phone in Union Pier would arouse his suspicions that she was doing something dangerous. It would be much wiser to hurry home and call him from there.

*   *   *

Toni stepped into her apartment, slipped off her shoes and tip-toed down the hall.

"Toni, is that you?" Her mother peeked into the hallway. She rushed up to give Toni a big hug. "I was worried about you. It's pretty late to be out on the road."

Toni relished her mother's tight hug and squeezed back with equal force. "Thank you, Mom. I'll tell you all about it in a second. How are the kids?"

"Oh, they're fine. They tried to convince me that they could stay up until 10:00, but I knew you wouldn't allow that on a school night."

"The little devils!"

She led her mom by the hand into the living room and whispered. "I'm going to send you home in a cab. It's too late to take the 'L'."

Her mom sat down on the couch. "That's fine dear, but first, we're going to boil some water and make some tea. Then, you're going to tell me what this mysterious trip to Union Pier is all about."

Twenty minutes and several white lies later, Toni gave her mother a good night hug and sent her downstairs to a waiting cab. She had given her a sanitized and slightly ambiguous description of her visit to Union Pier. "New developments" had required her to go to Union Pier to "make some statements." That was true wasn't it? She had stated some things to the B&B innkeeper, right? Her mom had assumed that the police had summoned her and the statements had been made to them. Toni had not bothered to correct those assumptions.

Was misleading one's mother a sin? Perhaps. But Toni took comfort in her belief that misleading was a lesser sin than outright lying. Anyway, there was no time for a thorough examination of conscience; she needed to call Mark before it got any later. Before she could pick up the phone, it rang. Maybe Markowski had finally gotten her messages.

"Hello?" she said.

"Hi, honey, it's me. I am so, so sorry for calling so late. Are you already in bed?"

She couldn't believe her good luck. Evidently, Mark hadn't tried to call yet. She said, "Ah, that's okay."

"Anyway, please accept my apologies. Today's court session went into overtime. There were some surprises from the plaintiff's side."

"What did you do to respond?"

"Oh, I asked for a short continuance to study the new evidence. I think I can refute the plaintiff's claims but I need a little time in the morning to do some research."

"Have you had anything to eat?" she asked and then realized that she hadn't eaten since lunch.

"Oh, sure. That's why I'm calling so late. I had dinner with some colleagues from Chicago, after which they insisted on talking business. God, I miss you! And, I am so sorry for missing a chance to say good night to the kids."

"Don't worry about it, Mark. When you get home, we'll do something special—all of us, together."

"That's sweet, honey. So, how was your day?"

Toni tried to stop herself from laughing but failed. She imagined herself saying, "Gee, honey, I dashed over to Union Pier and looked for clues in the murder."

"What's so funny?" Mark asked.

"Oh, nothing, really. It's just been a day of new and different things. I met with Ruth, the one who's our neighbor in Union Pier. Would you believe she's in charge of all the nurses in Chicago's Public Health Department? Mostly, she spends her time struggling to provide health care to low-income families in the projects. At first, she had been jealous that Simplified Data got a lucrative contract, depriving her office of money to hire new nurses. But I showed her that SDS can be good for her nurses and actually free up money to hire more. We have a lot in common."

"That all sounds good," Mark said.

"Then she took me out to Marillac House, an amazing, supportive resource for the East Garfield Park youth. They have a volunteer nurse on the staff who can benefit from our software."

"That's great, Toni. What a coincidence, huh? Ruth's a neighbor in Union Pier and also passionate about the same things as you. Hey, are there any developments in the murder investigation?"

"Well, I haven't heard anything from the detective." Toni was proud of her truthful but incomplete answer.

"Oh, well. Look, I've kept you up way too late. And, if the truth be known, I'm kind of beat. So, I'd better let you go. Sleep well. I love you very much."

"I love you, Mark. Good night."

Toni turned out lights in the living room, checked on the children and got herself ready for bed. She lay in bed, unable to sleep, reviewing what she would say to Markowski if he called. She couldn't prove PJ had actually committed the murder. However, she could prove he had been in Union Pier that night. What did they call that? Opportunity. And as for motive, all those payments to Page—they were big hints that something shady was going on. She would have to tell Markowski about the four thousand-dollar "campaign contributions," which meant she'd have to admit hiding them from the police. She was willing to take the heat for that if it meant getting at the truth. As a minimum, PJ was an embezzling scumbag. Worse than that, he might also be a murderer.

Chapter 27

PJ Conroy sang along with the tune on his car radio as he drove home from Old Town. It had been a great night. Technically, it was now Thursday morning; the midnight news was being broadcast. What a night! The redhead had been worth the one-week wait. He had chosen Steuben's Pub, at the corner of North and Weiland, for their late-night rendezvous. It had been packed, as usual, but he had gotten them a booth way in the back, where it was a little quieter and everything—the well-worn high-backed booths, walls and ceilings—was dark walnut. Okay, so it was a dive bar, but the food was good, the drinks were cheap, and the privacy had allowed for a little intimacy, a little unbuttoning of this and that, and a lot of kissing.

At this time of night, no one else was on the road in Highland Park. He turned off Sheridan Road onto his street. A few blocks later, he turned off the radio to ensure a quiet arrival, pushed the remote control button on his sun visor and, when the garage door had fully opened, drove his Mercedes 300SL into the garage. He got out of the car and took care not to slam his door closed. Heather would be asleep. This would be one of those increasingly frequent nights when he slept alone in Stacy's former room. He made his way to the staircase and had one foot on the first step when he noticed that the kitchen lights were still on. He walked over to the kitchen and reached for the light switch.

"Heather!" he said. "Gosh, you scared me! What are doing up at, what, almost midnight?"

"A detective delivered this for you." She walked up to him and handed him a business card.

"A detective? When was that?"

"About 5:00 p.m. Look on the back; he wrote a message."

PJ flipped the card over. *Need to see you in my office to-morrow at 4:00 p.m. sharp. Det. Caggiano.* The front of the card had the detective's full name: *Detective Paul Caggiano, Chicago Police Department, Bureau of Detectives, Financial Crimes Unit.*

"What did he want?"

"PJ, he knows about the $80,000. He knows you didn't loan that to the company."

"What do you mean he knows? Of course I loaned that to Simplified."

"The police have taken a statement from Roger, who—"

"You mean, our accountant, Roger Morton?"

"Yes. All I know is, the detective said that Roger asked for an investigation. You know how much I hate all this financial stuff. Why did you have to get us involved in this?"

PJ silently vowed to find out how that nosy bastard Morton had discovered the missing money. Then he would fire him. "Heather, I swear to you, there's been a terrible mistake. The money went to Simplified Data. Toni really, really needed it to get the company through some rough times. I don't know why my payments to Simplified are not showing up in their records. Maybe there's some reason why Toni didn't want it to show in the company's books. I can clear all this up tomorrow. And, like I said earlier, business is so good now that we will get our money back, with interest, very soon." He walked over to her and reached out for her hands; she didn't resist. He squeezed them and said, "Trust me, Heather, this will all be over in a day or two."

"PJ, please sit down and listen to me for a moment. This business with the girls' trust fund has really hurt me. It's just like that time, a year ago, when you told me this new merger would get you rich and you would never again be embarrassed by my father's wealth."

"Yeah, I didn't mean to make you cry that day; it's just that—"

"Why on earth would you feel that way after all the good things Mother and Daddy had done for all of us?"

Uh, oh. Now she was going to bring up how Daddy's money had gotten them this house, all the furnishings inside and so forth. Then she would go on to say how much she missed them, especially "Daddy," and ask yet again why they had to die so early. He felt a twinge of sympathy for her. She seemed incapable of overcoming her grief. Advice from family and mental health professionals had not helped. It was all getting a little tiresome. What could he say to make her feel better?

"Heather, I admit to being a little jealous of your dad's success. I just wanted to be successful on my own."

"Well, now look what you've done!" Heather said. "You *knew* that trust fund was for the girls' college tuition; we even planned on financing a Master's degree for both of them, if that's what they wanted."

He reached out to hold her hand and took a deep breath. This was going to challenge his acting ability. "I was wrong to do that, Heather. I am truly sorry for not consulting you when the company needed money. It will never happen again. And, I promise you, within a week, we'll get that money back and we will put it right back into the girls' trust."

"Oh, PJ, that's so good!"

He stood up and approached her. She hopped down off the kitchen stool and wrapped her arms around him. It felt good. All that yoga and tennis kept her body firm. It would be wise to shower her with some affection, perhaps even get her aroused and jump into bed with her. That would take her mind off the money troubles.

She rested her head on his chest and said, "I just feel . . . I don't know . . . lost? Inadequate? I spend all my time playing tennis or golf or attending board meetings for one charity or the other. I miss our daughters so much! With Bonnie and Stacy off at university and you gone so much, it doesn't feel like we're much of a family anymore."

He hugged her a little tighter and said, "Why don't I take you upstairs? I'll get these clothes off—I know you don't like the smoky smell of my late-night business meetings." He omitted the part about lingering perfume aroma from the redhead who had climbed all over him an hour ago. "I'll take a quick shower and we'll jump into bed—together." He kissed her, hoping there was none of the redhead's lipstick left on his lips.

Chapter 28

On Thursday morning, Bruce Markowski decided to look in on George Wilkens before heading to his office. He let the dispatcher know his plans. Traffic on Highway 12 was pretty heavy until he passed Highway 212, where most of the commuters peeled off to join the Interstate. He rolled up to Saint Ignatius Hospital's visitor parking at 8:45 a.m. After a short wait for an elevator, he rode up to the fifth floor and got the attention of the Psychiatric Ward's desk clerk.

"Good morning." He flashed his badge. "I'm Detective Sergeant Markowski, here to have a word with patient George Wilkens."

The clerk leaned forward to inspect his badge and said, "Sure, sergeant, let me make a quick call and then I'll buzz you through those doors." He pointed at two green metal doors off to the left. It's Room 7, down the hall. It's going to be a little crowded in there. Dr. Wilkens already has a visitor."

"Oh?"

"Yes, a neighbor; he's been here for about fifteen minutes. Excuse me." The clerk picked up a telephone and spoke to someone inside the ward. "Okay," the clerk said, "when you hear the door lock buzz, just pull it open and go in."

Markowski found his way to Room 7 and knocked on the partially open door.

"Come in."

He pushed open the door, saw who was inside and said, "I should have known. Jack O'Connor. Really, Jack—a neighbor? That's a pretty low way to talk your way in here. I hope you're not—"

"It's okay, detective," Wilkens said. "Mr. O'Connor called and asked my permission for an interview, which I granted."

"Nothing for publication," Jack said, "at least right now. I'm just here getting some background for a future story. And, in a manner of speaking, were are neighbors. We both have homes in Union Pier."

Markowski looked around and found a small wooden chair under a built-in unit that served as a desk and wardrobe. He pulled it over to the window, where the other two men were sitting in much more comfortable-looking upholstered chairs. "Well, don't let me interrupt you two. Please keep talking; maybe I can learn something." As he sat, he glanced down at his belt, where his pager should be, but wasn't. Had it come off in the car? He'd have to check later.

"Oh, Jack was just asking me about my relationship with Page and my connections to Ruth Smith, her nephew Bernie and Toni Harrington," Wilkens said. "Most of it, detective, I think you already know. I've already told you my reasons for hating Ed Page. But did you know that both Ruth Smith and Toni Harrington provided valuable data for several chapters of my book? The funny thing is—"

"Wait," Markowski said. "That book was published at least five years ago. Are you telling me that Ruth and Toni have known each other for that long?"

"Oh, no. No. I interviewed them separately for the book. As far as I know, they had never met until Toni and her husband bought their place in Union Pier, about a year ago. Now, what I was trying to say is, that's the funny thing about all this. Ruth's experience with inner-city health care was invaluable to me. At the same time, Toni's expertise with health care software inspired an entire chapter about technology's role in bringing more efficiency into the system. Her software could make Ruth's job so much easier. That's why this whole situation is so crazy."

Markowski resisted the temptation to comment on Wilkens's choice of words. "How so?" he asked.

"Ruth had her mind made up to hate Toni. Well, not Toni herself but her company, Simplified Data Systems. Of course, she also hated Page for his support of Toni's big city contracts while ignoring Ruth's pleas for more funds for her nurses."

"You said, 'Ruth *had* her mind made up.' Does that mean something has changed?"

"Yes, that's right!" Wilkens said. "And, ahem, I think I can claim responsibility for being a matchmaker for their new friendship. You see, when Ruth was visiting me the other day, I convinced her that Simplified Data's programs will actually be a good thing for Chicago's public health nurses. Now Ruth and Toni are becoming allies in the effort to get good medical care to the projects of Chicago. I just learned last night that they have been visiting each other's offices."

"Dr. Wilkens, you've been a busy man," Markowski said. "I thought you would be resting up over here, perhaps getting some therapy from Dr. Solomon, but—"

"Oh, I'll get to Dr. Solomon in a moment. But back to Ruth. I suppose you know she came over last night to try and bail out her nephew."

"Actually, no, I missed that somehow."

"Yes, well, she was unsuccessful. By then it was so late and she had no place to stay. Her place is all torn up. I didn't want her to stay at a motel or something, so I convinced her to save some money and stay at my house. She's there right now."

Jack said, "Wait 'till he tells you about his sessions with the doctor."

"Hold on, hold on," Markowski said. "Isn't this all private, privileged doctor-patient stuff? I'm not sure I should be hearing all this. Dr. Wilkens, you are still on my list as a murder suspect, although—"

"You can strike me off that list. I am going to recant my confession. I never really believed it myself, you know. Your friend Dr Solomon agrees with my decision to recant."

Jack was furiously writing notes.

Markowski glared at him. "Don't you dare publish a word about this until I give you permission."

Jack gave him a mock salute and said, "Yes, sir!"

"And so, Dr. Wilkens, if you are going to recant, can you tell me why you confessed in the first place?"

"Yes. I did it to protect Ruth."

"Do you think she murdered Page? Or had her nephew do it?

"At first I did. But after some reflection, I just can't see either her or Bernard as murderers."

Markowski said, "Well sir, off the record—" He glanced at Jack again. "—I don't think they did it either."

Wilkens looked past him at the doorway. "Well, what a coincidence! Hi Ruth."

Ruth Smith walked into the room. Markowski stood up, as did the other two men. He wondered how much of that last exchange she had heard.

"Mrs. Smith," Markowski said while gesturing at the chair he had vacated. "Please, have a seat."

"I just came back to return George's house key and sit for a bit," she said. "I hope I'm not interrupting anything important."

"No, ma'am, I'm just here to check on Dr. Wilkens's welfare and Jack—you know Jack, don't you?

Ruth nodded. "We met at the Harrington's Fourth of July party."

"Jack's a reporter. He's here to interview George."

Jack said, "Nice to see you again, Mrs. Smith." He stood and said, "Bruce, why don't you take this chair? My interview's complete and I've got to get going. I've got an interesting lead to follow up on."

"Does it by any chance relate to the Page murder?" Markowski asked.

"Yep."

"Jack, let me have a word with you out in the hall before you leave. Excuse us, please." Markowski walked out of the room and asked Jack to close the door on the way out. He said, "Is this lead of yours anything I should know about?"

"Well, that might fall into the category of privileged information that I am not required to—"

"Cut the bull, Jack. If you have information that would help me solve this crime, you'd better give it to me."

Jack sighed. "Okay, Bruce. Look, you're right. I want this cleared up as much as you do, if only to clear the names of my friends Mark and Toni. Plus it will be a hell of a story! I've got pages and pages of juicy notes and—"

"Jack! Just tell me what this lead of yours in all about."

"Right, okay. One of my sources says Chicago PD is very interested in Peter J. Conroy. Something about embezzling family savings and lying about investments in Simplified Data Systems. I'm researching that this morning."

Markowski said, "I'll check with Chicago. But Jack, call me the moment you learn anything. I mean it. I have a press conference scheduled for 1500 today—that's 3:00 p.m.—so I need all the info I can get." He made a note to double-check Peter J. Conroy's alibi; he hadn't yet seen the receipts that Conroy had promised to send.

Both the comfortable chairs were now occupied, so Markowski sat on the smaller and harder one. That was okay with him; he wouldn't be staying that long.

Mrs. Smith said, "Detective, since you're here, may I ask you a couple questions? Unofficially, of course."

"Sure, go ahead."

"Well, it's none of my business, of course. Actually, though, it *is* my business because Bernie's in jail and I suppose I'm still a suspect in Page's murder. Anyway, I've got to ask. Have you considered that Page's wife may have done it?"

This was a surprise; Markowski had expected questions about Bernard's bail. But he supposed it would do no harm to answer. "Yes, ma'am. I can't tell you the details, but I can say that she is being investigated as thoroughly as any of the others." In fact, he had interviewed Mrs. Nora Page by telephone several days ago and had verified that she had been in St. Louis on the day of the murder. He had run a background check on Mrs. Page and had found nothing incriminating. Could she have hired a contract killer? It was possible but very unlikely.

"Thank you," Ruth said. "Now, just yesterday I was over at Marillac House, a youth and senior center out in East Garfield Park. That's on Chicago's West Side, if you're not too familiar with the city. I overheard a conversation that may be important to this case. Shall I go on?"

Markowski pulled out his notepad, flipped it open and said, "Yes, please." Great; now he was taking advice from one of his suspects.

Ruth reached out and patted George's hand. "Sorry, George, this may bring up some bad memories, but I think it's important for Detective Markowski to know this. I overheard something Amanda Billings said—she's the mother of the boy who was 'allegedly' driving Page's car that fateful day. She was talking about a bribe that Page had offered to her and her son if Chuckie—her son—would lie about who was driving that car."

Markowski got some more details about this and promised to investigate. Just what he needed—another suspect! "Thank you, Mrs. Smith. I'll make sure to keep your name out of it. Now, about Bernard. I know you're really worried about him and I'm sorry that we're holding him without bail. But, after all, he and Rhonda Shain are suspects in a murder investigation."

Mrs. Smith stopped him with a wave of her hand. "It's okay. George told me you don't really believe he did it."

Markowski scowled. "Dr. Wilkens, what happened to that promise of keeping that off the record?"

Wilkens shrugged. "I thought we are all kind of family here."

"Family," Markowski said. This was his fault. He had let his personal opinions get in the way of proper investigative techniques and police procedure. He marveled at the absurdity of it all. He was in a room with two murder suspects, one of whom was the aunt of another suspect. Eight of the ten suspects were neighbors in Union Pier. He wouldn't be surprised if another suspect would walk through the door and claim to be part of the "family."

"Hello?" a female voice said.

Markowski swiveled to take a look at the door and breathed a sigh of relief. It wasn't another murder suspect but Alice Britt. "Trooper Britt, come in. Join the party."

She stepped in and said, "Sergeant, I'm sorry to bother you but I brought you this." She held out his pager. "You left this, ah . . ." She inclined her head toward New Buffalo. " . . . up north."

Bless her! She had been discreet. He had left it in *her* apartment, right on the bedside table. He took this as another sign he was falling apart professionally. First it had been becoming friendly with murder suspects. Now, it was letting romance—romance? Was that what it really was? He thought so. Whatever it was, it was interfering with this investigation. Alice was standing there, studying him.

"Thank you, Trooper Britt! Say, if you can afford the time, can you wait for me downstairs? I'll be just a few more minutes." He clipped the pager back onto his belt.

"Sure."

As he sat back down, Ruth Smith said, "She's very cute."

"Oh . . . well, I don't really notice those things," he said.

The corners of Ruth's mouth rose up just a bit. "Of course not," she said.

Crap, crap and triple crap. These women! They have some kind of sixth sense about romance. He said his good byes and, on the way out of the ward, left a message for Dr. Solomon saying that, from a law enforcement standpoint, George Wilkens was free to return home.

Alice was waiting for him in the lobby. "Thanks for waiting," he said. "Sorry if I looked awkward up there when you first arrived. I was angry with myself for forgetting the pager. But now I need some help. Do you have any assignments right now?"

"I'm not scheduled for patrol until 1800."

"Okay, good. Let's get back to the post and I'll tell you what I need. I'll stop and get us some to-go lunch on the way. What would you like?"

"Surprise me."

Chapter 29

Markowski leaned over his desk and used chopsticks to pick a piece of Mu Shu beef out of the takeout container. Meanwhile, Alice made very unladylike slurping noises while attacking her Kung Pao chicken with noodles. He wiped his mouth with a napkin and said, "I've got that press conference in about half an hour so I'm a little short on time. Can you do two things for me?" He handed her an envelope from his in-basket.

"First, this is from a Peter J. Conroy, a.k.a. PJ Conroy. You remember him from the suspect list?"

She nodded.

"Toni Harrington stated that he's quite a salesman for their company's software. She also said he is well-connected in Chicago city politics and has known the victim for, I think she said, 'quite a long time,' or something like that. That envelope has got Conroy's alibi for the time of the murder. Please check it out.

"Also, here's the business card for John Barron, a Chicago detective. He was there when I interviewed Toni Harrington in her office. Please call him, mention my name if you have to, and drop the hint that this is all critical to a murder investigation. Ask him to check out any ongoing investigations by Chicago PD on Conroy's finances."

"You got it."

"Oh, wait. Sorry, I guess there's a third thing." He gave her the details on Mrs. Billings and asked her to run a background check on her and her son Charles.

Alice picked up her box of Chinese food, her bottle of pop and went off to her tasks. Markowski finally got a chance to check the calls on his pager. The first number just said "Pay Phone" on caller ID. The second he recognized as Toni Harrington's office phone. He tried both her business and home numbers but got only voice mail on the former and a busy signal on the latter. He didn't recognize the third number. When he called it, he got Ruth Smith's answering machine. He hung up without leaving a message since he had just seen her at the hospital.

He finished his lunch and consulted his suspect board, hoping to get some inspiration on what to say at today's press conference. His first task was to rearrange the names based on a combination of facts and instinct. It was time to use his instinct, otherwise known as "guesswork." When he finished, he had eleven names on the board, none of whom could be totally excluded from suspicion. He would concentrate on the top three: Toni, Mark and this PJ fellow. The bottom eight all had a good alibi or had, in his judgment, little chance of being murderers.

Markowski decided to be very vague during his press conference, which would aggravate his superiors but would save him from speculating in public. The one exception to this would be about Rhonda and Bernard. He would intentionally leak the information that those two people were being held for theft but were not currently suspects in the murder itself. Once that news hit the streets, he hoped it would goad the murderer into doing something stupid. He jotted down an outline and rehearsed his brief statement. After a trip to the men's room to splash some water on his face and straighten up his tie, he walked out to face the press.

By 1545, the ordeal was over and he was back in his office. The press conference had gone as expected. After his brief statement, he had answered most of the questions with a "No comment." Alice came in with a stack of papers in her hand.

"Anything interesting?" he asked.

"Maybe. Let me give you the easy stuff first. She peeled off the top two pages of her stack and said, "First, I found nothing suspicious about Mrs. Billings. Her son, as we already know, is serving time for the accident and seems to be a model prisoner, or whatever they call juveniles at that facility."

She handed over a handwritten page. "I called Detective Barron in Chicago and left a message for him. He called back and these are my notes about what he said. Essentially, the Financial Crimes Unit stonewalled him. But they at least acknowledged that, yes, Peter J. Conroy is the subject of a current investigation. They wouldn't provide any details. Innocent until proven guilty, et cetera, et cetera.

"Finally, here's what I've learned about Conroy's trip to Detroit. He flew to Detroit on the 13th, checked into the Renaissance Hotel and listed a rental car license number on his hotel registration form. He flew back to Chicago on the 15th."

Markowski reached out to the murder board to move Conroy's name lower on the suspect list.

"Wait, wait! There's a little more to this story. Using my feminine charm and, ah, maybe mentioning possible letters of appreciation for his help, I managed to coax some information out of the rental car guy. When Conroy picked up his rental car, he made a second car rental reservation for *that same evening*, to pick up a car in South Bend, Indiana."

"South Bend? On the same night, the 13th?"

"Yes," Alice said. "I couldn't get any further without accessing his credit card records, but the extra trip made me curious. Why South Bend?"

Markowski glanced at the Michigan State map on the wall; it also showed the two adjoining states, Indiana and Ohio, plus Lake Michigan and a little slice of Illinois that included Chicago. "What's your guess?" he asked.

Alice didn't bother looking at the map. "I suppose there could be an innocent reason. Friends in South Bend? Connections to Notre Dame University? A business meeting? But . . . it's also the closest airport to Union Pier."

"My thoughts exactly. This is great work, Alice. Thank you. Let me have your notes; I'll get right on the phone and request a warrant for Conroy's credit cards, airline records, and car rental history."

*   *   *

Forty-five minutes later, after a spot of luck in getting a faxed warrant and a further lucky break to have reached all the appropriate people, Markowski said, "Let's write down what we've learned." He stood up from his desk and flipped over to a fresh page on his easel pad. He wrote as he talked.

"Friday, 13 October: Conroy arrives in Detroit at 1410, picks up a rental car at 1430 and makes a second car reservation for South Bend. Checks into Renaissance Hotel—a beautiful place, by the way; it's right on the river—at 1530. He returns to Detroit airport at 1625—parking garage records confirm this—and boards an ASAP Airlines commuter flight to South Bend at 1700." He handed the black marker to Alice. "Now, why don't you tell me what you've learned."

She took the marker and began writing. Markowski was a little embarrassed by her clear printing; his was more like a first-grader's scribbling. "Conroy's flight landed at 1805 on Friday the 13th. He picked up rental car #2 at 1820. Thirty-five minutes later, at 1855, he paid for a bottle of wine at G and J's Wine Shop on Highway 12 in Three Oaks." This time she did glance up and point at the map. On the next line below that entry, she wrote a big question mark.

"We don't have any record of what he did for the next seventeen hours and forty-five minutes. I've got a call in to the wine shop to see if they have a security camera that would tell us in which direction he departed."

"Good thinking," Markowski said.

"However, a person driving from South Bend to Union Pier would definitely have to pass through Three Oaks."

"Yes, I agree."

Alice said, "At 1000 on Saturday the 14th, he returned car #2 to the South Bend Airport. He put seventy miles on that car which, as it turns out, is roughly the distance of a round trip from South Bend to Union Pier. That's just one possibility, of course."

"But it's a somewhat incriminating coincidence."

She nodded. "Conroy's return flight arrived in Detroit at 1130 on the 14th. He paid for airport parking at 1140. The next time his credit card was used was at 1730 in the hotel restaurant. I assume that he attended his conference during the afternoon but have no proof of that. He returned rental car #1 at 1145 on the 15th; rental car records show that he put eighty-eight miles on it."

"Let me guess," Markowski said. "That equates to two round trips from the Renaissance to the Detroit Airport."

"Affirmative. He arrived back in Chicago at 1220 on the 15th." She swiped the black marker across bottom of the sheet and re-capped the pen with a flourish, as if she were sliding a sword into its scabbard.

Markowski picked up the phone. "I've got to call this guy or maybe I'll just call in a few favors and ask Chicago PD to pick him—"

"Bruce, hold everything!"

Markowski looked up to see Jack O'Connor in his doorway.

"You're gonna want to hear this right away," Jack said. He looked at Alice. "Uh, maybe in private?"

"No, Jack. Trooper Britt's in on this investigation too." He hung up the phone. "Go ahead."

"I'll try to be brief," Jack said.

Markowski resisted a sarcastic comment. Jack, brief? That'll be the day. "Please do that. There's a lot of breaking developments here."

Jack said, "About PJ Conroy's trouble with the law. My source led me to PJ's wife Heather and their accountant. Both refused to comment but my news-sensor alarm went off big time. Both of their voices betrayed them; they are worried about something. When I checked back with my PD source, he—I mean, the source, heh, heh—said the issue involved tens of thousands of dollars of possible embezzlement and falsifying records at Simplified Data Systems. Or something like that; I couldn't quite under—" ."

"Hold that thought," Markowski said. He picked up his phone and dialed the intercom for dispatch. When a trooper answered, he said, "This is Markowski. I need to commandeer Trooper Britt for an emergency related to the Page murder investigation. Can you get her off patrol duty today?" He waited several seconds, said, "Thanks," and hung up. "Alice, get your cold weather gear. We're going to Chicago." He stood up, removed his sport coat and grabbed a parka from the coat rack. He resisted the urge to pull his revolver out of its holster, pop open the cylinder and spin it to confirm it was loaded, like they did in the movies. If it had been loaded this morning, it still was now.

Jack followed them down the hall. Markowski looked back at him. The man had the sad expression of a puppy that knew he was going to be left behind. "What the hell. C'mon Jack; you might as well go with us. Alice, can you get him an extra parka, gloves and ski cap?"

Jack grinned. If he had been a puppy, his tail would have been wagging furiously.

Chapter 30

Freshly showered after her Thursday afternoon cardio workout, Toni walked out of the elevator feeling renewed in both body and spirit. She loved the fact that exercise seemed to stimulate her brain's creative thinking side. Today's inspiration covered two subjects. First, she had decided to treat PJ as innocent—well, not really innocent of *everything*,but concerning Page's murder, innocent until proven guilty. Maybe, just maybe, he'd be able to provide a reason why he had sneaked away to Union Pier in the middle of a business trip. He was gone for the day after a series of sales meetings so she'd have to ask him about that tomorrow. That's when she'd break the news that she couldn't work with him anymore. She could not associate herself or her company with a man who would rob his kids' educational savings. Could the company survive without him and his sales expertise? It would have to. She'd just bite the bullet and become a better salesperson. Or, maybe throw the idea out to one of the other employees; perhaps one of them had hidden sales talents.

The afternoon's second epiphany had come when she had looked out the fifth-floor gym window at the majestic lakefront view and said to herself, "What the heck am I doing in this over-priced office building?" Simplified Data Systems needed to move to a more humble space, and she already had a great place in mind.

Toni waved a "hello" to Margaret, who was on the phone, and walked over to Fred's cubicle. "Fred, can you come into my office for a minute? And, bring a summary of our office expenses, furniture rental costs and anything else that relates to this building, please."

She almost skipped down to her office; once she got her teeth into a good idea, she couldn't let it go. As Fred settled into a chair, she said, "Fred, can you add up our monthly expenses for these offices? Just a rough estimate is fine. I'm just doing some brainstorming."

"Let's see," he said. "Office rent is $5K per month and our rent-to-buy option for all the furnishings is costing us another $2.5K. Phone service is—"

"Oh, hold on, I apologize. I should have been more specific. I'm looking for expenses unique to this building. Things like phone service, fax lines and so forth, those will be a constant no matter where we are located."

"Uh, Toni, does this mean you are thinking of moving? You do realize that we just got settled up here. And, what will PJ think about this?"

"Fred, please keep this under your hat, but I'm seriously thinking about backing out of this partnership. I've researched it; PJ and I both have no-fault 'poison pill' clauses in our contracts. Either of us can terminate the partnership with two weeks' notice."

"But, things are just now beginning to get rolling. PJ's bringing in a lot of—"

"Fred, trust me; I have my reasons. Anyway, I am not going to do anything immediately. I am just trying to get some ideas, some options. That's why I beg you to keep this conversation confidential."

"Sure," he said. "Back to your original question, the only other expense for these offices is, we pay a monthly fee of $1,100 to cover 'building services,' which includes upkeep of the lobby downstairs, the doorman, elevator expenses, et cetera."

Toni added up the numbers on a note pad. Simplified Data was spending $8,600 per month for the privilege of looking out the window at Lake Michigan—oh, and having a prestigious mailing address and a doorman downstairs. "Thanks, Fred. We'll talk more about this soon and please, don't worry. I won't do anything irrational on my own."

Fred said, "Great." He pushed back his chair and stood up.

"Now that I mention it, would it be irrational to ask you this? What would it take to covert this LLC into a co-op? That is, an employee-owned company where everyone shares in the profits. Can you research that for me?

"Are you serious?"

She nodded. "Dead serious." Perhaps that was another bad choice of words.

"What in heaven's name gave you that idea?" Fred asked.

"I'm not exactly sure. You know how things just pop into your head sometimes? Well, my brain's been going a mile a minute lately on many different subjects. I'm fighting for my company's success, but how is success defined?"

Fred said, "I know how I'd define it. A positive balance sheet."

"Yes, I can see your point. But . . . now that I think about it, I was greatly influenced by my visit out to the East Garfield projects the other day. It both challenged and validated my passion for improving health care access, especially in low income communities."

"I understand the validation side, but what did you see that challenged you?"

"Yeah, I'm not expaining it very well. You know I'm motivated to help health care companies, which in turn helps their patients. But I got to thinking, do my employees really feel this same sense of mission or are they just sitting up here pulling down a paycheck? Would they be just as happy working one floor below at that architecture firm, or the import-export business? How do I get my passion for this company to rub off on everybody?

"My first thought was to get all our employees to do what I did—go out to the clinics or hospitals, especially those out near the projects, like Rockwell Gardens. Let them see first-hand how their work affects these communities."

"Not a bad idea," Fred said.

"But I was troubled by something. I work my butt off because I really believe in the social significance of what I do. What magic elixir did I drink to make me feel this way? And how do I get all of us at SDS to drink it? So I thought, what if the employees were more than employees? For example, Margaret out there at the front desk works hard to coordinate everything. When we sign up new business, the LLC's bank account grows, but does Margaret get a bigger paycheck? No! Her pay is the same whether we succeed or fail. What is she were a co-owner of this company and the more money we make, the higher her income goes? Would she enjoy coming to work more and once here work even harder? I've only heard of co-ops and I don't really know how they work, but I think the general idea is, when the business does well, everyone shares in the profits. I've heard that little phrase all my adult life. *'XYZ Company is employee-owned!'* Please look into it for me Fred. I think it's the right thing to do."

"You know, I kind of like that idea!" Fred said. "I'll get right on it." He put his fingers to his lips. "Confidentially of course."

Toni's next call was to Ruth, but she was not in her office. Who else could help her? She needed someone at Marillac House. Today was Thursday, so Nurse Grace would be there. She reached for the phone book to find Marillac's number, called, and got put on hold for what seemed like a lifetime but was probably less than thirty seconds.

"Marillac Health Room, Grace speaking."

"Hi, Grace, it's Toni Harrington. I was there with Ruth a few days ago. Remember me? I can't get ahold of Ruth, but I need a favor. You know that old vacant five-and-dime store right next to your building? It's got a "For Rent" sign in the window. Can you go out there and copy down the contact information for the rental agent?"

Twenty minutes later she had spoken to Top Shelf Realty, learned the square footage of the place and the monthly rent—$1,500. Simplified Data could work out of that place—it was actually larger than her current offices—and save $7,100 per month. She had an appointment to inspect the building tomorrow morning.

She needed to get home to the kids. Her mom was a saint for helping out while Mark was out of town, but it was time for her to get home to Dad. Her final official act of the day was to sign the checks that Fred had prepared and put them in each employee's cubby hole. Tomorrow was payday and there was nothing better than a paycheck in hand to improve employee morale. She signed all seven checks and distributed them. Toni shut down her computer, cleaned off her desk and picked up her purse. As she turned to leave, she saw PJ standing in her doorway, blocking her exit.

Chapter 31

As usual, he was dressed in a high-end suit, impeccable white shirt, silk tie and shiny black loafers.

He looked at his watch and said, "Wow, it's only 5:03 and everyone has cleared out? It must have been quite a stampede."

"PJ! I thought you were going straight home after your last sales meeting."

"I got done early, so I thought I'd drop in on my way home. Whew! It's been quite a week or two, hasn't it? Page's murder, the San Francisco earthquake, policemen in the office and, did you know that last Friday the stock market dropped by 190 points? That's a drop of about seven percent. They called it a 'mini crash.' Then on Monday the Dow gained half of it back. Crazy."

"Speaking of money," Toni said, "I just put your paycheck in your box."

"Oh, good. Now, here's another question about money. I was just wondering what you meant about that $25,000 reward when you said you might collect it."

She laughed. "I could use the money. Why, don't you think I can do it? I just want to solve this thing and be free of all connections to Edwin Page."

PJ smiled. "You and me both. Now, I hate to harp, but I'd really like to have those expense sheets. Where are they?"

"Safe," she answered.

"Safe where?"

"Just safe."

"Toni, what are you up to? I'd like to know."

His voice had changed pitch; the friendly chit-chat tone had hardened. She had never heard him speak like this.

"I'm beginning to distrust you, Toni. Why is that?'

"You've got me, PJ. Why on earth wouldn't you trust me?"

"I believe you are making some kind of deal with that detective." PJ stepped closer. She had to look up to see his expression. His jaw was clenched tight; she could see the small muscles on each side of his face bulging out. His eyes were narrowed as if he wanted them to drill into her brain and read her mind.

"I wish I could," she said. "I'd like to get him off my back. I'm probably his prime suspect."

"Don't make a joke, Toni."

"I'm not. Seriously, there's a lot of evidence pointing right at me."

"I suspect you *are* up to something," he said. "You'd better level with me."

"Are you threatening me, PJ?"

"Possibly."

"Well, don't you dare!" Her face felt hot; she was sure her cheeks were red. If PJ was smart, he would recognize this as a sign that he had gone too far. "What's going on here? I don't have to take this. What's up with you anyway?"

He stepped back and moved over toward the window. "Perhaps we should talk this out," he said in a lower voice and turned his back to her.

At least his rage had subsided. "Talk what out?" Toni asked. She moved a step or two closer to him.

He whirled around and shouted, "I want those expense sheets now, Toni!"

There he was, back into his angry-man mode. Well, she had a push-back mode of her own. "No way, PJ. My position on that hasn't changed,"

PJ turned abruptly toward the side window, reached down to unlock it, and raised the sash as far up as it would go.

"My God, it's cold outside," she called out. "Shut that window! Never mind, I'll do it myself." She walked to the window and reached for the handle.

Before she could react, he stepped behind her, grabbed the Venetian blind cord and whipped it around her neck. He pulled it tight enough to make her choke.

PJ said, "Don't make a sound or it will be your last. You know, Toni, your workouts haven't made you strong enough to fight me off. I locked the front door before I came in. You are just not going to turn me in."

"Turn you in where?"

"For the reward. For twenty lousy pieces of silver. For your 25,000 lousy city reward dollars."

She sucked in some air. This was not the voice of PJ, the smooth-talking marketing expert. This was the voice of a cold-hearted murderer. She should have followed her instinct and stayed away from him. "Did you kill Page?"

She felt one of his arms move. He threw something onto her desk and swung her around to look at it. It was the missing key for the Michigan house.

"Remember Friday the 13th? You shouldn't leave keys lying around, smart ass," he hissed.

"I know you went to Union Pier that night," she said, forcing the words out in a hoarse voice. Maybe she could scare him off with a lie. "And others know it too."

"It won't matter, Toni. As a special favor I am going to give you some information to take with you. Don't move or yell. I will snap your neck." His hands tightened the cord to an even more painful level.

Toni had never felt this alone or this frightened. What could she do? If she screamed, he would choke her. No one could hear her anyway; the place was empty. There were thousands of people down below on the streets, useless to her, unaware of her predicament. Bitter cold from the wind off the lake chilled her to the bone.

She willed herself to stay conscious, to breathe whenever he inadvertently loosened his grip on the cord—and to not hyperventilate. She allowed herself one brief prayer. *God, please hear me. It's Toni Harrington, on the twentieth floor of the People's Gas Building. Please help me!*

She decided to keep him talking. That seemed a much better option than being strangled to death. "You're not planning to let me go, are you, PJ?"

"You know better than that."

"But if you kill me," she ventured, "and you killed Page, you'd have two murders. I wouldn't be a suspect anymore. They'll be looking for you."

"I thought of that problem. I believe I have solved it."

"Oh, please, PJ," she cried softly. It was a change of tactics. "Please let me go. Think of my kids."

"It's nice to see you beg, Toni. You have always been just a shade too arrogant for me."

"No, you misunderstood. I never meant to be."

"I want those expense sheets."

His voice cut through her like a steel blade. "They aren't here; they're at my apartment," she lied, hoping she could convince him to take her there. An opportunity to escape or be rescued might pop up.

"I don't believe you. Where are they, really?"

"Forget the sheets. You're not getting them." She felt the cord tighten and needed to find a diversion. "How did you kill Page anyway?"

"I'll tell you. Then you will get me the sheets. I went to Detroit on Friday, checked in to the hotel and registered for the conference. However, I skipped the dull meetings. I drove the rental car back to the airport, flew to South Bend and rented another car for the trip to Union Pier. Those keys of yours? I used them to get into your house. I already had the alarm code."

"Why? Why our house?"

"Your house is elegant. It's upscale. I was looking forward to an exciting night in bed with your tenant, Rhonda."

"Ew! In our house? In our bed?" Toni was furious; she tried to turn around and scowl at him but he forced her back.

"What difference would it make to you?"

She tried to say, "That's disgusting!" but it gurgled out as "Ugh, ugh argh!" She coughed and tried again. "You wouldn't understand." Only a man with scruples would get it. How could she not have seen this side of him? Was he on drugs or something? Would he really kill her? She had never thought much about death—not her own, anyway. And she certainly had never imagined it happening in her own office at the hands of her business partner. Could this be a nightmare like the one with the spilled wine? At what point will I wake up? She could feel the veins in her forehead pulsing and the bile rising in her throat, symptoms of fear that she had only read about. She didn't think dreams were that detailed.

"You weren't due until the next day. I went in, turned up the heat and located some wine glasses. I even brought a bottle of fancy wine, a Château Clerc Milon."

Toni shook her head at the irony of PJ's wine choice. That was the same wine Mark had accidentally poured at Miller's Country House.

PJ's voice had changed. It was now emotionless, like someone telling a story but in a monotone.

"I never expected to see Page. I wish I had never opened the blinds. Shortly after I did that, there he was, standing at the front door."

Apparently, PJ wanted her to know every detail. He coughed quietly, which caused him to loosen his grip on the cord. She took a few deep breaths before he tightened it again.

"I had borrowed a good deal of money from my wife Heather's estate. I gave it to Page to purchase real estate on the West Side. There was going to be a new stadium built. He promised me a ten-fold return. He claimed there was absolutely no risk. He could buy the property for little or nothing, and even get around the back taxes due. When I saw him standing at the door, I said, 'Come on in, Ed. It's good to see you.'"

"'Good to see you too,' Page said. 'Did the Harringtons loan you their place?'"

Like an efficient bystander, PJ narrated the events. "'Oh, yes they did,' I said. "Page said, 'They have done a lot of work here. Mind if I look around?'"

"'Sure, go ahead.'" I said. He looked over the house carefully. He commented that you had done a nice job. 'It's always good to see places get fixed up,' he said. 'It helps the whole community. Every improvement is an asset to all of us.'"

So, I offered him a glass of Jack Daniel's. I knew you had some there in the cupboard. He accepted."

Toni shivered.

"Please don't do that, Toni. It makes me nervous."

Him nervous? What about her? She thought about her babies, Allen and Emily. Would she ever see them or hold them again? Would she see them graduate college? Who would raise them, mother them? Just as she had last Saturday,when she had gotten angry at the murderer for causing trauma to her kids, she vowed to make PJ pay for all this. The situation was different tonight, though. Last Saturday, the murderer had been some unidentified villain. Tonight, she had the bastard right here in her office.

Only she didn't exactly have *him*—he had *her* in a stranglehold. She was going to find a way to turn the tables by, uh, exactly what? She needed more time to come up with a plan. She only knew that she was not going down without a fight.

"Things at the house were going okay until Page lifted his Jack Daniel's for a toast. I noticed the gaudy Rolex trimmed with diamonds. I said, 'Page, you've been stealing my money. You're spending it on yourself. Look at that watch!'"

"'Beautiful, isn't it?' he said."

PJ snorted in disgust. "The guy was that arrogant! 'It cost ten grand and it looks it!' Page said. He actually flaunted it." He spat out the words bitterly. "Well," I said, "let's talk about money. Let's talk about *my* money."

"'Doesn't look good,' Page told me. 'The stadium might be falling through the cracks. The city isn't getting behind it.'"

I said, "You told me we couldn't lose."

"'Well,' he told me, 'I guess we could.'"

"We haven't lost it all, have we?" I asked him. You know what he said then? He said, "'Forget the *we* stuff. I think it's *you* who lost.'"

"Eighty thousand dollars?"

"'Every bit of it,' he said."

I yelled at him. "You bastard! You stole it."

"He says, 'Don't get harsh, PJ. I am getting you a lot of business.' Then he takes another drink. I was hot! I said, 'You'll never get me the million dollars I was promised. Are you saying I won't even see my eighty thousand?' He answers, 'Looks that way.'

"I hollered at him, 'You're nothing but a cheap crook!'" He laughs. Can you believe it? He laughs! And says, 'Maybe a crook but not a cheap crook. Excuse me while I take a leak.' He stood up and started up the stairs to your bathroom."

Toni felt another chill go down her spine. Strangers using her bathroom was another thorn in her side. This story was dragging on but at least she was still alive. She prayed that

PJ would come to his senses. The telephone rang, startling her. She made a move for it.

"Don't do it," PJ said.

Toni waited silently, with PJ breathing down her neck, while the phone rang about six times. Maybe it's Mark. Maybe he will come and find me. She was so cold.

"Please close the window, PJ," she pleaded.

PJ didn't seem to hear her. He went on with his tale.

"Page was at the top of the stairs. I grabbed the poker by the fireplace and lunged after him. I came down hard on his head. I was furious. He deserved it. I felt a crunch when the poker hit his skull. It felt good. I had done it; it was good."

Toni's trembling accelerated. If killing makes him feel good, I'm in real trouble. He must be a maniac, but he looks so . . . so normal! The cord was tightening again. How much tighter could it get?

"Page hardly made a sound, maybe just a little grunt." PJ seemed to be savoring the moment. "He staggered forward and fell into your tub. Kind of slid over on his back. I raised the poker. I was going to whack him again. Then I got worried. I ran down and looked out the windows; no one was in sight. I ran back up the stairs. He was breathing. I was going to beat him to death but then I thought there must be a better way."

PJ was panting, reliving the whole episode. "I ran to the kitchen, grabbed a sharp knife. Up the stairs again. I stabbed him, only once, but it was forceful and the knife went in deep. He got very still. I knew he was dead."

She couldn't handle all this. The story was sickening; she would surely pass out if she heard any more. How did he think he would get away with this? Killing her would double his crime. Then she realized that was not how a deranged killer would see things. After the first murder, what would be the harm in a second one? You could only go to the gas chamber or get a lethal injection once, whether it was for one murder or twenty. In fact, she wasn't even sure the death penalty was still enforced in Illinois.

"I closed the blind," he went on, apparently unable to stop. "Cleaned everything. The whiskey glasses, the knife, the poker. I never dreamed they could trace the weapons if I cleaned them. I wiped everything I had touched. Even my wine bottle. I put that in the wine rack in your kitchen. That's not bad compensation for the use of your house, right?"

PJ paused and took a deep breath. When he exhaled, she could feel his warm breath on her neck. His mouth was close to her ear. "PJ, it's not too late to—"

"Shhh!" he snarled while rearranging his grip on the cord. "I looked for some way to get Page out of the tub. I found a green tent in your garage, pulled Page out of the tub and wrapped him in it. I dragged him down into the garage. I wanted to pull him out of the house but it wasn't quite dark yet. Plus, Rhonda's car was parked out there. I knew she was in there getting ready for our date."

He stopped for moment, looking pensive. "There must have been blood in the bathtub. Apparently I forgot about it. I thought of everything else." He paused again, as if amazed at his error. Then he leaned around and sneered at her. "Somehow I no longer felt like fooling around. It would have been hard to have sex in your bedroom with Page dead in your garage."

He laughed, apparently finding this somewhat humorous. The thought just made Toni closer to being sick.

"After a while I called Rhonda. Told her I couldn't make it. Told her I was in Detroit. She really snarled at me. Pretty bitchy!"

How much worse could this have been if she, Mark and the kids had arrived in the middle of it all? What if the body had been there? Or this crazy killer?

"What if we had come in during all this?" she asked.

"Who knows? I would have improvised something."

He paused to breathe. His grip loosened just enough for Toni to resupply her lungs and her brain with air. She had to make a move, but how could she escape without him breaking her neck? On the other side of the glass partition, the clock on the wall read 5:25. Perhaps she should have taken martial arts. But how could she kick him in the groin without tightening her noose? She could not do anything but sit and wait. Was she waiting for death? She hoped God would absolve her from all her past sins. No time to think about those, though. She was pretty focused on the present. She hoped God would understand.

"When I told Rhonda I couldn't make it," PJ repeated, "I couldn't believe how nasty she was. She called me enough names to make a sailor blush. A few minutes later I saw her leave her house and drive away. I sure didn't want her to find me in your house. I waited for dark. That damned security light over the garage went on, so I threw some stones at it and finally broke it. The noise and the sparks scared me but no one else was around to see it."

He laughed.

It was more of a cackle—she was reminded of the Shakespearean phrase, " . . . *the crones cackled of evil deeds.*" What a silly thing to think about in this situation.

"I pulled Page over to the garage door, opened it and pulled him out. Then I locked all the doors and turned on the alarm. I dragged him into the house next door. The door was open. Inside, the floorboards were broken out. I shoved him into the space between the floor beams.

"All that exertion made me pretty tired, so I decided to stay at the Nine Cranes Inn, that B&B about a mile up the shore."

Toni said, "Yeah, I know."

"That's right, you already knew I was there! How did you find out?"

Despite her situation, Toni attempted a laugh but it came out as a squawk. "The B&B called here. You left your sport coat in your room. I drove over there and saw your name on the register." Some master criminal he was. PJ was going down for this, somehow, some way. The only question was, would she be alive to see him tried for murder? There was one thing she had to know.

"How can you get away with killing me?" she said.

"That's simple, Toni. You are going to leave a suicide note and jump out of this window."

"Thank God that can't happen," she said. "I won't do it."

"I think you will." He pushed her closer to the open window.

She struggled and tried to hit him but he pinned her arms against her chest. She was close enough to the window to look down twenty floors to the street below. One push by the stronger PJ and she would tumble out into the cold night. How long would it take her to fall before she hit the hard pavement below?

PJ used one of his hands to unwind the cord from around her neck. This was her chance; her right arm was free. She looked down, raised her right leg and stomped the thin heel of her right shoe down onto the top of PJ's right foot, the part unprotected by his fancy loafers. Then she rammed her right elbow back as hard and she could and was rewarded with an impact with the soft flesh of his belly.

His "Ow!" from the heel stomp was interrupted by a "Huhhh!" from the blow to his stomach.

She broke free and ran. One shoe had come off during the fight so she kicked off the other one. She rushed out her office door and headed for . . . what? The elevator? No that would take too long. The stairs? No, he would catch her. The bathroom? She could lock herself in but would then be trapped.

PJ shouted, "You bitch! Where'd you learn to fight like that?"

She could hear his footfalls behind her. She raced out to the main door, wasted one valuable second to unlock it and headed for the stairwell. Maybe she could outrun him.

As she approached the elevator door, it began to open but she didn't slow down. The stairwell door was ten feet away and she was going to make it there or die trying.

She heard a voice yell, "Freeze or I'll shoot!" but she had reached the door. She flung it open and was halfway down a flight of stairs before she heard a voice.

"Toni, Toni, stop!" It was Mark. "It's okay. They've got PJ. He's in handcuffs."

It took her another half-flight of steps to stop. She turned around, looked up and said, "Mark? What are you doing here?"

He jumped down the steps two at a time. He slid to a stop on the landing above her and opened his arms. She rushed up and hugged him tighter than she ever had before.

Mark said, "Your heart's pounding like a jackhammer." He released her and looked at her from head to shoulders. "Are you hurt?"

She touched her neck and winced. "Got a little raw spot on my neck, but that's all."

He wrapped his arms around her again and said, "God, I love you!"

They stayed in that position for what seemed like forever, and that was fine with Toni. Her heartbeat had finally slowed to only a hundred miles an hour when she noticed Jack on the next landing above them.

"Hi, lovebirds. It's safe up above. Come on up."

She and Mark, walking hand-in-hand, followed Jack up the stairs and across the elevator landing, where two Chicago Police officers had PJ up against a wall with his hands cuffed behind his back. They were frisking him. They reached the office lobby, where Toni saw a uniformed female Michigan State Trooper guarding her office door.

Mark said, "Sergeant Markowski's down in your office. Do you want to go tell him what happened?"

Go back to that cold office and hear the echoes of PJ's wild ranting? To see the open window and relive the threat of a twenty-story plunge to her death? Toni teared up, began trembling, and grabbed Mark's arm with both hands. Her legs were shaking so badly her knees knocked together. She was getting dizzy. Everything seemed to be swaying back and forth. She felt someone put a coat over her shoulders and a female voice said, "Get her to a chair, you guys! Can't you tell she's going into shock?"

Chapter 32

Toni smelled hot chocolate. She opened her eyes and saw a steamy cup being waved under her nose by an elegant woman's hand. An angel? "I hope I'm in heaven," she said.

"I don't think so. But you're not in hell, either." That was Mark's voice. She couldn't see him. Her head seemed to be drooping; all she could see was her lap and her legs. With great effort, she slowly raised her head and was rewarded with a sharp pain at the base of her neck. It felt better once her head was up in its normal position. She saw Mark, Jack, Sergeant Markowski and a man she didn't recognize. They were all lined up, staring down at her. Kneeling in front of her was the angel who held the cup of cocoa. Only this angel was a female Michigan state trooper.

"Mrs. Harrington, I'm Trooper Britt. You are safe. You're okay. Chicago EMTs will be here any minute to check you over, but I'm an EMT myself and I promise you, you're fine. Can you hold this cup?"

"Yes, I think so." Her hands shook a little, but she was able to get it to her mouth without spilling any. She took two small sips. Only then did she notice that she was wearing a heavy black parka with an embroidered police logo on the front. It fit too well to be a man's. Everyone else in the room had overcoats or parkas except the female.

"Is this yours? Aren't you cold?"

"You need it more than me," Trooper Britt said. "When you're ready, Sergeant Markowski would like to ask you a few questions. You don't have to go back into that office. We'll use your conference room."

"Okay." She took another sip of cocoa. "Thank you. Who made this?"

Trooper Britt smiled, leaned close to her and whispered, "I found your snack bar in the conference room. All these men were standing around being useless. As usual." She winked at her and stood up.

Toni's shakes returned. "PJ wanted me to jump out the window. He killed Page. Told me all about it. He almost killed me. He wanted me to write a suicide note."

Mark came over and said, "Excuse me." The trooper stepped aside and he bent down and hugged her. "You're safe now, Toni."

"Hey!" she said, "you never told me how you got here. You're supposed to still be in—"

"Your mom," he said. "She called and told me you had made a mysterious trip to Union Pier and were acting funny after that. I just got a bad feeling that you might have, ah, misled me when you promised to not do anything danger-ous. I jumped on the first available flight home."

"Thank you Mark. I love you."

When Mark stepped away, Markowski pulled up a chair and sat down in front of her.

"Mrs. Harrington, you've had quite a traumatic experi-ence. If you're not feeling up to it, you don't have to make a statement right now."

"Oh, I'm feeling better every minute. Would you mind holding this?" She offered him the cup and used both arms to push up off the chair. "Thank you." She took the cup back, brushed the wrinkles out of her blouse and skirt and headed for the conference room. "Let's do this." She did her best to walk down the hall without wobbling. She stopped at the thermostat and looked back at the others. "I'm going to turn this up a little. It's on a timer than reduces the temperature after hours."

She was the first to enter the room, with Markowski and the unknown man just behind. Markowski stopped in the doorway and said, "Mark and Jack, you guys will have to wait outside. Police procedure and all that. Sorry." He closed the door. "Mrs. Harrington, this is Detective Robbins from Chicago PD Homicide. He's here because this is his jurisdiction. If you are comfortable with it, he'll be the one to ask questions."

Robbins was a thick-set man with a large neck and the body of a wrestler or a pro football lineman. He put a brief-case down on the desk and took off his overcoat to reveal a rumpled grey suit. Robbins reached out for a handshake and said, "Henry Robbins, Mrs. Harrington. I will echo what Sergeant Markowski said. You've been traumatized tonight. Anytime you want to cut this short, let me know. You can go home, get some rest and we will continue later." His voice and mannerism was soft and considerate, in stark contrast to his rough-and-ready appearance.

"Thank you, detective, but I think I'd like to get it all done right now."

"Okay," he said. "Why don't we all sit down." He pulled a mini-cassette tape recorder out of his pocket. "Do I have your permission to record this?"

She nodded. Markowski pulled out his ever-present notebook.

Robbins said, "Why don't you tell me what happened here tonight?"

"Wow. Where to begin? I was the last person in the office, signing paychecks. It was, let's see—PJ himself mentioned the time—it was 5:03 p.m. I was already suspicious of PJ because I had discovered he had snuck over to Union Pier on the night of the murder. You know about that case, right?"

Robbins said, "Yes, ma'am."

"I had also learned that PJ had lied about investing his family's money in our company. Do you want me to talk about that?"

"No ma'am. I am aware of that too."

"Well, anyway, despite all of that, I had decided to give him the benefit of the doubt about Union Pier and was going to confront him about that tomorrow. But, just as I was leaving, he showed up in my office doorway. Now that I think about it, he was sort of blocking my exit. I suppose he didn't plan on letting me out of there alive."

She went through the entire conversation, trying her best to describe when it had shifted from normal business-related banter to a murderous assault. "He had some crazy idea that I already knew he was the murderer, when really I didn't. He thought I was after the $25,000 reward. Then he told me I was going to write a suicide note and jump out the window! If I hadn't been so scared, I would have laughed at him."

Robbins opened his briefcase, pulled out a typewritten piece of paper and passed it to her. "Is this your signature?"

She looked at the page and gasped. It was her signature, all right, at the bottom of a typed letter. She read every word of it out loud.

"Dearest Mark, Allen, Emily, Mom and Dad:

I am forced to do this with deep regret and sadness. I am sorry that it has to end this way. I killed Page. I was not alone. I hired two assassins. They were supposed to lure Page to our house, take him and kill him on the beach. I don't know what went wrong but they killed him in our house. I cannot give the names of the assassins because they might hurt my family.

Page was blackmailing me. I borrowed $80,000 from PJ and gave it to Ed Page to buy real estate on the west side where the Bears were going to build a stadium. I expected a million back. He either stole it or lost it all. He wanted another $50,000, so I had to shut him up. There seems to be no other way out. Good bye. Love, Toni/Mom."

"Yes, that's my signature at the bottom. But I didn't write that!"

"We assumed that." Robbins said, "Not many people type out a nice neat suicide note on their computer. But how did he get you to sign it? Did he force you?"

"No, the conniving bast—uh, sorry—PJ tricked me into signing two blank letters for some made-up business reason. Let's see, that was on the same day as Page's funeral, about a week and a half after his murder. I can't remember the exact date."

Markowski flipped through his notebook pages. "The funeral was on October 25th."

She wondered why Markowski would know that. "Okay, on that same day, PJ said his computer wasn't working and asked to use mine. I'll bet you could find that file on my computer and I'll bet it was written during the time I was out of my office at the gym."

Both detectives jotted down notes about this.

Toni told the rest of the story. When she described the maneuvers she did to break free, Robbins asked, "Where did you learn that? Do you have any training?"

She shook her head and grinned. "Training? Ha! No. I saw it once in a movie."

When she finished her story, Robbins shut off the tape recorder and put it back in his briefcase. "Oh," he said. "About these shoes." He pulled a clear plastic bag out of the briefcase and put it on the table. "These will have to stay in evidence."

"That's okay. I have gym shoes in my bag in the office."

Robbins held the bag of shoes up to the light. "Hmm. This one heel is broken. And, did you know you actually drew blood when you stomped him?" He held the bag closer to her.

She drew back and said, "I'll take your word for it." Seeing the shoes brought her back to that moment when she thought she might die and the fear and anger it had provoked. The fear was gone, but the anger still raged. She had to do something about that. This fight wasn't over yet. "Hey, are we done here? If so, I have a question."

The two detectives looked at each other. Robbins nodded and opened his briefcase.

"Wait," Toni said to Robbins. "Don't put the shoes away. Is PJ still here? I want to say some parting words to him."

Robbins and Markowski exchanged more looks. She could not read their expressions.

"You know her better than I," Robbins said to Markowski. "It's your call."

Markowski leaned forward, rubbed his face and groaned. "Mrs. Harrington, the law enforcement side of me is saying no. That would be a bad idea. However . . . this is your office, after all. You are free to go. If you were to leave this room before we do, perhaps while we are reviewing some of the case details, and if Mr. Conroy were still out there, we couldn't be responsible—"

"Say no more!" Toni jumped out of her chair, grabbed the bag with her shoes and said, "I need this for a second."

Robbins called after her, "Just don't open the bag!"

When she reached the outer office, she found PJ sitting on Margaret's office chair with his hands cuffed in front of him and two Chicago PD officers standing guard, one on each side.

She strode up to him and said, "Stand up."

He looked up at her but didn't move.

"Get up out of that chair!" she shouted. "Do it now!"

Trooper Britt rushed down the hall, followed by Markowski, Robbins, Mark and Jack.

Markowski said, "Is everything okay out here?

PJ said, "Officers, do I have to take this kind of—"

The officer on his left looked down at him and said, "Buddy, if I was you, I'd stand up."

PJ did.

"You bastard!" Toni screamed at him. She gulped in some air. "You invaded my house! You killed someone in my bathtub. You stole money intended for your own kids' education. And, you tried to kill me." She leaned in toward him. He was taller, but she stretched herself as tall as she could. She wanted to grab him by the lapels of his suit coat and shake the living daylights out of him. But the police would probably frown on that.

"But you know what the worst thing is? The thing that made me want to hunt you down? You made my kid cry. You gave him nightmares. A word of advice, PJ. Whatever you do, never, ever, harm a mother's child. There is nothing more dangerous than an angry mother!"

She turned around and took two steps toward the conference room but stopped. Her chest was heaving. She swung around to face PJ. It took all she had to resist flinging the evidence bag into his face. She settled on shaking it at him with the ferocity of a killer holding a loaded gun. "One more thing. You made me break my favorite shoe. For that alone, I would have hunted you to the ends of the earth."

She watched as PJ was led away. She turned to the detectives, Trooper Britt, Mark and Jack and said, "I'm sorry, everyone. I got a little hot under the collar there."

Markowski and Trooper Britt looked at each other. Markowski shrugged. Trooper Britt gave her a thumbs-up. Mark and Jack were grinning.

Chapter 33

Epilogue

The sun had just set on the lake. After an afternoon of frolicking under clear skies on Union Pier's somewhat chilly public beach, their two tired kids were already showered and in their pajamas. Mark was busy reading them a bedtime story. Jack and Jeri, who had invited themselves over for the evening and brought pizza, salad and wine, had volunteered to clean up the kitchen. That left Toni with nothing to do but bask in the glory of taking a rare Friday afternoon off.

"So," Jeri said, "tell us what everyone's reaction was at the office."

"Do you mean about PJ's arrest, getting the afternoon off, the office move, or the co-op thing?"

To no one's surprise, Jack produced a note pad. "Do you mind if I take notes? Unless that was just wine-induced euphoria, I think you and Mark just gave me permission to document all this for a magazine article. Hey! Maybe even a book!"

Jeri shook her head and looked at Toni. "Do you know how many times I have rued the day when I decided to marry a journalist?"

"Well, hey, dear," Jack said, "it does help put bread on the table and, in this case, pizza, wine, et cetera."

Toni waited for Jeri to punch him.

Instead, Jeri said, "I'd like to hear about all four of those things."

Before she could answer, Mark returned to the living room and said, "The kids are all tucked in." He sat down next to her.

Toni said, "Well, this morning I called a meeting and told everyone about PJ's arrest and the fact that he'd confessed to murdering Page. I told the two employees he had brought to the merger to listen to the rest of my speech before they decided what to do next. Then I explained my vision to turn Simplified Data into an employee-owned co-op."

"What is a co-op, exactly?" Jeri asked.

"Let me answer that with four words: Place people over profit. Doesn't that kind of say it all?"

Toni looked at the others and knew her concise explanation had failed. She picked up her wine glass and drank the last few drops, hoping that Mark would get the hint and run to the kitchen to find another bottle. "Okay, okay," she said, "four words is not enough. A co-op serves the community." She tried to blink away a little attack of tears. "Members of a co-op don't just want a paycheck, dammit, they want to build a better world!"

She sniffled a bit and had to wipe her nose before continuing. "From now on, everyone at SDS gets an equal vote on what we do and where we go. I might be the CEO, or the chairman, or whatever you want to call it, but my vote carries no more weight than anyone else's. If there is profit at the end of the year, everyone gets a proportional share."

"My God, it's communism!" Jack shouted.

No one said a word for several seconds.

"Hey, I'm only kidding!" he said.

"My heart in really in this, Jack," Toni said. "But I was worried. Would others at SDS share my passion? I stood there in the conference room and told them that we were going to leave the ridiculously expensive high-rise offices and set up shop in a run-down defunct dime store, using thrift store furniture, down in the gang-infested projects of East Garfield Park. I went on to explain why I thought it was important to be there. That's where the community lives that we want to serve. Finally, I announced that I, the person who has been terrible at making sales pitches, was ready to take over the sales job." She paused and, since Mark hadn't taken the hint, said, "Honey, is there any more wine?"

He jumped up. "Oh, so that's what that look was, a moment ago. I'll be right back."

Toni continued, "I half-expected all the employees, PJ's side and my own, to jump up and run for the nearest exit. But . . . but you know what? They . . . they . . . I'm sorry." She reached for a napkin to dab her eyes; she hadn't expected to get teary about this. She said through tear-clouded eyes, "They actually . . . actually applauded—all of them—and shouted things like, 'Right on!' and 'Let's do it!' and 'Where do we sign up?'"

Mark hurried back from the kitchen to come behind her and wrap his arms around her shoulders. He leaned down and kissed her on the neck. "Yeah," he said. "I was there for that great moment. She got even more applause when she said everyone was getting the rest of the day off!"

"What about the lady next door's nephew," Jeri asked, "and your tenant, that Rhonda Shain? What's going to happen to them?"

"I can answer that," Jack said. "Bruce Markowski says they have been charged with theft and transferred to the county jail up in St. Joseph. Since they returned all the stolen items, he thinks the prosecutor will not be too harsh on them. Bernard may not get even jail time but he's not sure about Rhonda."

"Rhonda's already voluntarily broken her lease on our cottage," Mark said. "If we're lucky, we won't be seeing her again."

"And what about your neighbor Ruth? How is she doing?"

Toni said, "Well, the good news is we've become close friends and I will be seeing her quite often over in Chicago, since we are now on the same team, so speak. That is, we collaborate on how to provide health care to low income areas. But the bad news—which turns out to be not so bad after all—is that she's selling her house." She pointed at the house next door. "The sight of Page's body in there will haunt her forever."

"That's too bad," Jack said.

"Not really. It turns out that the house a few doors up from George Wilkens's is up for sale. Ruth plans on putting in an offer on that one, contingent on the quick sale of her current house. So, we'll still be neighbors, just a few blocks away from each other."

"Who would want to buy a house where someone has been murdered?" Jack asked.

"Believe it or not, Ruth said there's a local contractor, Robert Zee—ah, Zee-something; it's a long Polish name—who's interested in buying it. Evidently he thinks that, by the time he finishes the remodeling job to his high standards, everyone will have forgotten about the murder and it will be easy to sell."

"Speaking of creepy things like murder," Jeri said, "How are you guys dealing with that jetted tub?"

"Oh, my God!" Toni said. "I thought Mark had already told you! You should go see that bathroom."

"Uh, no thanks. I'm sure I don't want—"

"No, no, Jeri, don't worry, the tub's gone. It's history! We now have a brand new, spacious, walk-in shower with a gazillion showerheads. Mark had the contractors rip out that tub as soon as we got access to the house."

"It was expensive, but now we have peace of mind," Mark said. "Plus, all the work was paid for out of the reward money. Hey, you guys want to buy a jetted tub? Used only once!"

Jack grimaced and Jeri said, "Ewww."

Mark went over to the fireplace and added a log to the fire using one of the brand-new fireplace tools. He said, "I'll get another bottle of wine. We need to make a toast." He walked off to the kitchen.

Toni watched him examine the small wine rack on their kitchen counter. He slid out a bottle, brought it over to the table and sliced the foil wrapper off the top. As he positioned the corkscrew for opening, he examined the label, looked at her and then back at the label. He said, "Toni, wait a minute. This is not our wine! It's another bottle of that expensive stuff I accidently poured at Miller's—Château Clerc Milon 1989. How did it get here?"

Toni hesitated. Then she said, "You wouldn't believe me even if I told you. Just enjoy it. We deserve every ounce." She noticed Jack leaning forward, about to push himself up and make one of his theatrical salutations. "Sorry, Jack," she said. "Sit down, please. It's my turn."

After Mark had opened and poured the wine, she swirled it around in her glass, raised the glass high and said, "To friends, to justice . . . and to this bloody wine!"

Kay and Terry Hallagan

In 1949, Kathryn Malatesta and Edward Terrence Hallagan met on a blind date at Chicago's Union Station. Kay told Terry she planned to enter a cloistered convent, and Terry convinced her to marry him instead. That marriage lasted 63 years yielding: 12 children, 34 grandchildren and countless great grandchildren.

In their free time, Terry created Hallagan Business Machines to support his expanding family and HBM is now 60 years old. Kay mothered a dozen children while writing her weekly "Promises To Keep" column for the Chicago Daily Defender and working as a social worker at Marillac House on Chicago's Westside.

During their golden years, Kay and Terry spent time in Union Pier, Michigan, writing *This Bloody Wine.*

Acknowledgments

We would like to thank our editors (all family members!) for helping us get this book into print. Keeping in the spirit of this "family affair," our granddaughter Norah K. Noonan created the art work for the cover. Also we are grateful to the Michigan State Police, Chikaming Township Police and the New Buffalo Police for their valuable advice on law enforcement procedures.